MAYBE THIS CHRISTMAS

She glanced up at Logan, glad that her cheeks were reddened by the nippy morning air and wouldn't reveal the warmth she felt just from looking at the glow in his eyes.

"I love the way the snow swirls around, like whipped frosting on a cake."

"Hmmm. So you like snow," he said, setting the logs on the ground with a devilish gleam in his eye.

"Logan Taylor, don't you dare!" she squealed as she watched him pick up a clump of snow and ball it in his gloved hand.

She turned just as he threw it, and it splattered on her back. He kept on pelting her with snowballs as Jennifer fought desperately to retaliate. In seconds she was laughing and stumbling toward the cabin. Then a well-aimed snowball hit her in the leg, and she fell headlong into a towering drift. With Logan's assistance she rolled breathlessly over onto her back, giggling happily while he brushed the snow off her face. Her hood had fallen back, revealing the shining red-gold of her hair.

The corners of his eyes were crinkled into deep lines, his smile much too sexy as he rested for a moment above her. Then his lips covered hers, persuasively, demanding a response. . . .

BOOK YOUR PLACE ON OUR WEBSITE AND MAKE THE READING CONNECTION!

We've created a customized website just for our very special readers, where you can get the inside scoop on everything that's going on with Zebra, Pinnacle and Kensington books.

When you come online, you'll have the exciting opportunity to:

- View covers of upcoming books
- Read sample chapters
- Learn about our future publishing schedule (listed by publication month *and author*)
- Find out when your favorite authors will be visiting a city near you
- Search for and order backlist books from our online catalog
- Check out author bios and background information
- Send e-mail to your favorite authors
- Meet the Kensington staff online
- Join us in weekly chats with authors, readers and other guests
- Get writing guidelines
- AND MUCH MORE!

Visit our website at
http://www.kensingtonbooks.com

JANET DAILEY

Maybe This Christmas

ZEBRA BOOKS
KENSINGTON PUBLISHING CORP.
http://www.kensingtonbooks.com

CONTENTS

DARLING JENNY

Chapter One

"Please fasten your seat belts," a flight attendant said briskly, pointing to the red sign that flashed above the arched doorway of the coach section. Jennifer Glenn obeyed the instruction, then brushed back a strand of the red-gold hair that had strayed to the corner of her eyes, tilting her head upward toward the fresh, cooling air from the vent and letting the breeze play lightly on her face.

She should have put her hair up, in the feminine but businesslike style she wore to the office. Her mouth compressed painfully. But Brad had liked it this way, loose and waving gently to her shoulders. Jennifer liked it this way, too, but it made her look young—and right now she felt old, much older than her twenty-two years. Her brown eyes were sadly contemplative.

Just two years ago she had graduated at the head of her class in business school. Beaming and full of confidence, she'd kissed her parents good-bye, climbed aboard the bus in Alexandria, and headed for the big city—Minneapolis! For three weeks, she made the rounds, in and out of executive offices, her certificates and recommendations proudly carried in her hand. And the results had always been the same.

She would walk into the room and see the impressed and interested look on her interviewer's face change to one of doubt. After the second week, Jennifer could almost predict their reactions. They studied her petal-smooth complexion, her bright eyes, her button nose, and her wide, nervous smile. There was always the same unasked question: *Are you really twenty? You look more like sixteen.* But instead they murmured about her lack of experience.

Finally, at the end of the third week, with her limited funds running short and facing the prospect of returning to her inexpensive hotel again that night without a job, Jennifer had practically pleaded with her last interviewer to give her a chance to prove she was as good as her credentials said. With a fatherly look in his eyes, the man had reluctantly consented to at least let her try, noting that her computer skills were useful in a legal firm. Jennifer could tell he regretted his decision the minute he made it, but at last she had a job. The software they used was no match for the complexity of the legal documents she was typing, but Jennifer did her best.

For a year and a half she had stifled her naturally exuberant personality so that she would appear efficient and businesslike even amid the gaggle of women. Legal secretary positions in the attorney firm Smith, Katzenberg, Petersen, and Rohe, occupying two full floors of a downtown office building, were few and far between. At last, after months of dull legal forms and hundreds of hours in front of a computer, Jennifer got her chance. Mr. Bradley Stevenson's secretary had abruptly left her job, and a replacement was needed immediately.

The flight attendant walked by, offering magazines to the passengers. Jennifer declined politely when he stopped by her seat. She preferred to stare out of the plane's window at the misty fog of clouds that enshrouded it, her thoughts drawn back again. The memory was very fresh. It might have been yesterday instead of six months ago. . . .

Jennifer had known the minute she stepped into his office that things were going to change. After repeatedly being told that she had to be lying about her age, she had begun wearing her hair up in an effort to appear sophisticated and older. She had known exactly what to expect of Bradley Stevenson. He had been called one of the more brilliant young lawyers in the state and was undoubtedly one of the most attractive bachelors in the firm. Although she'd seen him several times in the building, this was the first time she had actually met him.

She stepped into his office, noticing the wayward lock of black hair that drifted over his forehead as he glanced up from his papers. The full force of his dark eyes almost melted her, as did his wide, extremely charming smile.

"Well, Ms. Glenn," he said. "You have a very impressive record. Mrs. Johnston, your supervisor, speaks highly of you."

He'd asked a few questions about her qualifications, but Jennifer had known all along that the job was hers, that she was going to be the private secretary to this compelling, handsome attorney. The Minnesota farm girl had landed the most coveted job in the firm.

With a stubborn determination born of self-will, Jennifer had set out to make herself indispensable to Bradley Stevenson. For three months she sacrificed precious minutes of her lunch hour, stayed after hours typing and printing out crucial briefs, or followed up on important correspondence. In the beginning, she put in extra effort simply to prove that she was capable, but she couldn't deny that she looked forward to his smile and brief words of appreciation. One particularly late night, he insisted on taking her out to dinner despite her protests.

"Hey, I'm your employer," he finally told her, "and you have to let me take you out now and then. It's no big deal." Laughing, he added, "If it upsets your strict code of ethics to dine with your boss, pretend we're talking about our latest case over a glass of wine."

"You really don't have to do this," Jennifer said, embarrassed at the growing color in her cheeks and the pounding of her heart.

"If you have a date, say so. I don't want to fight off a jealous lover." His dark eyes had studied her intently as she replied.

"Oh, no, nothing like that. I don't go out very much." Immediately she regretted her words. To Jennifer, they sounded too much like an invitation, so she added brightly with a teasing glance, "Besides, I've been working so hard."

It had been a wonderful evening in a cozy, dimly

lit restaurant with Brad—he insisted that she call him that—as he asked what seemed like really interested questions about her home life and background. When he drove her to her apartment, and she'd thanked him for the evening, he touched her arm and said, "If you really enjoyed the evening, do me a favor. Have lunch with me tomorrow, that is, if I don't have another appointment. Do I?"

"No, you don't," Jennifer laughed happily before getting out of the car and dashing into the building.

"And wear your hair down!" she heard him call. She looked back to see him leaning out the car window for one last look at her, grinning lustily.

So it began. Occasional lunches and dinners had become nights out at exclusive clubs and plays at the Guthrie, and first-row seats at sporting events until it had ended . . . Was it only two nights ago?

"I bet this is the bumpiest ride I've ever had on a plane," the lady seated next to Jennifer said, bundling up her knitting and placing it in her tapestry bag. "I dropped three stitches in the last two minutes. I hate turbulence."

Jennifer was suddenly aware of the plane's bouncing around, and murmured something reassuring. Taking Jennifer's reply as an invitation for conversation, the woman rattled on.

"I was in Salt Lake City with my daughter and her new baby. It's her first, and I told Richard—that's my husband—that it wasn't right for her to cope with those first few weeks on her own. Of course, it's our first grandchild and we were both dying to see her. Her name is Amy, a nice, old-fashioned name, I think."

Jennifer nodded and smiled politely, wishing the

woman would stop talking and at the same time grateful to get her mind off that painful night.

"Are you going to Wyoming to ski?" the woman asked. "The weather's perfect for it."

"No. I'm going to stay with my sister for a while," Jennifer answered.

"Oh, does she live in Jackson? I'm from outside Alpine myself. What does her husband do? Wouldn't it be a coincidence if I knew them? I know quite a few people there."

"Sheila manages a motel in Jackson, but she's only been there a couple of years. Her husband was killed on active duty in the Middle East a few years ago," Jennifer replied.

"Oh, that's too bad." With a sudden movement, the woman turned toward Jennifer. "Was it the Jeffries boy?" At the answering nod, she continued, "I know his parents well. It was so difficult for them when he was listed as missing in action. They held out hope for so long."

"Yes, the confirmation of his death was a terrible shock. That's why my sister moved to Jackson. She felt the children should get to know their grandparents better. And it would ease their grief, too."

"You say she runs a motel? It's coming up on the busy time for her now with the holiday season just a few weeks away. Of course, the skiers don't seem like much compared to the hordes of tourists that descend on the Grand Tetons and Yellowstone in the summer. Will your sister be waiting for you at the airport?"

"I think so," Jennifer replied.

"I hope she won't be too upset when we don't get there," the woman said.

"What do you mean?" Jennifer raised an eyebrow curiously.

"The weather, dear. Before I left Salt Lake, the radio said there were heavy snows in the Jackson Hole area," the woman answered prophetically.

"Good afternoon. This is your captain speaking," a pleasant masculine voice said over the PA system. "I have some good news for you skiers. The temperature in Jackson Hole is thirty-two degrees, I've been told there's six inches of new powder on the slopes, and it's still coming down.

"Unfortunately, the wind is blowing and the visibility at the airport is below the required minimums for landing. That means we'll be landing at Idaho Falls instead. The airline will provide ground transportation for passengers to Jackson. You can check at the ticket counter when we arrive at Idaho Falls. Our arrival time will be twelve-fifty-five P.M. Thank you and happy skiing!"

Jennifer leaned back against her seat, turning her head toward the window to hide her misting eyes from the inquisitive woman at her side. She had been looking forward to being with her sister again, especially after their brief phone conversation the day before. Despite their age difference— Sheila was five years older—they had always been close. A steady flow of letters and E-mails had kept Sheila posted on her sister's growing romance with Brad Stevenson. After that fateful night, Jennifer turned to her sister rather than burden her parents with her heartbreak and humiliation. Jennifer's eyes cleared as she remembered with a smile Sheila's reaction to that last evening with Brad.

"Bradley Stevenson, brilliant, bold, and a brute,"

Sheila had stated caustically, sympathetic anger lacing her words while recalling a favorite word game of theirs as youngsters. "You can't work for him now, and going back to the farm and Mom and Dad isn't the answer. You need a complete change of scene. Come and stay with me. I always get lonely at Christmastime for some of my own family, and I can use the extra help this time of the year, what with all the skiers. Catch the next plane out—and I won't take no for an answer. Besides, you've never seen snow until you've spent winter in the Tetons."

Happily and tearfully Jennifer had agreed.

"Write the folks a letter telling them your boss is sick and in the hospital or something, and that you're taking a leave of absence to come visit me," Sheila went on in a take-charge voice. "They'll understand."

What a blessing it was to have a sister like Sheila, Jennifer thought, always knowing the right thing to do. Her sister had been the beautiful one of the family, with raven-black hair and amazing blue eyes framed by thick, dark lashes. Jennifer had been the cute one, mostly because she looked like a perennial child.

The flight attendant's voice interrupted her thoughts. "We've begun our final approach to Idaho Falls, and will be landing shortly. After landing, please remain in your seats until the plane has come to a full stop at the gate. Those passengers going to Jackson, Wyoming, are to report to the airline ticket counter. We do apologize for the inconvenience, and on behalf of the entire crew, we want to thank you for flying Western Airlines."

Jennifer hugged her beige suede coat around her as she hurried down the plane's steps into the building, amid dancing snowflakes and an icy wind. They should have been landing in Jackson right now, and she would have been rushing to meet her sister. Now she was faced with yet another journey and more time to think about what had happened—and to feel sorry for herself.

Most of the other passengers had disembarked before her and were already huddled around either the ticket counter or the luggage area. She stood back in a less crowded area, waiting for the lines to shorten. Absently her fingers dug into the white sheepskin that lined the coat and its upturned collar as she gazed uninterestedly at the other passengers arguing impatiently with various clerks. She was suddenly looking into another pair of brown eyes that were inspecting her with interest.

The unconcealed appraisal in the man's glance was unsettling. Jennifer felt as if each curve and feature of her body were being inspected and assessed. She straightened her shoulders and surveyed him, not finding much fault with what she saw. Even leaning back against a closed ticket counter, she could tell he was tall, over six feet, and the width of the brown suede Marlboro-man jacket across his shoulders couldn't be all sheepskin. The thumb of one hand was hooked in the waistband of his jeans, holding open the coat to reveal a white sweater.

His broad, strong face was ruggedly sexy; his brown hair, thick and wavy, she noted with dismay. His eyes had a devilish and knowing gleam under thick, dark lashes and gold-tipped brows, with crinkling lines at the corners. He had definite cheekbones and a strong, chiseled nose. His lips had curled into a mocking smile by the time Jennifer noticed them, revealing a disconcerting dimple in his cheek.

Embarrassed that she'd even returned his stare, Jennifer looked away, missing the last detail: his chin had a slight cleft. Her instinct told her all she needed to know: he was lawless, lordly, and a Lothario. And she'd had enough of that kind of man for a lifetime.

The line had thinned out at the baggage carousel, and Jennifer quickly stepped toward it and away from the stranger. She was just reaching down to pick up one of her bags when a low baritone voice said, "May I help you?" Then an arm reached past her and picked up her suitcase.

She straightened to glare angrily into the mocking eyes of the stranger she had seen only a few seconds before.

"I can manage, thanks," Jennifer replied frostily, reaching for her bag.

"You are Jennifer Glenn, aren't you?" he said with a knowing smile. "I didn't see any other redheads get off the plane."

"My hair isn't red. It's strawberry blonde," Jennifer asserted.

"Sheila called my hotel and told me your plane was being rerouted here. Is that yours, too?" He was reaching down for a blue suitcase that matched the one in his hand.

"Yes," Jennifer answered, momentarily surprised to hear her sister's name. "Who are you?"

"I'm sure Sheila's mentioned me in her letters. The name is Taylor, Logan Taylor."

So the *L* was right after all. *Lawless, lordly, and a Lothario,* Jennifer thought with a triumphant gleam in her eye.

His hand had taken her elbow, and he was guiding her through the crowd. Sheila had mentioned him in her letters, but Jennifer somehow got the impression that Logan Taylor was much older. He wasn't more than—she glanced at his face from the corner of her eye—thirty-one, thirty-two? He owned the motel that Sheila managed, and a lot more, from what her sister had said in her letters.

"I thought you might like to have a cup of coffee and relax a little before we leave," Logan was saying as he ushered Jennifer into the café area.

"Leave? Leave for where?"

"Jackson Hole, of course." He pulled out a chair at one of the tables for Jennifer before seating himself.

"But the airline . . ."

"I already let them know that I was meeting you. Good thing your sister caught me just as I was checking out of my hotel. She knew I was driving back today. Since you'll be staying with her, the ride will give us a chance to get acquainted." His drifting glance once more swept over her face in appraisal. "What'll you have? Coffee?"

"Yes, that's fine. Black, please," she ordered as the waitress approached their table. Jennifer waited until the girl had moved away before she replied a little icily to his previous statement and his glance. "I doubt we'll see very much of each other, Mr. Taylor."

"It's Logan, and Jackson Hole isn't that big. We'll see each other." He leaned back against his chair as the young waitress brought their coffee and set it in front of them on the table. He smiled up at the girl warmly, but only Jennifer saw the waitress blush under his glance. *Sickening* was her immediate thought and it must have shown on her face, because Logan Taylor glanced at her with a puzzled expression.

"Logan!" a feminine voice cried. "Logan! So you didn't leave after all!"

Jennifer looked up just as a pair of gorgeous girls descended on their table, one of them a blonde wearing a fur coat that looked like it cost a year of Jennifer's salary.

"I came to pick up Rachel, and I find you. If you'd told me this morning, we could have come out together." She pouted as she glanced over her shoulder at the long-haired brunette who was staring seductively at Logan. "Isn't this great, Rachel? I was going nuts because Logan left, and here he is at the airport. I should've known you would change your mind about driving back in this weather, especially after the late night we had."

Jennifer nearly sighed in disgust at the blatant way they were throwing themselves at him. And he was sitting there enjoying it all immensely.

"Who's the little girl, Logan?" Rachel asked huskily, her dark eyes never leaving Logan's face.

"This is Sheila Jeffries's sister. Jennifer, this is DeeDee Hunter and Rachel Scott." Logan made the introductions as Jennifer sat in fuming silence.

"It's only the second week of December. I didn't know school vacation started so early," DeeDee said.

"I'm twenty-two. Not exactly a schoolgirl," Jennifer retorted sharply.

"Are you really that old? You look much younger." DeeDee answered in disbelief as Jennifer met Logan's teasing look. But the blonde's interest in Jennifer didn't last long before DeeDee turned her rapt face back to the man beside her. "We're having a welcome-home party for Rachel tonight. Can you come?"

"I'm driving back to Jackson Hole this afternoon," Logan said quietly, ignoring the petulant expression on the blonde's face. "I stayed just long enough to pick up Jennifer. We'll be leaving in a few minutes. Next time, maybe."

Keep them hanging on the string, Jennifer thought disgustedly.

"You really shouldn't drive in this weather," Rachel protested. "Why don't you stay until it lets up?"

"No, I'm sorry," he said firmly.

"You are mean, Logan Taylor," DeeDee said sulkily. "But don't you forget to make reservations for us. A party of eight, the weekend after Christmas."

"I won't forget." Logan nodded.

"We'd better go. See you soon, hot stuff." DeeDee smiled, disentangling herself from his arm, then blowing him a kiss as she began to push Rachel toward the door. "Nice meeting you, Janet."

"You too, Dumbelina," Jennifer mumbled.

"What was that you said?" Logan asked, seating himself once again in the chair beside her.

"Nothing. Listen, if I'm keeping you from something, I'm sure I can still catch the airline's transport." Jennifer sipped at her coffee before pushing a strand of her copper-gold hair behind her ear.

Strong fingers captured her chin and turned it toward him. Quickly she jerked herself away, her heart hammering in her throat.

"I thought for a minute your eyes were green," he mocked, picking up his coffee and raising the cup to his mouth. His eyes twinkled at her. "They're still brown."

Jennifer rose from the table. "If you're ready to go, I'd like to leave now and get this trip over with," she snapped.

"For someone who's not a redhead, you sure as hell have a short temper!" Logan laughed, and she wanted to smack him.

Chapter Two

Snowflakes fell thick and fast, obscuring everything in sight. The only other occupant in Jennifer's snow-surrounded world was the last person she would have chosen, the man behind the wheel, Logan Taylor. She glanced over at his profile, glad that his attention was concentrated on the slippery road in front of them. The speedometer needle hovered at the thirty mark.

"Well, Jenny Glenn, are you going to stay silent for another two hours?" His hand flexed on the steering wheel as he scowled out at the falling snow.

"My name is Jennifer," she corrected, her mouth setting itself in a firm little line as she spoke.

"I like Jenny Glenn better. So easy to say, I have to smile. Jenny Glenn." The dimple appeared once again as he repeated her name, glancing over at her with an irritating twinkle in his eyes.

"I hate the name Jenny," Jennifer protested, even though it sounded rather nice the way he said it. "It sounds like a donkey or a mule!"

He glanced at her again. This time his smile was wide and unmistakably teasing. There was so much fun and warmth in his gaze that Jennifer had to look away or be drawn by his magnetic charm. She shivered slightly as she wondered if she was always going to be susceptible to men like this.

"Are you cold? There's a blanket in the back if you want to cover your legs," Logan offered, his swift gaze taking in the pantyhose-covered legs beneath her olive skirt.

"No, I'm fine. Just a ghost walking over my grave, I guess," Jennifer shrugged. She stared out at nothing. "Do we have much farther to go?"

"Twenty—thirty miles, I imagine."

"I hope Sheila isn't worried about me," Jennifer mused.

"She won't be. You're with me," Logan asserted. The devilish gleam in his eye mocked her.

"And that makes everything all right, doesn't it?" she retorted sarcastically.

Logan didn't reply as he slowed to negotiate a curve in the road. The snow had begun to drift, covering the highway until it was difficult to see it. But the reflector poles on the side of the road gave some idea of where the paved road ended and the shoulder began.

"You don't like me very much, do you?" Logan commented, his eyes never leaving the road as a crosswind pushed at the Jeep.

"Don't be ridiculous. I hardly even know you," Jennifer lied.

"Who's being ridiculous? I think you've already got me pegged. Don't I fit the picture that Sheila described?"

Jennifer glanced at him coolly, taking in his rugged profile and the strong, chiseled jawline. He was all man—powerful, virile, arrogant, and no doubt very experienced in the art of love.

"No, my impression was of someone older, more settled, a family man," she replied honestly with a hint of rebuke in her voice. "How long has my sister known you?"

He laughed lightly.

"Quite a while. Eric was my best friend. As a matter of fact, we both met Sheila at the same time. Your sister is a very beautiful woman. We both tried to date her, but Eric won. I couldn't make it to the wedding, or I probably would have met you. When Sheila moved out here, I went to see her and the children. Little Eric is pretty grown-up for a seven-year-old, and Cindy sure tries hard to be like him."

"Sounds like you see them often," Jennifer commented, wondering if he still had any feeling for her widowed sister.

"I do. Your sister's the independent type, but once in a while she likes having a man around to lean on. Paul and Katie, Eric's parents, like to spoil the children, which is only natural for grandparents, so I step in occasionally to keep them in line a little and help Sheila out."

"Sounds awfully cozy," Jennifer said sarcastically.

"What's that supposed to mean?" he asked with ominous quietness.

"Don't get me wrong. I appreciate your concern for my sister and her kids," she retorted, giving him an innocent smile.

"How long has it been since you visited her?" His eyes narrowed as he glanced at her.

"I saw her when she was home this past spring, but if you mean coming out here, this is the first time."

Jennifer tossed her red-gold hair out of her eyes with a defiant movement of her head.

"You haven't seen her spend all her afternoons with those kids, and then work late into the night on everything else she needs to get done. Or the way she looks at her sketchbook and only dreams of putting her ideas on canvas. You haven't seen Eric and Cindy fighting for her undivided attention, or the way they act too grown-up sometimes so they won't be a burden to her. Even if I'd never known her husband, I would still do everything I could to help her. Nothing you or anyone else says is going to stop me."

Jennifer flinched at his piercing look. She *had* meant to provoke him, unsure as she was at the exact nature of his interest in her sister. But she had troubled the still waters of his easygoing outward personality and revealed the hidden and possibly treacherous depths of his indomitable character.

"I should have known. You may be Sheila's sister, but you're nothing like her," Logan muttered. His meaning was clear—she didn't measure up.

Jennifer realized she had asked for that unflattering assessment of her character. She made a silent vow to be as much of a help as she could to Sheila, at the very least.

The Jeep fishtailed slightly as she started to apologize. One look at Logan's face was enough to tell her that now wasn't the time for talking. The section of road visible in front of them was glazed with ice. Then the road began to curve.

"Hold on, Jenny. I don't think I'm going to make this turn."

Silently, intently, she could almost feel him will the Jeep around the corner. For an instant it looked as if he was going to make it; then a spray of snow flew onto the windshield as they careened off the road. They bumped and bounced to a halt, the snow on the windshield slashed away by the pulsating beat of the wipers until the white world outside could be seen. The snow cushioned the impact, and the airbags had not inflated.

"Jenny? Jenny, are you all right?" Logan's hand was brushing the hair away from her face while his eyes examined her intently.

"I'm f-f-fine," she managed in a shaky voice. With a nervous laugh, she added, "I was scared though."

"So was I." He smiled. "Nothing's broken? You didn't hit anything?"

"No," she reassured him with a smile. His anxious concern made her feel warm and safe inside, and she was sorry when he moved away.

"Well, let's see what the damage is."

He opened the door to a flurry of snow and biting cold wind. His form was strangely dark in the white void as he moved first to the front, then disappeared to the rear of the Jeep. Seconds later he was back inside with snowflakes covering his head and coat, and his breath making smoky puffs in the cold.

The audacious twinkle was back in his eyes as he met her serious gaze. "I have some good news and some bad news. Which would you like first?"

"Give me the good news first," Jennifer smiled.

"We're stuck."

"Okay, what's the bad news?" she asked with a note of alarm.

"There's a building a few hundred feet back up the road with smoke coming out of the chimney," Logan grinned.

For a brief moment, anger rose inside her before her innate sense of humor took over and she burst into laughter.

"So you have a sense of humor." His laughter finished into a satisfied smile. "This would be a lot worse if we were at each other's throats." His gloved hand patted the steering wheel thoughtfully. "Well, you'd better bundle up. It's going to seem like a long hike in this weather."

Jennifer nodded and pulled the hood of her suede coat over her head, fastening it securely around her neck. Taking her fleece-lined gloves out of her pocket, she swiftly slipped them on her hands, glancing over at Logan as she finished.

"Get out on my side. The snow's tramped down some."

She slid behind the wheel as he clambered out of the Jeep. Logan was standing calf-deep in snow beside the door as she swung her legs around to get out.

"Those boots aren't going to do you much good when you're going through these snowdrifts," he laughed as he looked at her short, fur-trimmed snow boots.

"They're meant for city streets," Jennifer said ruefully, fully aware of how much bare leg was going to be in the snow just standing where Logan was now.

He slid an arm under her knees. "Put your arm around my neck. I'll carry you to the road," he instructed as his other arm encircled her back and waist.

For a second, Jennifer wanted to protest. She didn't want that much close contact with this man, but protesting would be foolish. After all, it was the most practical thing to do. So she relented, her arms encircling his neck.

They were only twenty feet from the road, but the wind was blowing directly into them. Jennifer was glad that she could hide her face in the brown suede of his coat, not just to protect her face from the icy blasts of the wind, but also to keep Logan from seeing the rising color in her cheeks. Then he was placing her on her feet, keeping hold of one hand while huddling down toward her in the flurry of snowflakes and wind.

"We'll walk now," he nearly shouted as the wind tried to whip his voice away. "Hang onto my hand so I don't lose you in a snowdrift."

They struggled against the blizzard while the falling and blowing flakes danced maliciously around them. The drifting snow slowed their steps, making a short walk into an arduous trek. Then Logan stopped.

"We'll cut across here." He pointed to the shadowy gray outline of a building. "The snow's really deep. I can carry you."

"No, no," Jennifer protested. "It's too far. If you go ahead of me and break a path, I'll be okay."

He grinned at her but didn't argue. Then he stepped into the untouched snow, his legs moving in close, scissorlike motions to leave behind a white furrow for her to walk in. The wind pushed at her as she tried to concentrate on staying in the narrow lane, steeling herself not to feel the flurry of cold snow Logan kicked up. She felt like a tightrope walker balancing on the high wire.

It seemed like they had covered miles as Jennifer looked over Logan's shoulder to see the house still some distance ahead of them. She was out of breath, and the numbing cold grabbed at her legs, making her steps awkward and clumsy. Then she stumbled, falling on her knees into the snow.

"I'm so cold," she panted as Logan pulled her up and brushed away at the snow clinging to her skirt and legs. "I can't really catch my breath."

"That's the altitude," he muttered, looking worried. "We're probably at seven thousand feet."

Without asking permission, he swept her up into his arms. Jennifer had no strength to refuse. She was just grateful to hold exhaustedly onto his shoulder as he carried her to the house.

She was disappointed when they were finally close enough to see that it was just a log cabin, not a house—a forlorn little building sitting isolated amid the pine trees that towered over the roof. She glanced at Logan's face to see his reaction, but there was none. They had barely reached the doorstep when the door swung open.

Standing in the opening was a lean, gaunt old man, his chin covered by pepper-and-salt stubble with matching strands sticking out from the cap on his head. His shoulders were stooped and bent beneath the red flannel shirt he wore. As Logan stepped closer, Jennifer saw a youthful spark in the old man's dark eyes, as if the fire of life wasn't even close to dying. There was anything but welcome in his expression as he glared at them.

"What in tarnation do you want?" he fairly roared at Logan.

"My Jeep got stuck in the snow out by the road," Logan replied easily, ignoring the hostility in the other man's voice. "I saw the smoke coming out of your chimney, and I thought we might impose on you for some shelter tonight."

"You two are damn fools to be out in weather like this!" He grudgingly opened the door wider and stepped to one side so they could enter. "Might as well come in before she freezes to death in that getup."

Logan thanked him sincerely as he stepped through the door and set Jennifer on her feet. His eyes twinkled merrily as he saw the apprehensive expression on her face.

"Ain't much, ain't got nothin' much, but you're welcome to stay." The grudging invitation was given in a growly and irritated voice.

Jennifer's eyes adjusted to the dimness of the cabin, and all she could think was, *This is it, one room, four walls, that's all?* Then the immaculate cleanness struck her. The wood floors reflected the flames burning in the fireplace across the room, and the little table sitting in the middle was covered with a bright red checked cloth. On the wall to the right of the fireplace was a sparkling, white-enameled, cast-iron monstrosity, its chrome handles shining from the light of the fire. Even the black circles on top seemed to glow from hand-rubbed care. It was an old-fashioned, huge wood-burning stove. The wood cabinets, on the wall where the door was, gleamed with fresh varnish. The bed on the left had a brightly colored quilt thrown over it.

"Want some help with your boots, Jenny?" Logan offered, his voice tearing her attention away from the cozy room.

"No, thank you." She shook her head, bending down to her task as Logan turned back to their host.

"Name's Logan Taylor. I own the Box T spread on the south Gros Ventre Range. This is Jenny Glenn. We really appreciate you taking us in like this."

"Taylor, you say? Say, I know your old man. Used to hunt, didn't he?" the man commented, inspecting Logan closely. "I don't hold with huntin' for pleasure. They oughta make people eat what they kill."

"My father died several years ago, but yeah, he used to hunt," Logan said, shedding his coat. "He always said there was nothing better than a juicy venison steak."

"Humph!" the old man snorted. "S'pose that's a hint that you're hungry. Get yourselves warm by the fire, and I'll go get us some steaks from the ice-house. Name's Carmichael," he stated, thrusting a gnarled hand reluctantly toward Logan. "She cook?" At the amused expression on Logan's face as he glanced toward Jennifer, the man shuffled over to the rack beside the door, where his coat hung. "Only two things I can't abide," he said, "a woman that can cook and one that can't."

Logan walked over to the fire and extended his hands to the flames as Jennifer joined him. He smiled down at her reassuringly.

"Cantankerous old coot, isn't he?" he said very softly, glancing down at the shimmering copper highlights in her hair. She nodded agreement as he turned back to the fire. "You'd better change into warmer clothes. I'll go back and get your suitcases."

"You really don't need to," Jennifer protested. "I can get by in what I'm wearing."

"Yeah, right," Logan retorted firmly. He stepped away from the fireplace to draw up a cane-backed rocker. Taking Jennifer's hand, he led her to the chair and sat her down. "You wait here. I'll only be gone a minute."

"At least wait until you've warmed up some more."

"No. It's almost dusk now. If I wait any longer I'll be fumbling around in the dark."

Jennifer watched reluctantly as he buttoned up his coat and pulled on his gloves. With a cheery wave, he opened the door and went outside.

He was being awfully nice, Jennifer thought, leaning back in the rocker to rest her feet on the hearth and wriggle her toes in the warmth from the fire. Of course, that was his game, being charming. Still, he was probably a lot of fun just as long as you didn't take him too seriously. But what about Sheila? As a widow, she probably couldn't resist a man like Logan. He undoubtedly had an uncanny knack for appearing to be what a woman wanted and needed most. Luckily, her experience with Brad Stevenson had taught Jennifer to recognize men like that—and avoid them. She almost saw an amber caution light flashing when she looked at Logan.

A whoosh of snow and wind announced the return of the grizzled old man as he stomped in through the door. He dropped his loosely wrapped package on the counter with a thud, ignoring Jennifer's smile of welcome.

"Would you like me to help you with something?" she offered as he busied himself at the old range.

"Nope, can't stand women in my kitchen."

At that moment Logan came hurrying in the door.

"Brrr! It's really blowing now!" He shuddered, knocking the snow off his jeans and boots as he set the suitcases down before walking over to warm himself by the fireplace.

"Most likely it'll get worse," the old man remarked. "One thing about Wyoming weather in the winter—you can be sure it's gonna snow until you swear the mountains got a bad case of dandruff, or it's gonna be colder than your wife's feet on a winter night, or the wind's gonna blow until your teeth chatter right out of your mouth. It's really hell when it does all three!"

The rich, deep chuckle from Logan brought Jennifer's laughing eyes around to him.

"Mr. Carmichael's right. You don't know what winter is until you've spent it in the Tetons, Jenny." Logan smiled down at her warmly. "Is there a place for her to change clothes?"

"Over there. That door on the left of the fireplace." The old man pointed. "Promised Margaret forty years ago I'd get her indoor plumbing, but she up and died before I got it all put in. Those frozen pipes are a damned nuisance."

She opened the door to an extremely small room and squeezed herself behind it. An enormous cast-iron bathtub took up most of the room, leaving her only about two feet of clear space for maneuvering. But she finally succeeded in getting pants and a heavy sweater on without seriously banging herself into the wall.

* * *

Later, Jennifer was inspecting the titles in the makeshift bookcase sitting in the far corner of the cabin as Mr. Carmichael bustled around, setting the table by the light of a kerosene lamp.

"Have you ever considered hooking up to electricity?" Logan asked. "It runs right outside your cabin by the road."

"Too expensive," the old man snorted. "Besides, what do I need it for?"

"You have some wonderful old books," Jennifer interrupted, picking up a worn copy of Mark Twain's *Tom Sawyer* nestled snugly between Shakespeare's *Romeo and Juliet* and Dickens's *Oliver Twist*.

"Didn't ya think I could read?" he grumbled, shuffling over to the fireplace to fish out the potatoes from the coals.

"Oh, that's not what I meant," Jennifer apologized quickly. "I just thought . . ."

"I know, that a crotchety old buzzard like me wouldn't be readin' good books," he growled. "Well, sometimes I get so desperate for entertainment that I even read the labels on my tin cans. Come on over and sit down. Supper's on the table."

The meal was delicious. The steaks were tender and juicy, and Mr. Carmichael informed Jennifer that it was elk and not deer venison. There were thick slices of sourdough bread toasted so the unique flavor came through, baked potatoes, stewed tomatoes with a savory blend of seasonings, followed by a steaming cup of the blackest coffee Jennifer had ever seen. She sipped the bitter brew hesitantly and watched in astonishment as Logan and Mr. Carmichael drank it down.

"Coffee's kinda weak," the old man grumbled.

"It's really good when you can slice it with a knife."
Then he guffawed loudly at the startled expression
on Jennifer's face and winked at Logan. "This here
is man's coffee. It'll put hair on your chest. None
of that watery stuff you women fix." Turning to
Logan, the old man's eyes burned fiery bright as
he added in a more serious tone, "That's a right
purty female. 'Course I knowed many a woman in
my glory days. She's gonna be one of those that always look young. Her skin ain't gonna be crinklin'
up into a prune face." He glanced back at Jennifer
as if to reassure himself of his opinion, then returned his gaze to Logan. "And she's got a fine
pair of hips, wide and strong. Oughta have some
healthy babies."

Jennifer's mouth opened in astonishment, but
she closed it quickly as she met the mocking gleam
in Logan's eyes.

"Let me do the dishes, Mr. Carmichael," she offered, hoping to change the subject and hide her
growing embarrassment.

"Nope, I'll do 'em," he said quickly as he pushed
his chair away from the table. " 'Course, if you want
to make yourself useful, you can get them old quilts
out of the trunk and make up a bed on the floor
beside the fireplace."

Anything to keep busy Jennifer thought, sending
Logan a withering glance. The trunk was sitting at
the foot of the narrow bed. A wave of fatigue swept
over her as she looked longingly at the quilted
bedcover. It was—what—only eight o'clock? she
wondered. But she was exhausted. She lifted the
heavy wooden lid of the trunk and tilted it back
until it rested against the bed.

There was one extra-thick quilt that Jennifer decided she could use to cushion the wood floor. The other two, lighter quilts could be used for covers. A little smile flitted across her face as she imagined Logan crawling under the covers with their grizzled host. Minutes later she had the blankets spread on the floor, the top two covers turned back invitingly.

"I couldn't find any pillows, Mr. Carmichael," she said, turning toward the counter, where he was putting the last of the dishes in the cupboard.

Grunting indignantly, he shuffled over to the dresser, pulled open one of the lower drawers, and removed two square pillows. He walked over and handed them to Jennifer with a gruff "Use these."

Needlepointed on the front of one was a charming picture of a log cabin with blue smoke rising from the chimney, and the words *Home Sweet Home* beneath it. But it was the other one that really caught Jennifer's eyes—a large red heart framed with lace and the words *My Darling* embroidered inside. She choked with silent laughter as she wondered mischievously which one of their heads was going to rest on it. Without a word she placed them side by side on top of the quilts.

Finished, she curled up in the rocker by the hearth and stared into the hypnotic flames. She glanced over at Logan, but he was watching the old man at the counter with the most peculiar, calculating expression on his face.

"Well, dishes are all done," Carmichael announced, his shuffling feet taking him over to the cot. "If you folks don't mind, I'll go ahead and turn in. You're welcome to go to bed whenever you've a mind to."

Jennifer sat in horrified silence, barely hearing Logan speak up quickly.

"Ah—I was wondering if Jenny could sleep in your bed tonight."

"In my bed?" their host exclaimed incredulously, his gnarled fingers digging into the mattress as if he thought they were going to steal it from beneath him. "What's wrong with the one she made ya on the floor?"

Jennifer stared from Logan to Mr. Carmichael to the quilts on the floor. Hysteria welled up inside her. It was a dream! A nightmare! It couldn't be true!

Suddenly it wasn't an old brick fireplace she was in front of; it was an ultramodern white one. The quilts on the floor became a plush fur rug, and she was lying on it in the arms of Brad Stevenson. She was kissing him . . . No, she was fighting him, pushing off the hands that were trying to slip under her sweater, twisting, struggling to free herself from his embrace until at last she had wrenched herself away. Brad was shouting at her.

"Don't pull that innocent routine with me!" he was saying, his lips curling in anger. "You knew exactly what was going to happen when I invited you here, baby-face. I've been coming across with evenings out, spending way too much money on you for weeks now. So guess what. You're going to come across tonight!"

She remembered looking down at him, filled with disgust that she had actually wanted to fall in love with this man. Then she had run. And now, by sheer coincidence, she was thrust into almost the same situation.

"That's my bed!" the old man was saying. "It's got my lumps in it. You two are young. Your bones aren't brittle like mine. A night sleepin' on the floor ain't gonna hurt her."

"But you don't understand," Jennifer whispered in a strained voice. "We aren't married."

"Ya will be. I seen the way you two been lookin' at each other." He glanced at Logan with a conspiratorial smile before adding belligerently, "Because it's my house and I say I'm sleepin' in my bed!"

Chapter Three

Logan rose from his chair by the table to walk over by the fire. Tears misted Jennifer's eyes as she looked pleadingly at Logan. When he refused to return her glance and continued to stare somberly into the flames, she rose to stand by his side.

"Please," she whispered, touching his arm lightly, "you've got to do something."

He studied her face and the anxious, almost fearful expression in her eyes. He shook his head in puzzlement. "I don't know what we can do," he said, flashing a swift glance behind him at the man sitting on the bed.

"I can't possibly sleep in the same bed with you!"

"Don't get hysterical about it," Logan said, calmly and softly. "There's nothing that says we can't go to bed in the clothes we have on. And I can sleep on the side here by the fire and just use the one cover. You can sleep on the other side under both covers."

Jennifer hugged her arms about her. It would work. It wasn't as if they had any real choice.

"He's an old man, Jenny," Logan continued, "and it's not as if I were going to try anything. After all, there's a witness," he finished with a gleam of mischief in his eyes.

She studied his face intently. Except for the dimple in his cheek, he seemed sincere enough. But could she really trust him? Obviously, when he had previously shared a bed with a woman, it had not been for sleep.

"Okay," she gave in grimly. "But stop calling me Jenny. And so help me, if you . . ."

"Don't worry," he grinned, holding up his hand in a mock promise. "I swear I won't lay a hand on you."

"You'd better not or I'll scream so loud there'll be an avalanche," Jennifer said firmly.

"I'll try to control myself. You might as well crawl under the covers and get some rest." Logan pushed her lightly toward the quilts. "I'm going to sit up for a while and relax."

Jennifer didn't argue with that. Although as she slipped under the covers, she glanced at him distrustfully. Then she noticed the bright red heart pillow at her head. Quickly she reached and exchanged it for the one closer to the fireplace.

"Good night, Jenny Glenn," Logan laughed, amused by her defiant gesture.

"Good night," Jennifer replied in an unfriendly voice.

She turned away from the fire to the darkness of the cabin. The silence of the room enveloped her until the night sounds took over: the slow stirrings

of their host in his bed, the slight creaking of the
rocker where Logan sat, and the crackling and pop-
ping of the fire. The loudest of all was the howling
of the wind outside as it shook and rattled at the
door. Jennifer felt like one of the little pigs with
the wolf outside huffing and puffing to blow the
house in.

As tired as she was, sleep eluded her. The hardness of the floor under the heavy quilt pushed at
her bones while the needlepoint pillow felt like a
lumpy rock under her head. She felt as if she was
waiting for something to happen, for Logan to crawl
under the covers with her. Her muscles tensed as
she heard him rise from his chair. She listened to the
ominous clunk of his boots coming off and hitting
the floor. Then there was the muffled sound of his
stocking feet as he walked toward her. She closed
her eyes quickly. He was lifting the top cover and . . .
that was all. Just the top cover, as he had promised.

She listened to his even breathing, holding hers
in apprehensively. But he just lay there on his back.

"Go to sleep, Jenny," he whispered softly. "Everything's going to be all right."

As if on command, her muscles relaxed and she
drifted off to sleep, feeling strangely safe and se-
cure.

"You sure are bright-eyed this morning," Logan
chided, studying her rapt face with interest.

"I can't believe how beautiful it is out here," Jennifer murmured, gazing around her at the white
wonderland of snow-covered trees and buildings.
"I don't even feel the cold. It's as if it were powder
instead of snow."

"There's no wind to bite into you," he said as he stacked a pile of firewood on his arm. "And snow is a pretty good insulator."

"What does that song call it?" she mused. "Oh, yes, a marshmallow world. Just look at the trees, all sugared up—and the pines up the hill have giant white gumdrops weighing down their branches!" There was no masking the delight in her face or voice. "Logan! Check out the size of the snowdrift by the shed!" she exclaimed with a joyous laugh.

"I was beginning to think you didn't remember my name," he said provocatively, walking over to stand by her side as she pointed out her latest find.

She glanced up at him briefly, glad that her cheeks were reddened by the nippy morning air and wouldn't reveal the warmth she felt just looking at the glow in his eyes.

"I love the way the snow swirls around the corner, like whipped frosting on a cake," she said quickly.

Logan smiled affectionately at her happy face, framed by the beige hood of her coat. "You either have a very sweet tooth or you didn't eat your breakfast this morning."

"Who wants oatmeal?" Jennifer grinned impishly. "A big dish of fresh snow with milk and sugar sounds much better!"

"Hmm. So you like snow," said Logan, setting the logs on the ground with a devilish gleam in his eye.

"Logan Taylor, don't you dare!" she squealed as she watched him pick up a clump of snow and ball it in his hand.

She turned just as he threw it, and it splattered on her back. He kept on pelting her as Jennifer fought desperately to retaliate. In seconds she was laughing and stumbling toward the cabin. A well-aimed snowball hit her in the leg, and she fell headlong into a towering drift. With Logan's assistance she rolled breathlessly over onto her back, giggling happily while he laughingly brushed the snow off her face. Her hood had fallen back, and the red-gold of her hair was accented by the whiteness of the snow she lay on. The corners of his eyes were crinkled into deep lines, his smile infinitely sexy as he paused above her body.

Suddenly the suggestiveness of her position struck Jennifer, and her smile slowly sobered at the same instant his did.

"No," she whispered. She began to struggle to get to her feet, but he quickly pinned her arms to her side.

"You've been expecting something like this ever since you met me," he said quietly with a look in his eyes that Jennifer had never seen before. "I wouldn't want to disappoint you."

Then his lips covered hers, persuasively and yet demanding a response that she wasn't willing to give. She fought her own desire to surrender to the rising, hungry feelings in her body, to yield to the erratic beat of her heart. She didn't want to enjoy the possessive tenderness of his kiss. He was like Brad; she should be revolted by his embrace. But resistance only increased her need to return the warmth and fire he was bestowing on her. Thoroughly ashamed of herself, she realized her lips were moving, responding to the exquisite pressure of his. Instinct had taken over, despite the tough lessons she had learned from experience.

Swiftly she turned her face away, tugging and pulling her arms free.

"Someone hurt you not too long ago." Logan studied her grimly as she moved farther away from him, scooting in the snow.

"What are you talking about?" Jennifer asked in a hoarse whisper.

"The man you left behind you."

"No," Jennifer answered firmly, anger flashing in her eyes. "He didn't hurt me—my stupidity and ignorance did. I didn't recognize a wolf when he was standing in front of me. I was blindsided by charm and good looks."

"And now?"

"And now I can see through any disguise. I just hope my sister can," she answered sarcastically.

He stepped toward her threateningly, then halted when a jingling noise pierced the winter air. Logan turned his head away from her, exhaling slowly before turning back to study her defiant expression.

"That'll be Carmichael. He's hitched up his horse to pull the Jeep out of the snow," he told her. "Better get your things together." As Jennifer started to walk away, he added, "Don't expect an apology. You enjoyed that kiss as much as I did, and you might as well admit it."

She stared at him, tears stinging her eyes. Why had she let him know she was attracted to him? Why had she given him that weapon?

She raced toward the cabin, not prepared to engage in a further battle of wits with Logan Taylor. She had salvaged some of her pride, and she was content with that.

* * *

After the Jeep was finally freed from the snow-bank, the short distance into Jackson, Wyoming, was covered in less than twenty minutes. Patches of sunlight filtered through the thick, billowy clouds to allow Jennifer to see the breathtaking mountains. As the highway made its last curve through a pass into town, she turned toward Logan, her thoughts full of questions she longed to ask even as she dreaded to break the silence. He beat her to it.

"Ready for a history lesson? The town got its name from an early trapper named Jackson," Logan informed her. "In those days, all valleys surrounded by mountains were called holes by the mountain men. Since Davey Jackson preferred trapping here over any other place, his partner referred to it as Jackson's Hole. Gradually the *S* was dropped to make it just plain Jackson Hole."

"What about the mountains, the Grand Tetons?" Jennifer asked, too interested in finding out more information to worry about the source. "Did they get their names from the Indians?"

"No, as a matter of fact," Logan replied, maneuvering the Jeep off the main street onto one of the side streets, "the three highest peaks in the range were named by French fur trappers. You're looking at Les Trois Tetons, which means the Three Breasts. The biggest one is Le Grand Teton."

"Oh." Jennifer's reply was an embarrassed murmur.

Logan grinned. "I'll take you to Sheila's house. She's probably down at the lodge, but at least we can drop your suitcases off." They turned a corner and slowed down in front of a picturesque pine log house. "There's her car," Logan went on, nodding toward a small blue car parked directly in front of them. "Looks like you're in luck."

A huge St. Bernard dog came bounding around the corner of the house, barking ferociously while its tail wagged frantically.

"That's the first member of your welcoming committee," Logan smiled as he opened his door and stepped out. His smile was so sexy, so disturbingly *male* that Jennifer remained temporarily motionless even after he turned away from her. She suddenly knew that this would not be the last time his stunning virility would get to her. At last, his "Down, Rags, down!" brought her hand to the door latch, and she walked around the Jeep to join him.

From the same side of the house that had produced the dog, now ecstatically licking Logan's face, came two more racing bundles, one in red and another in blue.

"Uncle Logan, Uncle Logan!" the blue one cried. He was larger and faster than the red one, who just reached them as the blue one flung himself into Logan's arms. "We was so worried!"

Jennifer watched with a mixture of disbelief and wonder at the exuberant welcome, as Logan scooped the red bundle up in his other arm, gazing laughingly into the bright eyes of both children.

"Mommy thaid you would come latht night," the red one announced. The lisp immediately brought a smile to Jennifer as she recognized the sweet face under the hood. It was Cindy.

"Your Aunt Jenny and I got stuck in a snowdrift," Logan explained, glancing over at Jennifer with a twinkling gleam in his brown eyes. "We had to wait until this morning before we could be pulled out. Now, where's your mother?"

"She's in the house," said Eric as Logan set the two of them onto the ground. "Did you stay in the snowdrift all night?"

"No, we stayed at a house nearby," Logan answered patiently, rubbing the red hood of the other affectionately. "Better say hello to your aunt before she decides you're not even glad to see her."

Dutifully the colorful pair turned to Jennifer and murmured their greeting. Well, she certainly couldn't expect much more, Jennifer thought. The children had only seen her a few times since Sheila had moved here. How were they to remember the hours she had held them as babies when her sister had stayed with their folks while Eric was overseas? She watched wistfully as they raced to the house, followed by the ungainly St. Bernard. She felt Logan's gaze on her and turned.

"A little surprised by their enthusiasm?" he mocked.

"Why should I be?" Jennifer shrugged lightly.

"They say dogs and children are instinctively right about people."

A stinging retort rose to Jennifer's lips but was held back as her sister came running from the house. Logan was amused at how well she stifled her annoyance as she turned to exchange hugs with Sheila.

Jennifer was grateful that Sheila took over the conversation, asking questions too fast to allow more than a yes or no answer. She had time to cool down and ignore the expression of faint triumph on his face. They were ushered into the house together, and the suitcases were dumped unceremoniously in the center of the tiny living room.

"There's coffee and sweet rolls in the kitchen," Sheila announced. "I'm sure you could do with a snack before lunch."

"Thanks, Sheila, but I have to get going," Logan replied. "I'm sure Mom is worried about me, so I'd better run over there before heading out to the ranch."

"Oh, you can call her from here," Sheila insisted, a pleading sparkle in her striking eyes.

"As she would tell you, hearing a voice over the phone is not the same as seeing someone in person," Logan said, his soft gaze trailing over Sheila's black hair to the teasing smile on her face. "Besides, you and Jenny will want to spend some time together before you have to go to the lodge."

"Jenny?" Sheila laughed, glancing mischievously at her sister when she heard Logan's nickname for her. "Oh, that must have endeared you to her heart."

"Jenny Glenn and I," he paused, gazing speculatively at the smoldering expression on Jennifer's face, "have made quite an impression on each other. It was a trip I wouldn't have missed for anything." One corner of his mouth curved mockingly. "I'd really better go now, Sheila."

"Don't go, Uncle Logan," Eric begged. "Cin and me want you to build a snow fort."

"Another time, maybe," he answered firmly but with a promising nod.

"Well, if you really must leave," Sheila sighed, taking his hands in hers, "then let me thank you for picking Jennifer up and bringing her here."

Jennifer watched with disgust as her sister reached up and brushed Logan's cheeks lightly with her lips.

So her worst fears were apparently true. Her sister was emotionally involved with this man. She longed to reach out and scratch his eyes when he finally turned to her in his round of good-byes.

"Good-bye, Jenny Glen. I'll see you," he promised.

"Jenny Glenn," Sheila echoed with a twinkle as the front door slammed behind the departing man.

"Please don't start." Jennifer made a face.

"Hey, it has a ring to it," her sister teased. "I wonder why we never called you that before."

"Probably because Mom didn't like nicknames, and neither do I." A frown creased her smooth forehead as she turned away from Sheila. It looked as if it didn't matter what Logan did; it was all right in her sister's eyes.

"Aunt Jenny, do you want to thee my room?" Cindy asked, "I have lotth of toyth and thingth."

"Later, Cindy," Sheila hushed her quickly, sensitive to her younger sister's pensive mood. "You and Eric run out and play for a while. And please take Rags with you."

In seconds she had them bustled out the door and had turned back to Jennifer.

"Come on. Let's go into the kitchen and get some of that coffee. Then you can tell me everything," Sheila said sympathetically, taking Jennifer by the arm and leading her through the living room.

Jennifer didn't tell her everything. She wasn't about to mention her misgivings about Logan Taylor or say anything about the embarrassing situation the previous night and the following scene in the morning. Sheila seemed to hold a high opinion of him, one that Jennifer didn't want to alter. As quickly as possible she changed the subject of their conversation to Sheila, the children, and the lodge where Sheila worked.

Her sister explained her reluctance to constantly shuffle the children to Eric's parents on the weekends and during school vacations. His parents were elderly, and her two live wires were a handful for them. Jennifer gladly volunteered to take care of them and fill in occasionally at the lodge to give Sheila more free time.

In the days that followed, they developed a casual routine that brought Jennifer and her sister closer together, as well as Jennifer and the children. It was fun messing around in the kitchen again, fixing meals for a family, taking care of numerous little household chores that had become a burden for Sheila.

Jennifer almost never thought about Brad Stevenson, but getting Logan Taylor out of her mind wasn't that easy. Cindy and Eric were forever saying, "Uncle Logan this" or "Uncle Logan that," or Sheila chimed in with "Logan suggested" or "Logan said."

Unwanted reminders of that aggravating man were ever present. But in the eight days that she'd been in Jackson, Jennifer had not been subjected to his unwanted presence. She decided she should be grateful for that. At least she wouldn't have to put up with that knowing smile of his, although she couldn't deny that his image haunted her.

When Sheila had a free afternoon, she insisted that Jennifer spend some time taking care of her personal chores. Since she hadn't even started her Christmas shopping, Jennifer reluctantly agreed. The children would be easy to buy for, but she wanted to take more time selecting just the right present for her sister. Her previous expeditions into town had been in the company of Cindy and Eric, who got impatient with idle wandering through the stores. As it was, Jennifer went to three shops before she found a sweater and pants in blue that were perfect for Sheila.

With the gift-wrapped package under her arm, Jennifer dashed across the street to the town square, pausing briefly in front of the antlered archway that marked the entrance. She had seen it several times, but to Eric and Cindy it was nothing new, not worth the extra time that Jennifer had longed for to study it.

The intricate network of interlocking antlers that formed this strange arch amazed her. She had soon learned that antlers and trophy heads were commonplace decorations in Jackson; even the lodge where Sheila worked had several large trophies of bighorn sheep in the lobby, appropriately, since its name was Big Horn Lodge. But this arch was a magnificent work.

"Don't try to count them, because there's too many," a voice behind her spoke.

Jennifer spun around to see Logan Taylor standing beside her, gazing down at her with a speculative gleam in his eye.

"I wasn't counting," she replied abruptly.

"Just admiring our quaint Western novelty?" he retorted just a trifle sarcastically.

"Yes, if you must know. I find it fascinating," Jennifer answered.

"Most people do. They're all elk antlers, you know."

"How did they find so many?" she mused, looking once again at the arch.

"The winter refuge of the elk is just north of Jackson Hole. The males shed their antlers once a year, just like deer," Logan explained.

She was uncomfortably aware of his eyes on her, feeling again the quickening of her pulse.

"Oh, right. I heard someone mention the refuge, but I hadn't really thought too much about it. How many elk are out there?" Her voice had a nervous lilt to it as she tried to keep the conversation on an impersonal level.

"From six to eight thousand."

"That many?" Jennifer exclaimed. "What do they do with all the horns?"

"Only the bull elk have antlers," Logan replied. "Each spring the Boy Scouts gather the antlers and have an auction here on the town square, with the proceeds going towards scouting activities." He stopped abruptly as she turned to face him. She felt caught by his demanding gaze. "It's cold standing here on the corner," he finally said. "Come have a cup of hot chocolate with me?"

"I . . ." She shook her head hesitantly. She didn't want to be with him or get any closer or his maleness would arouse that physical attraction she tried to stifle.

"Afraid?"

"Of course not!" Jennifer retorted, suddenly finding the voice that had forsaken her a minute ago.

"We'll go to the public restaurant down the street," Logan said, with an emphasis on *public*. "You can see the skiers come down Snow King Mountain."

"All right," Jennifer gave in reluctantly, unable to think of an excuse not to go. It occurred to her that secretly she wanted to go with him, but she quelled the thought.

His arm rested lightly and naturally across her waist in back. Despite the thickness of her coat she could feel the flat of his hand guiding her along.

"I see you're still wearing those useless boots," he said, his smile teasing.

"The sidewalks are all shoveled, and it didn't seem necessary to wear my new ones," Jennifer replied evenly.

"Then you did get some real boots." His eyes took in her rosy red cheeks. . . . Was she blushing?

"They're so big I feel like a lumberjack in them," she laughed.

"And you once accused me of being vain, Jenny Glenn," Logan baited her lightly as he turned her toward the restaurant door.

"Stop calling me that!" she answered in a lowered voice, annoyed that she had succumbed to his easy charm and hating herself for even reacting to his affectionate abbreviation of her name. *"Arrogant* is a better word than *vain* for you."

"Geez, I thought that you had mellowed towards me," he said with false regret as he pulled out a chair for her, facing the window near the front. "Absence makes the heart grow fonder, right?"

"I wish," she retorted frostily as soon as Logan was seated opposite her. At the quizzical rise of his eyebrow, Jennifer explained, "Sheila always talks about your many virtues, and the kids just go on and on about their 'Uncle Logan.' Why do they call you uncle? Whose idea was that?"

The waitress came at that moment, delaying Logan's answer until after he had ordered for them.

"That was Cindi and Eric's idea. Sheila didn't see any harm in it and neither did I." His expression was solemn as he answered. "I think they want me to be an honorary member of the family. They take it seriously, and so do I."

The waitress returned, setting down two cups of hot chocolate with swirling dabs of whipped cream floating on top. Wordlessly Jennifer concentrated on hers, feeling rebuked by his statement and knowing her question had been asked almost as a defense against his magnetism. She glanced at him, taking in the light brown sweater with the band of white circling the brown stag's head. There was a suggestion of hard muscle underneath the knitted image, and beneath the smiling face, a determination to succeed. Brad had been ambitious, too, but with a streak of cunning in him that Jennifer had just now recognized, because she suddenly realized it was absent in Logan.

"You try so hard to figure me out, Jenny. Why don't you just accept what you see?" Logan asked softly.

"Once bitten, twice shy," she answered brightly, trying to laugh at the wariness he always aroused in her.

"Well, I'm not trying to bite you." Jennifer tried to catch where the slight inflection of his voice placed the emphasis, on *bite* or on *you*. A strange sinking feeling told her it was on the latter.

"Are you saying that you don't try to score with every girl you meet?" she asked, using a smile to hide the cutting tone of her voice.

"Are you asking specifically about strawberry blondes or girls in general?" His knowing smile lit an angry fire in her brown eyes. "Don't tell me you think that kiss in the snow made you a fallen woman. It was only a kiss, nothing more."

She longed to reach across the small table and slap that mocking smile off Logan's face. At his amused laugh, Jennifer flashed a burning glance toward him.

"Poor Jenny Glenn." Logan smiled, a dancing gleam in his own eyes. "So much righteous indignation and no one to blame but yourself. All I did was kiss you once. But I really enjoyed erasing that prissy look from your face."

"Oh, please. Find someone else to tease, because I'm really not amused." Determinedly she controlled her temper as she gathered up her bag and gloves to leave.

"Finish your hot chocolate, Jennifer." Logan's expression was unchanged, but there was a hardening in his gaze. An eyebrow raised at her indecision. He would probably think it was funny if she stomped out the door right now, in spite of his order for her to stay, Jennifer thought. With deliberately controlled movements, she replaced her gloves and purse on the table. She directed her attention to the window, where she watched the swift lines of skiers coming down Snow King.

"Do you ski?" Logan asked.

"Yes," Jennifer replied calmly, her gaze remaining on the skiers as she sipped the hot chocolate.

"Do you ski well?"

"I'm an experienced amateur," she answered.

"We'll have to make sure you get the chance to try the slopes while you're here." Logan's voice was friendly, but Jennifer wasn't about to be drawn out by him.

"I don't need an escort to go skiing." Her glance as it flicked over him was coolly dismissive.

She felt the amused speculation of his gaze as he replaced his cup in its saucer.

"What you're really saying is that you don't need me, Jenny Glenn. But don't hit the slopes alone the first time. Go with someone if you can." For all the concern in his words, the tone of his voice was completely indifferent. "If you're ready, let's go. My car's outside, and I wanted to talk to Sheila. Believe me, that's my only motive for taking you home."

His suddenly casual attitude irritated Jennifer. Logan Taylor seemed to want to make it clear to her that she wasn't all that important to him. Her cheeks were flushed with anger and embarrassment as they left. She silently vowed to treat him as lightly as he treated her.

Chapter Four

"Here's the car," Logan said, steadying Jennifer's elbow as they stepped off the pavement onto the snow-packed street.

Her gaze rose from the path of her feet to the brand-new white Mercedes parked beside them. She had been expecting the Jeep, and her surprise must have registered on her face.

"I store it in the winter just taking it out a few times to keep it in condition. Besides, I can't find it in a snowdrift," he joked, opening the car door to assist Jennifer inside.

She couldn't help admiring the opulent black interior as she slid into the low seat. Her hand trailed lightly over the leather upholstery as Logan walked around the car to enter on the driver's side. Quickly Jennifer placed her hand primly in her lap. She knew he was waiting for her reaction to the car. He obviously expected her to be impressed.

"I don't see how you could possibly have trouble finding it." Jennifer smiled with saccharine sweetness. "All you have to do is look inside to see it's as black as your heart."

His rich, warm laugh filled the car. His gloved finger flicked her cheek lightly as he spoke. "I knew you couldn't keep that tongue of yours still for long."

The deeply creased lines of amusement remained in his cheeks as he started the car and backed it out of its parking place. As she stared out the side window, Jennifer mentally cursed herself. She should have known he couldn't care less whether she was impressed by the car. He had only wanted to get a rise out of her, and he had succeeded.

Minutes later they had arrived at their destination and Logan was instantly pounced on by the children as he assisted her with her packages.

"Are you bringing our Christmas presents already?" Eric demanded, his blue eyes wide as he inspected the brightly wrapped gifts in Logan's arms.

"Nope. These are presents Jenny's bought. I'm just carrying them for her," Logan replied, ruffling the dark hair on the boy's head.

"We got our tree, Uncle Logan," Cindy chattered brightly. "It'th out in the waundry room. Mommy thaid it had to get warm before we could decorate it. Come thee it, please."

"You come too, Aunt Jenny," Eric pleaded, tugging her hand.

"Jennifer," she corrected him, with a trace of exasperation at the children's insistence on copying Logan.

"Yeth, Aunt Jenny, you come, too," Cindy added her voice to her brother's.

"Later," she promised. The last thing Jennifer wanted was to be stuck in the small laundry room with Logan.

"Logan!" Sheila's startled voice came from the hallway. Her raven hair was piled under a towel with a few wet locks peeping out underneath. "I didn't expect to see you this afternoon."

"There was something I wanted to tell you." His expression was serious as he faced Jennifer's sister, not the mockingly amused one that he invariably showed her. "But first, I'm going to be dragged off to see your tree."

"Such as it is," Sheila murmured to Jennifer as she watched him being hustled out of the room by her children. She glanced at Jennifer with a resigned and loving smile. "The kids picked it out. On one side there's a two-foot-wide hole with no branches. The rest of the tree looks as if it's suffering from malnutrition. Cindy said nobody would buy that tree, and it would be all alone on Christmas if we didn't take it. Naturally we did."

"Naturally," Jennifer laughed, yet touched by the totally unselfish gesture of the young child.

"All your shopping done?" her sister asked, busily putting away some of the scattered toys as Jennifer removed her parka and hung it in the closet. "I never dreamed you'd bring Logan home with you or I would have waited to wash my hair."

"I ran into him downtown," Jennifer explained hurriedly, lest her sister think she had intended to meet him. "He insisted on giving me a ride home."

"That was nice of him."

"Yes," Jennifer agreed with a noticeable lack of enthusiasm.

Her sister stared absently at the door of the laundryroom, her head tilted to one side in contemplation. Jennifer tucked her red-gold hair behind her ears and out of her face as she walked into the small kitchen.

"You know, sometimes I feel guilty about the way the children demand so much of Logan's attention," Sheila mused aloud. "But he seems to enjoy it." She turned abruptly toward her sister. "Remember that game we used to play where we took the first letter of a person's name and thought of adjectives to describe them? Every time I think about Logan, it's always *loyal,* and *loving.* He's done so much to help the children and me."

The words were so far from Jennifer's *lawless, lordly,* and *a Lothario* that she nearly choked.

"How about a cup of coffee?" she hurriedly asked her dark-haired sister before the subject took a firm hold of the conversation.

"Okay. I'll take half a cup," Logan said, stopping in the kitchen doorway.

"What did you think of that magnificent specimen of a Christmas tree?" Sheila laughed as she seated herself at the small wooden breakfast table in the kitchen.

"Cindy thinks it's perfect," Logan said with a dubious shake of his head. "But some of those branches aren't heavy enough to even hold an ornament."

He lowered his tall frame onto one of the table's chairs, spreading his legs in front of him so that Jennifer had to step across them to set the coffee down. Her hand trembled as she did so, but she refused to meet his glance. The two children entered the room as his last sentence died away.

"Let's decorate the tree and make it pretty," Cindy insisted, hurrying over to stand beside Logan.

"But if the branches snap when we put the lights on," Eric began fearfully, "how can we decorate it?"

"We can make garlands of popcorn and berries, and paper chains," Jennifer spoke up quickly as the corners of Cindy's mouth began to droop.

"Just make sure that Rags doesn't decide to snack on the popcorn," Logan teased.

"Ragth hathn't theen our tree yet," Cindy lisped with a yelp. "Come on, Eric, let'th go get him."

A silence crept lightly into the room after the children had dashed outside to find their St. Bernard. Logan straightened, leaning his elbows on the table, holding his cup with both hands. Jennifer watched him glance speculatively at her sister before his head turned back to the table. He took a swig of hot coffee before his low baritone voice broke the growing silence.

"I dropped into the lodge this morning." Logan studied Sheila out of the corner of his eye. "You'll never guess who was checking in—Dirk Hamilton."

Sheila's face grew as white as the towel around her head. Her hand trembled slightly as she raised her cup to her mouth in a struggle for nonchalance.

"Really?" her voice broke. "I wonder what he's doing here at this time of the year?"

"He said he wanted to do some winter landscapes of the Tetons." Jennifer was struck by the concern that was etched in his face as Logan watched her sister's reaction. "Listen, Sheila," he went on quickly as she rose from the table and walked over to the sink, "if you want me to, I'll ask him to stay somewhere else."

"Don't be ridiculous, Logan," put in Sheila— too quickly, Jennifer thought, and with forced lightness. "Why should he pay some other motel when he can pay us? Besides, it just doesn't matter to me anymore. As a matter of fact, I was going to take Jennifer down to the lodge with me tomorrow, to sort of show her the ropes. It's been a while since the children spent a day with Eric's parents." Sheila paused; then she turned away from the sink and toward the intense gaze that was now fixed on her. "Jennifer could take over some of the front desk duties."

Jennifer suddenly felt Logan's eyes on her, his expression harsh and forbidding. She realized she was practically gaping at Sheila's statement. After all, they had only discussed her filling in on an emergency basis, if one of the maids became ill or something. Now it sounded like a full time job. And who was Dirk Hamilton? Glancing at her sister, Jennifer saw the almost pleading expression in her blue eyes. Logan continued to stare at her, waiting for her to make some sort of comment.

"It . . . it sounds fine to me," she stammered as Sheila silently breathed her relief. Logan didn't seem convinced of her enthusiasm, so she added, with an effort at lightness, "I was beginning to wish for something else to do anyway. I spent an awful lot of money on that business degree. Don't want to waste it."

"Is that the way you want to handle it, Sheila?" Logan asked, quietly but with sharpness.

Jennifer noticed that Sheila seemed visibly nervous under Logan's scrutiny.

"She just said so, Logan," Jennifer said quickly before her sister lost her composure.

Logan's mouth closed in a grim line, accenting his firm jawline.

"I think you're making a mistake," was his only comment as he rose from his chair. "But I don't have the time to discuss it now."

Jennifer was aware that Logan was walking to the door, even managed to murmur her thanks for the ride home, but her attention was focused on the obvious turmoil that her sister was experiencing. As the sound of the door closing behind Logan echoed into the kitchen, Sheila's movements became more anxious.

"I'd better set my hair before it dries," she said quickly, a fluttering hand touching the towel briefly.

"Who's Dirk Hamilton, Sheila?"

"Just an artist," her sister replied—very casually. "He was here this last summer, doing some painting." At that moment the two children and the St. Bernard came bursting through the door. "How many times have I told you to keep that dog out of the house when he's all muddy!" The unusually strident tone of their mother's voice stopped both children. "You heard me. Get him out of here at once," she ended in a more controlled voice.

The children were quick to obey. But Jennifer's heart was tugged painfully by the crestfallen and confused expressions on their young faces. A glance at Sheila told her that her sister regretted the outburst.

"Sheila?" Her hand brushed a straying strand of her red-gold bangs away from her eyes.

"Look, he was interested in some of my portraits, that's all," Sheila said sharply, with bitterness in her words. "I've never asked you to tell me about Brad, so please . . . I just don't want to talk about it!"

For the first time that Jennifer could remember, there was a strained silence between them, one that she didn't know how to bridge and her sister refused to.

Jennifer's front desk duties weren't exactly difficult, but the flow of holiday skiers was never-ending. She couldn't suppress her curiosity about the occupant of Room 228, Dirk Hamilton, but so far, he hadn't appeared at the desk. She had just paused during a lull to chat with Carol, whose switchboard had also ceased to light up insistently, when a noise from the counter drew her attention.

A stocky man neither tall nor short, with thick black hair, was studying her with analytical thoroughness. She stepped toward him, a polite smile curving her lips, when she noticed Logan enter the lodge. His brown eyes scanned the lobby quickly, coming to rest on the man in front of her. Immediately his purposeful stride brought him toward them.

"Morning, Dirk." His tanned hand reached out toward the other man in polite greeting.

So this is Dirk Hamilton, Jennifer thought in a rather stunned silence. Although Logan was several inches taller, the other man's hand was nearly as large as his—hardly the hand and fingers of an artist. Their eyes fixed boldly on each other, holding a clear challenge. Jennifer was struck by the assured way that Logan measured the man, neither openly friendly nor hostile, but he seemed to be weighing his advantages and disadvantages, as if they were about to do battle.

"I just thought I'd check to see when you wanted

to set up your trip into the Tetons," Logan said casually.

"Whenever's convenient." The answer was indifferent, as was Dirk's face as he turned it back toward the silent Jennifer. His gaze traveled over her face and hair once again, cool, without any apparent interest in her. "You're Jennifer."

"Y-yes," she managed, surprised that he could possibly know who she was.

"I saw your portrait. Sheila didn't capture the color of your hair—golden like the sun with a few streaks of a fiery sunset. Copper's too brash a color. Yours is much softer. Sets off your angelic features."

Jennifer flushed lightly at his appraisal, but flashed a warning look at the mocking gaze of Logan Taylor.

"The features may be angelic, Dirk," Logan drawled, "but not the girl. Well, maybe she's half angel. The rest is pure elf."

"I'm Dirk Hamilton. Maybe Sheila mentioned me?" There was more than a hint of a question as the artist offered his hand to Jennifer.

"No, I'm sorry she hasn't," she answered, placing her own slim hand in his politely. A flicker of something that resembled pain crossed his face, causing Jennifer to add, "That is, she did say you were interested in some of the portraits she's done. Is that where you saw mine?"

"Yes. Your hair was in pigtails then, much longer than it is now. There was expression of hidden laughter in your eyes that captivated me," he answered. He studied her features, as if sizing them up against a remembered painting.

"Oh, yes, Sheila did that one several years ago,"

Jennifer smiled widely. Now that Dirk had turned toward her, it was her turn to study his face. His features weren't handsome, but strong and powerful, yet lacking the magnetism that was so apparent in every line of Logan's face. He looked—Jennifer hesitated—dependable. Yes, that was the word, *dependable.*

"I take it Sheila isn't working the desk anymore." Dirk cast a quizzical glance toward Logan.

"She asked Jenny to take over," Logan replied, "for now, anyway."

Neither Dirk nor Jennifer missed the casual emphasis on the last phrase, which left no doubt that the artist was the cause of the change.

Dirk's glance returned to Jennifer. This time his inspection was more personal, including a fast look at the ringless fingers on her left hand.

"What's your opinion of artists, Jennifer?" Dirk asked.

"I'd better like them," she answered with a flustered wave of her hand. She was irritated by the way Logan was watching her with a disapproving glint in his eyes. She knew from the conversation between Logan and Sheila yesterday that Dirk's sudden appearance at the lodge had upset them both. After all, she was old enough to make her own judgments about people, and she was beginning to like this man. "After all, my sister's an artist," she finished before the lull became too long.

"Is she?" Dirk retorted with unexpected sarcasm. "Gee, I was under the impression that she was a struggling widow with two young children. I understood painting was a frivolous pastime to be indulged in when there was nothing left to do."

"Dirk, why don't we go into the café and discuss your trip?" Logan suggested, intervening quickly before Jennifer could reply. "You can give me an idea of some of the places you want to go."

Dirk removed a cigarette from his pocket and tapped it lightly on the No Smoking sign before placing it between his lips. He didn't light it, but it was clear he'd done it to annoy Logan.

"Yes, why don't we? Then you can begin to use your vast organizing abilities and persuasive charm to get me packed up and on my way, huh?"

Logan chuckled at Dirk's reply. It was a warm, deep sound, with no trace of anger. "Your bitterness is showing," he said as he moved aside for Dirk to precede him into the coffee shop.

A rush of pity surged through Jennifer's heart for the overmatched artist, despite his biting criticism of her sister.

In the week that followed, Jennifer was surprised at how skillfully her sister avoided Dirk Hamilton. She decided Sheila had a sixth sense about the man, usually disappearing minutes before he entered a room. As for Dirk, the name *Sheila* wasn't even in his vocabulary. He always stopped and exchanged some brief conversation with Jennifer when he saw her—nothing ever personal, just passing the time of day.

What little information Jennifer had came from Carol, the switchboard operator. She was about Jennifer's age, with light brown hair and a plump figure. The two often chatted during the slower hours, and one afternoon, after Dirk Hamilton had dropped his key off at the desk with Jennifer,

Carol asked her if Sheila was glad that Mr. Hamilton had come back.

Jennifer replied that she really didn't know, and asked why Carol wondered if she was.

"Well, last summer she seemed to be having such a good time with him. I mean, you'd see them having coffee or lunch together during the day, and he usually took her home at nights. For a while, some of us thought maybe there was something going on between them," Carol answered rather hesitantly. "Not that we gossiped about them or anything. It's just that your sister is such a nice person and so easy to work for. It's so sad to think about her being a widow with two children, you know, and it would be nice for her to find someone again."

Jennifer agreed, and waited for Carol to tell her more.

"But one day he just checked out and that was it. Of course, Logan—I mean, Mr. Taylor"—the girl blushed fiercely over her error—"was away most of the time that Mr. Hamilton stayed here."

"What's that got to do with it?" Jennifer asked bluntly, wanting to find out more about her sister's involvement with this man.

"Probably just coincidence." Carol shrugged lightly before leaning back in her chair to sigh. "Mr. Taylor really is something, though. I couldn't blame your sister if she had a crush on him. Practically everyone within a hundred miles has at one time or another, whether they admit it or not. I mean, every female who notices him tries to get him to notice her back."

"And if he does?" Jennifer had difficulty hiding the sarcasm in her words.

"Then there's lots of dates, and the lucky girl gets to enjoy those gorgeous smiles of his and that sexy way he has of looking at you as if you were the only person in the room." Carol gazed dreamily at nothing while Jennifer shivered, remembering her own reaction to his attentions. "Lately," she continued, snapping out of her romantic reverie, "since your sister took over the lodge, there haven't been so many girls around. Not that anyone has conceded victory to her, you understand."

"Of course," Jennifer replied, grateful that the switchboard had begun to light up, which ended the uncomfortable conversation.

She tugged viciously at her hair, twisting the rubber band around half of it before glancing down at the St. Bernard dog sprawled in the doorway. Lifting an eyelid, he gazed at her sadly through bloodshot eyes.

"Please don't tell me how babyish I look with my hair in pigtails, Rags," Jennifer said, stepping gingerly over his legs, hoping he wouldn't suddenly decide to get up and send her sprawling with his bulk. "I have to wash those sweaters, and this hair just falls in my face."

She hurried on past him into the kitchen, where her sweaters were piled up beside the sink. Lethargically the dog rose, padded into the kitchen, and flopped beside her feet.

"So you decided to keep me company." She looked down into his mournful face, cocking her head to one side. Sighing deeply, Jennifer turned back to the sink and immersed the olive sweater in the sudsy water. "What a way to spend my day off, doing hand laundry talking to a bored dog. Well, thanks for the show of interest anyway, Rags." The dog thumped his tail twice before closing his eyes again.

It was midweek, time for a break before the week-end warriors descended on the lodge for a few days of skiing. She had planned to take care of all the time-consuming tasks that she'd put off. But now that she was actually getting started, they all seemed so pointless.

The jingling of bells outside drifted into the house. It didn't seem possible that Christmas was just next week. Cindy and Eric reminded her often enough, and with the snowfall this season, a white Christmas was a sure thing. But her holiday spirit just wasn't there. She couldn't deny her inner empti-ness or ignore it. Those jingling bells put nostalgic pictures in her mind of childhood sleigh rides in the snow behind her father's two plowhorses. This was her first Christmas away from her parents. Maybe that's why she felt so depressed, Jennifer decided.

Refusing to let herself succumb to melancholy, she immediately began singing "Jingle Bells" with as much enthusiasm as she could muster. A knock-ing at the front door reduced the sound to a hum as she hurriedly wiped her hands dry and followed Rags to the door.

She opened the door and stopped humming. There, parked by the curb, was a dark bay horse with a blaze face, hitched up to a shiny black swan sleigh. Her rounded eyes turned to the man who braced himself casually on one side of the door with his outstretched arm. Logan's brown eyes were studying her lazily.

Large flakes of snow drifted down between them

while Jennifer looked at him with amazement. His light brown hair was ruffled by the breeze, and she felt an inexplicable longing to reach out and smooth it into place. But the way his eyes were regarding her from beneath the gold-tipped lashes frightened away that thought. The wind-blown hair might have looked boyish, but the strong, tanned features were strictly male.

"Well?" Jennifer breathed unevenly, trying for a frosty indifference and settling for a melting warmth.

"Aren't your ears on straight, or is it your pigtails that are crooked?" At his grin, Jennifer's hand rushed up to her hair.

"The pigtails, I think," she answered, feeling a blush of embarrassment rush into her cheeks. She glanced toward the sleigh. "Is that yours?"

"I borrowed it from a friend," Logan replied. His eyes twinkled with amusement at her astonishment. "I thought it would be fun to go for a ride out to the elk refuge."

"Oh, but the children aren't home from school yet. They won't be home for several hours. Vacation doesn't start until the weekend."

"I know."

"Well then, why . . ." Jennifer began, only to be silenced by his laughter. She straightened indignantly. "I don't see what's so funny."

"I know I'm good and kind and loving," Logan mocked, "and a perfect example for the children. But this afternoon I decided to play the role you chose to case me in—the wolf to Little Red Riding Hood." He tugged a red-gold pigtail mischievously. "Or would you prefer to be Rudolph and guide my sleigh?"

She hesitated, her gaze on the horse and sleigh, picturing a ride through the snow. But with Logan? Wasn't that asking for trouble?

"Well, Jenny Glenn? Dolly's getting impatient. Will you come with me?" His low voice added its own persuasive magic.

"Yes," she answered breathlessly before she could change her mind.

"Hurry up, then. Get your coat. I'll wait for you by the sled." He settled a brown Stetson firmly on his head before he retreated from the door.

With a quickness that surprised her, Jennifer grabbed her coat out of the closet, stuffed a pair of mittens in a pocket, pulled on her snow boots, and even snagged earmuffs as she bustled out the door. Logan was waiting beside the sleigh to give her a hand up to the seat. She was pulling her mittens on as he crawled up beside her from the opposite side. He reached down and unfolded a heavy blanket. The seat wasn't very wide, and Jennifer stiffened as his arm brushed her. With a barely concealed smile, he handed her a corner of the blanket, taking in the apprehensive expression on her face.

"Here, tuck this in around you," he instructed. "It'll keep your legs warm."

She did as she was told while he took the opposite side and tucked it around himself before taking the reins and clucking to the horse. For the first few blocks, Jennifer was uneasily aware of the man beside her, and the pressure of his arms and legs against hers, but she relaxed, gradually, enjoying the cheerful ringing of the bells on the horse's harness. Huge flakes of snow seemed to float in

the air around them, mixing with the puffy clouds
from their own breath. Then they were out of town,
the sleigh's runners skimming effortlessly over the
snow-packed road.

Chapter Five

The soft silence of the falling snow gave Jennifer a magical feeling of going back in time. The foothills of the Tetons closed in around them, their tops hidden by low clouds. She didn't even have to close her eyes to capture the feeling of days gone by.

"Can't you just picture what it was like years ago?" Jennifer whispered very low, not wanting to break the spell. "Before cars and civilization moved in?"

"Mother Earth," Logan agreed quietly. "In all its untouched beauty. Would you have enjoyed being a pioneer?"

"Only if I were a boy!" She made a playful face at him.

Logan eyed her with apparent dismay. "Don't you know that Wyoming was the first state in the Union to grant political, civil, and economic equality to women? And that was back when we were still a territory. You'll find that Wyoming men respect and appreciate women, and that's not just some line, either."

Jennifer remained silent when he finished, stunned by his unexpected speech.

"What's the matter, Jenny Glenn? Didn't expect to hear that from a womanizer?" She couldn't help turning crimson at his astuteness. "Despite all the big talk, men need women more than they even admit. Body and soul." A shiver raced up Jennifer's back at his words. Could he feel that way about a woman? she wondered, glancing at him from the corner of her eye.

His profile beneath the wide brim of his Stetson was deeply etched against the snowy backdrop. His expression was pensive as he sensed her gaze and turned to meet it, and his brown eyes seemed much darker when they looked into hers. Her pulse increased at an alarming rate as the corners of his mouth curved into a tender smile. She looked quickly away before she revealed too much of what she was feeling.

"That sounds like a description of love, Logan." She spoke brightly in an effort to stop the tumultuous hammering of her heart. "Are you actually familiar with this emotion?"

His answering chuckle was short but laced with amusement.

"What if I said I was waiting for the ghost of someone's former lover to fade before revealing my feelings to the woman I cherish and adore? No, I can see you wouldn't believe a tale like that. Not that you wouldn't like to see me brought to my knees by a woman." Logan pulled the horse to a halt, then turned sideways in the seat, settling an arm along the back near Jennifer. He winked at her. "My mother says I'm sampling the fruits so that at harvest time I'll be able to pick the most delectable one."

"And she made you into the man you are today," she said pointedly. Her mind returned to his remark about the ghost of someone's former lover. Did he mean Sheila's late husband, Eric? It wasn't a question she wanted to ask.

"Oh, it's not so bad. Isn't that what the battle of the sexes is all about? Someone wins, someone loses." His wolfish grin left no doubt as to who he thought was winning.

Anger swept through Jennifer, stiffening her back and tilting her head defiantly.

"Mind if I ask if you've been in love before?" Logan continued. "Or was that man back in Minneapolis just an experiment?"

"That's none of your business!"

"Couldn't have been love, because I only see anger in your eyes." He seemed to be amused once again by her display of temper.

"How could Sheila tell you about that?" Jennifer fumed.

"Believe me, I only got the sketchiest details, and that was because I was there when you phoned in the middle of the night."

She eyed him skeptically, and in spite of his exaggerated air of innocence, she believed him. Mostly because she didn't think her sister would ever reveal the entire story to a complete stranger.

"What were you doing with Sheila at that hour—sampling fruit?" Her voice held an edge.

"Darling Jenny," Logan sighed, "that statement hurts your sister's reputation more than mine."

"You seemed to be saying that there wasn't any

double standard in Wyoming for women," Jennifer observed with deadly calm. Inwardly she seethed at his remark about her sister, but outwardly she couldn't resist another jab at his male ego.

"We recognize equality, but we honor propriety." Logan's amused exasperation was beginning to show the edges of anger, even though carefully controlled. "That's from the pioneer days, too, I guess."

The mare moved restlessly against the traces, no longer content to stand patiently in the snow. Logan slapped the reins lightly on her rump, and the horse started off at a slow trot. The sleigh passed several sheds filled with hay before Jennifer was able to swallow enough pride to speak.

"I apologize. I spoke out of line back there, and I just want you to know I'm grateful for everything you've done for Sheila—and the children."

"And I apologize for teasing you." He turned on the full charm of his smile as his hand, resting on the back of the seat, reached out and tugged her hair. "But then, you were being pretty sassy." His hand rested momentarily on her shoulder, sending a sensual heat through her before it returned to the reins as he slowed the horse to a walk. Logan's gaze was now directed in front of them. "We've reached our destination, Jenny. There's your elk."

She had been so engrossed in their conversation and aware only of the man beside her that she had paid no attention at all to their surroundings. Looking forward, Jennifer saw a large blotch of brown in the distance. Nearer to them was another hay shed and a smaller building with two wagons and teams of horses standing beside it.

"The Jaycees and the refuge operate a sleigh

ride to the elk herd," Logan explained following her questioning gaze. "Tourists love it."

A man walked out of the small building and waved a friendly hello to them. Logan reined their horse to a halt and waited until the man walked up to their sleigh.

"Hi, Frank." Logan smiled. "Thought I'd take Ms. Glenn for a closer look at the herd."

"Sure, go ahead." The man smiled. "Probably won't be able to get too close, though. They're kinda skittish, especially around a strange sled."

"Okay, we'll be careful," Logan nodded before clicking to the horse.

As they drew closer, Jennifer was able to distinguish individual elk amid the sea of brown. Some were lying down, some were standing, some were grazing, and some were simply watching them approach. She sat in awed silence, and then two females reared at each other, hooves striking out, disputing ownership of a salt lick. A big bull elk with an enormous rack of antlers eyed them haughtily.

"Impressive animals, aren't they? The males stand about five feet tall at the shoulder and top out around a thousand pounds. The females are smaller. The males with the short, spiked antlers are usually one or two years old. The older bulls have five or six points on each antler." Logan's low voice came from just behind her ear.

"Where do they all come from?" Jennifer wished her unsettling awareness of his closeness would go away.

"Mostly from Yellowstone and Grand Teton, the national parks to the north. At the first good snow they migrate down here to the refuge."

"Have they always come here?"

"No, they used to travel farther south to the plains around Rock Springs. In the 1880s, when ranching operations cut their winter forage to practically nothing, they began starving to death. One spring it was said you could walk for miles on the carcasses of dead elk. Plus the elk had to contend with hunters called tuskers, who killed them only for their teeth, which were prized by the Elks Lodge. That was finally outlawed and the refuge established by Congress in 1913."

An eerie, yapping wail broke out from the hillside, joined by several other equally mournful voices. The uncanny howl, like an animal in pain, sent shivers down Jennifer's spine. She glanced at Logan apprehensively.

"Don't like the serenade? It's coyotes. They're useful scavengers, cleaning up the carcasses of dead animals."

"Don't they attack the herd?"

"They don't need to. There are always crippled and wounded elk that make their way to the refuge after hunting season. Some make it through the winter, but others are too weak to survive. Others die simply from old age. The coyotes and other scavengers like the raven live well."

"How horrible!" Jennifer shuddered.

"Just the balance of nature," Logan reasoned, but with a sympathetic smile. "Look there on the hillside." His arm reached around her to point. She trembled, but this time not because of the coyotes. "There's the choir by that stand of pines."

She looked obediently in the direction, knowing that he must be able to feel the quaking of her body even through her coat.

"Are you cold, Jenny?"

Her heart leaped at his words and the sudden tightening of his arm around her shoulder. Although she stiffened slightly, he pulled her closer to him, his hand rubbing her shoulders briskly.

"We'd better head home and get you in front of a warm fire," he said calmly, either ignoring her resistance or unaware of it as he urged the mare into a trot. "You don't see other large animals in the refuge very often," Logan continued conversationally. "Deer and moose usually forage in the park or migrate south. Sometimes you see a trumpeter swan or two on the refuge waters. They spend the year here. There's a fish hatchery as well, but we'll skip that this time."

Jennifer nodded a silent agreement, resolving inwardly that she wasn't going out with him again any time soon. He was too physically attractive for her peace of mind.

They made the circle in silence past the small building housing the concession ride, with Logan waving good-bye to Frank. Once again the jingle of the horse's harness bells was the only sound that broke the stillness of a wintry afternoon. The shiny black sleigh with its curving sides seemed to snuggle its two riders in its lap. Jennifer romantically pictured herself resting against Logan's side, his arm hugging her to him, then blamed the notion on the old-fashioned setting and not any desire on her part to get close to him.

His gloved hand moved to rest on the side of her neck, caressing it affectionately.

"You can rest your head on my shoulder if you want," Logan suggested. Jennifer's eyes flashed sparks of anger. Trust him to know that she had just thought of the inviting idea herself.

"I'm fine where I am, thank you," she said firmly, moving as far away from him as the small seat would allow, which wasn't very far.

"What's the matter? Afraid I have designs on your virtue?" His seductive glance played havoc with her pulse.

"No, I just want you to know that I don't need your—your . . ."

His sexy grin melted her attempt at cool composure, and he finished her sentence for her. *"Shoulder* is the word."

"I know," Jennifer retorted indignantly. She was only too aware that he knew exactly what effect he had upon her senses. She was silent for the rest of the ride back to the house.

"Well, Jenny Glenn, here we are, safe and sound," Logan said teasingly as he reined the horse to a stop in front of Sheila's.

He stepped down off the sleigh and turned to place his hands firmly around her waist before lifting her to the ground. She stared crossly up at his bemused expression when he didn't release her from the circle of his arms. Breathlessly she saw his gaze fasten on her lips. For one dizzying moment she thought he was going to kiss her. His sensuous, masculine lips hovered invitingly above hers, reminding her how vulnerable and responsive she had been the last time that had happened, and of the wild sweetness of his kisses.

"Thanks, Logan. I had a very nice time," she said hurriedly, knowing her inner confusion made her words sound stiff and insincere.

"It's easier than you think," Logan laughed. He looked at her with amused detachment. His hands returned to his sides and she was free.

"It never hurts to be on guard," Jennifer retorted, stepping away from him before he changed his mind about letting her go.

"Tell Sheila that I'll be out of town for the next day or two, will you?" he asked without rancor. "When I get back, I'll probably have to spend a few days at the ranch. Unless there's a change in plans, Mom and I will be over about seven on Christmas Eve."

"Christmas Eve?" Jennifer asked with stunned surprise. "What are you coming over for?"

"Well, we usually do." He frowned. "It's been a tradition in our family since Eric and I were kids."

"I didn't know." Jennifer's reply was an apologetic whisper. The sudden resentment in his eyes had startled her. She was so accustomed to his charming side that she had forgotten until this moment how irate he could be when he didn't get his way, and she didn't like being the object of it. "Okay. See you Christmas Eve, then," Jennifer said calmly.

"Till then," Logan agreed with a polite half smile.

Jennifer passed on Logan's message to Sheila that evening. Her sister said offhandedly that it was something they'd done every year, confirming Logan's words.

"The children and I always get them a gift every year—nothing too expensive—but we can add your name to the card," Sheila suggested.

"No . . ." Jennifer hesitated, a rebellious idea forming in her head. "I think I'd rather pick out a gift for Logan myself."

"As for Mandy, Logan's mother, you can always play it safe by getting her the latest best-seller."

"Mmmm, thanks," Jennifer replied absently, deciding to keep her devilish little plan to herself.

Three days later, she finally had a free afternoon. Finding Mrs. Taylor's present was easy. Taking Sheila's advice, she went to the local bookstore, where the clerks were unpacking the latest bestsellers, and chose a biography, selecting a delicate filigreed metal bookmark to go with it. With that scratched off her mental list, she went in search of Logan's present. Several stops later she finally found what she was looking for. She was nearly bubbling with laughter as she watched the skeptical clerk wrapping it up for her.

Leaving the store, Jennifer glanced at her watch. Sheila would pick her up in less than an hour. Time enough to have a leisurely cup of coffee at the restaurant.

She chose the little café that Logan had taken her to, for no other reason, she told herself, except that it was close by. It was crowded with skiers who were ready to call it a day on the slopes. The only free table she could see was a small one for two off in the corner. She was almost finished with her coffee when she happened to look up and notice Dirk Hamilton walk in the door. He spotted her at almost the same instant, glanced around the full tables, then back at Jennifer, and hesitated before coming over.

"Would you mind sharing the table with me, Jenny?" Dirk asked politely, almost steeling himself for her refusal.

"Of course not," she smiled.

He managed a half smile of gratitude before he settled his stocky frame in the chair opposite her. For some reason his calling her Jenny didn't annoy her. But the way Logan said it was simply too personal.

"You don't mind me calling you Jenny, do you?" Dirk asked after ordering a cup of coffee. "The name Jennifer sounds so sophisticated—not like you at all."

"I'll take that as a compliment, thank you," Jennifer laughed. "But it's only since I got to Jackson that people started shortening my name. I did resent it at first."

"I've noticed that Logan Taylor calls you Jenny." A bitter smile played across his lips. "Was it the nickname you resented or the person using it?"

"Since he's so important to my sister, I think I'll let that question pass."

"Hm. Sounds like you don't approve of Mr. Taylor." Dirk eyed her curiously. "Doesn't his charm work on you?"

"I'm just not taken in by it," Jennifer asserted. Her basic honesty refused to let her lie about the physical attraction he aroused in her. "Sheila is another question."

"Sheila needs security," Dirk sighed. Exasperation and anger mingled with his words. "As in financial security, which Logan certainly can offer her."

"Raising two children alone isn't easy. She's worried about money. Anyone in her shoes would be." Jennifer spoke up firmly, not liking Dirk's implication. Her sister was no gold-digger.

"Guess an artist doesn't seem like a good bet, huh?" It was a rhetorical question that she didn't answer as Dirk stared moodily at the table. Finally, when the waitress returned with his coffee, Dirk looked up at Jennifer, a determined expression on his square-jawed face. "When I first started out, I did a lot of paintings that weren't very good. But I sold enough of them to survive. I'm thirty-five years old, Jenny. Between exhibits and commissions, I don't have to struggle anymore. I make an adequate living, believe it or not."

His big fist slammed the table to emphasize his words. He glanced around him in embarrassment, then ran his hand through the dark thatch of his hair.

"But your sister doesn't seem to care. I don't know what I expected to happen," Dirk added grimly. "There's no painting I particularly want to do here. It's all just an excuse. I take it she never talks about me to you?"

Jennifer shook her head.

"I fell in love with her last summer, and I thought Sheila fell in love with me, too. I mean the kind of love where you accept the person the way they are. But all of a sudden she was talking about me getting a job and painting on the side. The financial future of an artist was too uncertain for her. She wanted to be sure there would be money coming in every week, but I couldn't guarantee that." He let out a long sigh. "It didn't matter to her that painting was my life and my future. All we did was argue so I left, telling myself I was lucky it was over, that she was better off with Logan, and in time, I'd get her out of my system."

"But you couldn't convince yourself," Jennifer said softly.

"No," Dirk agreed in a quiet, resigned voice. "I had to come back one last time. So far, I haven't even seen the back of her head. I'm sorry!" he said suddenly, "I shouldn't burden you with this."

"You have my sympathies." Jennifer's heart went out to her unhappy companion. "Maybe I can help. I am her sister, after all."

"I couldn't let you do that." The hope that had flickered in his dark eyes faded. "I can't put you in the position of being disloyal to your family."

"Oh, I won't," she said. "But I can't stand the idea of Logan as Sheila's husband. I'd just be looking out for my sister's best interests if I introduced someone more suitable back into her life."

"How? She's made it clear that she doesn't want to see me." Dirk shook his head ruefully, gradually being drawn into Jennifer's plot despite his misgivings.

"Well, she can't stop me from having friends over, unless she kicks me out of the house, which I doubt. And if she should happen to be at home when you arrive, well . . . ?" Jennifer ended with a mischievous twinkle in her eye.

"You're a conniving little witch." But the smile on his face was so wide and such a marked change from the sullen, sober expression that Jennifer broke into a lilting laugh.

"I found her, Mommy!" a childish voice cried just before two red-clad arms flung themselves around Jennifer.

"Cindy, I didn't expect to see you," Jennifer exclaimed in surprise.

"We wath lookin' all over for you," Cindy admonished as Jennifer glanced up to see Sheila and Eric making their way over to the table. Sheila didn't notice Dirk until he spoke.

"Hello, Cindy," he said softly.

The little girl turned startled blue eyes on him before breaking into an enormous smile and dashing over to his side.

"Dirk, I mithed you," she lisped, her sweet voice trembling with emotion. "Mommy thaid you'd never come back."

"I thought I taught you how to say your *S*'s," Dirk stated, a mock reprimand in his dark eyes.

"Sssss," Cindy said. A sad, almost lonely, expression came onto her face as she enunciated very clearly, "It didn't seem very important after you left us."

Dirk didn't reply, because he had just glanced up into Sheila's white face. Jennifer was amazed at the lack of expression in his tone as he greeted her quietly.

"Hello, Sheila. How are you?"

Sheila glanced desperately at her sister before mumbling that she was fine. Dirk turned to a sulky-looking Eric.

"And how's my little man?"

"I'm not your little man!" Eric retorted, stepping away from the hand reaching out to him.

"Aren't you glad Dirk is back, Mommy?" Cindy cried, then turned excitedly back to him. "You should thee Ragth. He'th real big and fat now! You know what we bought him for Chrithmath? A toy pork chop! Ithn't that nithe?"

"Hush, Cindy!" Sheila's face was red as she met Dirk's glance. "I'm sure Mr. Hamilton isn't interested in that."

"Yes, he ith tho, aren't you, Dirk?" Cindy insisted.

"Of course," he answered calmly, raising an eyebrow in Sheila's direction.

Cindy flicked her mother an I-told-you-so look before continuing. "You should thee what I bought Eric. We're gonna open our prethenth Chrithmath Eve. Oh, I wish you could be there. Our tree ith tho beautiful."

"Strange you should say that, Cindy," Jennifer inserted quickly. "I was just asking Dirk what his plans were for Christmas Eve, and he said he was going to be all alone."

She knew it was an unfair way to further her plans, but Jennifer would do anything to get her sister away from Logan Taylor.

"Jennifer!" Sheila exclaimed in a whisper with an accusing gleam in her eyes.

"Come over to our houth, Dirk. Pleathe!" Cindy begged.

"Of course I'll come," Dirk said, then looked over at Jennifer. "You sure it's all right?"

"Seven o'clock, in your holiday best!"

"It's a date," Dirk smiled.

"Good. Well, looks like you're ready to go," Jennifer said to Sheila. "I'll probably see you tomorrow, Dirk."

Her sister and her nephew were quiet, despite the chorus of good-byes exchanged among Cindy, Jennifer, and Dirk. They were out on the street when Sheila managed a very angry "How could you?" to Jennifer, which she shrugged off indifferently. After all, she'd invited Dirk for her sister's own good. It had nothing to do with distracting herself from Logan's presence. Or did it?

Chapter Six

It was the night before Christmas Eve, and Jennifer had tucked Cindy and Eric into their beds more than a half hour ago. Sheila was still at the lodge, working.

She had expected her sister to explode with fury after the invitation to Dirk, giving Jennifer a reason to use all her well-thought-out arguments. But her sister had discovered a better weapon: silence, a much more eloquent accusation of betrayal, one that didn't allow Jennifer the opportunity for discussion.

With a sigh of annoyance, Jennifer closed the book that had failed to capture her attention. She gazed at the twinkling lights on the Christmas tree. They really had done a good job of decorating the spindly thing. It had taken hours of stringing popcorn before the two children and two sisters had enough garlands to circle the tree. Many of the ornaments had been too heavy, as Logan had predicted, but there had been some that they were able to use, plus paper snowflakes and artificial snow to hide the worst of the bare spots. With the twinkling fairy lights, the tree looked fine.

Restless stirrings from Eric's room brought her thoughts back to Sheila and Dirk. It hadn't taken Jennifer long to discover that her nephew's sullenness might get in the way of her plan to bring her sister and the artist together. But the little boy's dislike of Dirk was all the more confusing when compared with his sister Cindy's wholehearted acceptance.

She rose from the armchair and tiptoed quietly to his door to check on him. As her shadow filled the doorway, Eric turned his head toward her, his wide-awake, questioning eyes studying her.

"Can't get to sleep?" she asked softly, hoping their voices wouldn't wake Cindy in the next room. "What's on your mind, Eric?" He still didn't reply. "Sometimes problems don't seem so bad when you share them."

He rolled over to face her as Jennifer walked in to sit beside him on the bed. She could tell he was mulling over her words, trying to decide if he wanted to tell her.

"I'd be happy to listen."

He looked at her solemnly.

"Does God really hear everybody's prayer? Even a little kid's?"

"Especially a little kid's," Jennifer asserted with a smile.

"Does He always answer them?"

"Oh, yes. He always answers them, but sometimes, Eric, the answer is no." His shoulders drooped at her words, and his chin settled down on his chest. "What was your prayer for?"

Two very sad blue eyes looked up at her—with an unmistakable hint of rebellion lurking in the depths.

"I prayed that Logan would marry Mommy." There was no missing the defiance in his voice. "And that Dirk would go away and never come back."

Jennifer managed to conceal her dismay and reply calmly. "That wouldn't be very fair to your sister. She likes Dirk, you know."

"She's just a baby." Eric's chin trembled at his effort to hold back the tears in his eyes. "The only reason she likes him is because he gave us Rags. He was just a dog that nobody wanted."

"That's not true anymore. Rags has a very good home here. I know Cindy loves him, and I think you do too."

"I do not! He's ugly and goofy and he's scared of everything! I want a dog like the one Logan has at his ranch. He's got a job and he's important. Uncle Logan says he could never take care of all those cattle without Ranger!"

Logan again, Jennifer thought silently.

"St. Bernards are brave dogs, Eric. They're trained to rescue people lost in the snow in the Alps. You should be proud of Rags, because his ancestors saved people from blizzards and avalanches."

"I guess I like Rags all right," he admitted reluctantly. But the brief flicker of interest her words had sparked was replaced quickly by sullenness. "But I still don't like Dirk!"

"But why?" Jennifer wondered at his vehemence.

"Because the last time he was here, he made Mommy cry! And I don't want her to cry again." His last words ended in a painful sob.

"Oh, Eric," she murmured, reaching out her arms to the little boy as he hurled himself into them. Holding the sobbing small body close, Jennifer wondered how she could possibly explain to her nephew that Logan was capable of making Sheila cry, too. As his weeping subsided gradually, she smoothed his tousled hair and began to explain. "People cry for all sorts of reasons. Because they're hurt or lonely or even because they're happy. I don't know why Dirk made your mommy cry, but I know he could make her very happy. That's what you want, isn't it? For her to be happy?" His dark head nodded slowly while his little hand manfully brushed away his tears. "So why don't we just wait and see what happens, okay?"

"Okay, Aunt Jenny," he agreed quietly, moving out of her arms and back onto his bed.

"Do you think you can go to sleep now?"

"Yes." He snuggled under the covers. "I feel better now."

"I'm glad," Jennifer smiled, silently wishing that she did. "Good night, then. Sleep tight and don't let the bedbugs bite," she teased, dropping a light kiss on his forehead.

"Good night."

At the rap on the door, Jennifer removed the practical apron that she was wearing to protect her long green velvet gown. The flowing lines of the dress accented her slender curves, and the deeply cut V-neck showed off her swanlike neck. The long sleeves, fitting the upper portion of her arms before fanning out gracefully around her wrists, gave the gown a slightly medieval effect. She had done her hair into a pretty coronet of curls, which added to the romantic look.

She opened the front door to admit Dirk, whose arms were filled with brightly wrapped Christmas presents.

"Merry Christmas!" he grinned.

"You must be Santa Claus," she teased as he managed to transfer a few of the presents into her arms. "Eric! Would you come here? You have some more gifts to put around the tree."

With the gifts safely distributed between Eric and Cindy, Jennifer helped Dirk off with his coat.

"I kept expecting you to call me this afternoon and tell me not to come," Dirk began nervously as he looked into the front room, where the two children were placing the presents around the tree, with their grandparents' help. "Where's Sheila?"

"In the kitchen, keeping quiet." She raised her shoulder in an expressive shrug just as there was a knock at the door.

"That'll be Logan," said Dirk. "They were just driving up when I knocked at the door."

Jennifer reluctantly opened the door and exchanged holiday greetings with Logan and his mother, before calling out to her sister.

"Sheila, Logan and Mrs. Taylor are here!"

There was a flurry of footsteps as Cindy and Eric descended on the pair, saying hello and relieving them of their packages. During that time, Jennifer had a few seconds to study Mrs. Taylor. She had half expected to meet an autocratic woman who doted on her son to the exclusion of everyone else, but her opinion was quickly revised when she looked into the warm brown eyes above the dimpled smile.

Jennifer turned, hearing a sharp intake of breath from Dirk as her sister entered the room. The clinging knit outfit she wore was only a shade lighter than her brilliant blue eyes. Even her hair, which tumbled glamorously over her shoulders, glistened with a blue-black sheen. Jennifer couldn't help glancing at Logan to see his reaction to her sister, only to find him inspecting her. She took an involuntary step closer to Dirk, as if needing his protection, only half hearing Logan introduce her to his mother.

"Jenny Glenn. What a pretty name!" His mother's voice called her back to reality. "But it suits you perfectly. Now, perhaps Logan told you that I consider your sister as an adopted daughter, which makes you part of our family, too, so please call me Mandy."

It was impossible for Jennifer to dislike this woman. In her own way, Mandy Taylor was just as charming as her son. Jennifer knew instinctively that she was sincere, though she still had her doubts about Logan's motives.

Taking Mrs. Taylor's fur-trimmed coat, Jennifer added it to the one already draped over her arm and led the exodus into the living room. She was nearly to the hall doorway that led to the bedroom when she noticed Eric tugging Logan's arm insistently. She had a feeling that his reason for whispering in Logan's ear had nothing to do with childish talkativeness. She and Logan both looked to where the small finger was pointing: at the sprig of mistletoe that hung from a velvet ribbon above

Sheila's head. Jennifer's lips compressed tightly. Her nephew didn't miss a trick.

"Your romantic son won't let me forget a certain Christmas tradition," Logan declared after he had walked over to Sheila, tapped her on the shoulder, and pointed above her head. "And I don't pass up any invitation to get next to a beautiful woman."

In the brief moment that Logan touched Sheila's lips with a tender kiss, Jennifer was jolted by a surge of jealousy. Despite the teasing cheers that marked the end of the kiss, Logan's eyes met hers. All too aware that her emotions must be written on her face, she turned quickly away and hurried into the hallway and on to the bedroom. She dropped the coats quickly on the bed and clutched at the footboard to support her suddenly shaking legs.

How could she be jealous of Logan kissing her sister? It was out of the question! She despised the man—it had to have been anger. Yes, anger—brought on by a combination of Eric's childish machinations and Logan's tomcat tendencies. Oh, God, please let it be anger! she cried silently to herself.

"Is this where the coats go?"

Jennifer turned around to face Logan. His glance flicked past her to the bed.

"I guess it must be." He answered his own question with a faint smile. She watched him warily as he walked closer, stopping in front of her while tossing his coat onto the bed. "I had the distinct impression a few minutes ago that you wanted to scratch somebody's eyes out. Mine or Sheila's?"

"I think your ego is showing," Jennifer retorted, fighting the breathlessness in her voice.

"Could be." His head moved to one side indifferently, but his gaze remained on her pale face and trembling lips. "I decided you were too shy to share a kiss under the mistletoe in a room full of people. But it seemed to me that you might do it in a more private place, though." At her angry indrawn breath, he added, his tongue definitely in cheek, "Then again, maybe not. You're much too prim and proper. Did you know that shade of green makes your hair seem more red than gold?" he commented with a lightning-fast change of subject.

"I'm sorry you don't like it," Jennifer retorted sarcastically. He was going too fast for her and she couldn't keep up with him. No longer capable of meeting his unsettling gaze, she looked away.

"I like it." His low voice had a smooth, seductive quality to it now. His hand suddenly began caressing the back of her neck lightly. "I've heard that the nape of the neck is a great place to heighten a woman's desire. Is that true?"

His fingertips were leaving a trail of fire that began to course through her body with irresistible intensity.

"Stop it!" she hissed, turning quickly around to face him before she lost control. His hand rested now alongside her throat.

"Your pulse is racing," he drawled with irritating calmness.

She stared into his mocking brown eyes. He knew exactly what he was doing to her, and that infuriated her.

"Stop it!" she sobbed as she shoved his hand away. "You're . . . you're everything I hate in a man. Especially your oversize ego!"

"Oh? You're so sure that I'm bad to the bone,

and still you're attracted to me." His tone was provokingly cool.

"Attracted!" Jennifer cried. *"Repelled* is a better word."

"I can see we're going to have a stormy relationship," Logan laughed.

She spluttered for a moment before flouncing out of the room. By the time she reached the living room, her temper was under control and only her hands, clenched into tight fists, betrayed her inner feelings. She quietly shifted Cindy from her seat on the sectional couch to her lap, avoiding Logan's amused glance when he followed her into the room after a discreet pause. The soothing sounds of "Adeste Fidelis" and other Christmas carols on the CD that Sheila was playing eventually calmed her to the point where she could join in with the rest of the festive group. Sheila and Dirk, although seated on opposite sides of the room, were talking to each other, she was relieved to see.

Peace on earth? Maybe this Christmas, she thought, thankful for the lack of hostility between her sister and Dirk. She glanced at Logan, who was listening attentively to Mr. Jeffries, Sheila's father-in-law. She certainly didn't feel any "goodwill towards men" tonight.

"Ithn't it time to open our prethents?" Cindy asked for the sixth time.

"I agree with Cindy." Mrs. Taylor spoke up from the chair on Jennifer's right. "It's time to end the suspense."

"All right, all right," Sheila laughed as she was hugged by two eager children. "Grandpa Paul, will you do the honors?"

As the gifts were passed around, the small living

room became a chaotic confusion of brightly colored wrapping paper, ribbon bows, and a babble of laughter and delighted voices. Jennifer's hand closed on the square package from Logan to her. After a brief flare of curiosity, she buried it beneath another from Sheila.

"Oh, Jenny, thank you!" Mrs. Taylor exclaimed exuberantly. She held up a new best-seller. "Someone must have told you how much I like to read."

"Yes, someone did," Jennifer admitted.

Then Jennifer's attention was drawn by the excited voice of her sister. She was holding up a beautiful turquoise and silver necklace.

"It's magnificent, Logan," Sheila said softly as she hurriedly clasped it around her neck and lovingly fingered the delicately stamped silver chain.

Logan was gazing at her with undisguised tenderness and admiration. "The Navajo Indians believe that happiness and good fortune come to those who wear turquoise. I hope you'll wear it as a symbol of all the things I wish for you."

Embarrassed by Logan's heartfelt declaration, Jennifer turned to his mother, only to see Mrs. Taylor gazing at her son with a light of dawning wonder in her eyes. She glanced at Jennifer with a bright twinkle in her eyes and a tremulous smile. Jennifer realized that there was some significance to the necklace that Sheila had received. That smile on Mrs. Taylor's face had a knowing look to it that made her nervous.

Things were happening too quickly for Jennifer to have any control over her own plans. She turned to Dirk, whose mouth had set into a grim line as he left the couch to help Cindy assemble one of her toys. He had picked up the unspoken message, too. She covered her confusion by fumbling with a package.

Logan slid silently into the seat beside Jennifer, replacing Dirk. In his hands was her present to him, still wrapped.

"This is heavy. Do I dare open it?" he mocked her.

All of the impish pleasure that buying it had given her was gone. All she wanted right now was to snatch it away from his hands. But he was busily unwrapping it and it was only a matter of seconds before the contents were revealed. Jennifer nearly cringed, awaiting his reaction, feeling none of the malicious amusement she had anticipated. After staring at it almost incredulously, Logan threw his head back and roared with laughter. Every person in the room turned their attention to him as Jennifer colored furiously beneath his laughing eyes.

He tore away the rest of the paper to show everyone the large basket of fruit. Since no one else knew of their conversation that day of the sleigh ride, they didn't see the point of the gift and stared in puzzlement at Logan.

"Only you would think of this, Jenny Glenn." Deep amusement filled his voice as his gaze shifted from her to his mother. "I once told Jenny how much I liked fruit," he explained, "so now I get to sample everything from oranges to the proverbial apple of temptation."

Mrs. Taylor's melodic laugh inspired more hesitant ones from the rest of the group. Gradually everyone's attention returned to their own gifts, allowing Jennifer's scarlet face to return to its normal color. She took her time unwrapping her present from Dirk and inhaling the scent of the expensive per-

fume, knowing there was only one package left—
Logan's. She was reluctant to open it with him sitting right beside her. But at that moment Sheila
enlisted his help in the kitchen and Jennifer began
to unwrap it without his embarrassing presence.

It was a black, rectangular jewelry case. She
opened it and barely stifled a gasp of surprise and
pleasure. Nestled on a cushion of white velvet were
two strands of delicate gold chain holding a jade
pendant, encircled by antique filigree studded
with diamonds. She didn't know too much about
gems, but this was obviously very expensive jewelry. She closed the lid quickly on the exquisite
piece, knowing she should refuse it, yet longing to
see how it looked on her.

"Jenny, would you give me a hand with the
eggnog?" Sheila asked as she passed a tray to Mrs.
Taylor, not noticing her sister's stunned silence.

"Of course." Jennifer was all too glad to put Logan's present down. She escaped as quickly as she
could into the kitchen, avoiding any contact with
Logan's searching eyes as she darted past him. But
minutes later, his footsteps muffled by the clinking
of crystal glasses, he entered the kitchen.

"Sheila makes really good eggnog," he remarked
as he stopped beside her.

Jennifer paused before filling another glass. She
tried to breathe naturally while smiling in agreement.

"You're not wearing the necklace." He glanced
casually at her unadorned neck. "I thought it would
look nice with that gown."

Jennifer placed the ladle back in the bowl and
turned toward him with a determined lift to her
chin.

"It's beautiful," she said sincerely, "but I just can't accept it."

He lifted an eyebrow at her as his half smile faded away. "Why not?"

"It's much too expensive." She suddenly found it difficult to explain why she wanted to refuse it. "It just wouldn't be right for me to wear it. What would everybody think?"

"Jenny, we're not exactly strangers—after all, we spent a night together in the same bed. A piece of costume jewelry can't be classified as a compromising gift after that."

"Costume jewelry?" Jennifer whispered, taken aback. "I thought it was jade."

"It's jadeite," Logan informed her with a grin.

"Oh!" Her voice sounded very small. That must be some synthetic form of jade, she thought. How humiliating for her to believe he was giving her an expensive gift. "Well, in that case, I guess it is all right to accept it."

"I'm glad. After all, I accepted your gift in the spirit in which it was intended." His teasing voice brought a fresh wave of pink into her cheeks as he continued, "Sheila told me you were the one who invited Dirk here tonight."

"Yes, I did."

"It's only been a week. I didn't realize that you two were friends already."

"Well, not close friends." Jennifer answered him casually, but there was a defiant gleam in her eyes. "But I do hope that my sister—well, I think Dirk would make an excellent husband and father."

"You do? So you've decided you know what's best for your sister, huh?" His look of amused indifference was simply irritating. "Just don't tell her that.

I've found subtlety works best with Sheila. But I agree with you on one point—I think it's time she remarried."

His words hung in the air as if his sentence was unfinished. Mentally Jennifer finished it for him: *but not to Dirk*. To Logan?

"Are you going to interfere?" She tilted her head back to glare coldly into his face.

"I would never stand in the way of Sheila's happiness. But whatever happens should be Sheila's decision, not yours or mine, Jenny Glenn." A dimple appeared briefly in one cheek as Logan answered with an air of assurance. He reached around her and picked up a tray of glasses filled with eggnog. "I'll take these in before they send a search party for us."

Jennifer stared after him blankly, feeling utterly forlorn as he walked out of the kitchen. She was sure that Dirk loved her sister deeply. But could Logan's love be even greater? He had practically said he was willing to step aside if it meant Sheila's happiness. Just the thought made her heart constrict painfully until her hand reached up to clutch her dress, as if to tear away the ache. A vision of Logan and Sheila in an embrace flitted across her mind.

Her heart sank. Jennifer suddenly realized the true reason behind her betrayal of her sister. She had fallen in love with Logan Taylor herself. And her feelings for him were much deeper than a mere physical attraction, as Logan had once suggested. No, not when she could be consumed with jealousy of her own sister and overwhelmed by heartrending pain at the discovery that Logan loved Sheila to the exclusion of his own happiness. Could she be that unselfish? Jennifer wondered, blinking at the tears that were threatening to overflow down her cheeks. One thing was certain—she couldn't ever let Sheila or Logan know her true feelings.

The rest of the evening would be her first test. Calling upon her almost depleted reserve of will-power, Jennifer fixed a smile on her face and began the long walk into the living room, determined that no one would know the secret that haunted the depths of her soul.

Chapter Seven

Jennifer made it through Christmas Eve and Christmas and the four days that followed them, but the morning of the fifth day seemed to hold a prediction of the future.

The upcoming holiday brought more guests than ever, taking advantage of extra vacation time to hit the slopes. Logan had been around the lodge much more than usual, helping Sheila out. Jennifer took precautions to avoid him whenever possible, practically hiding in Dirk's shadow if he was around, trying to erect a barrier against Logan's magnetism. But she couldn't stop the fluttering of her heart when his gaze rested on her, nor could she ignore the pangs of jealousy when she saw him with her sister.

Oh, she managed to keep smiling, but she knew exactly how brittle her facade was, and how easily it could be shattered. The arrival of DeeDee Hunter, the platinum blonde Jennifer had met at the airport with Logan, had very nearly put a crack in it this very morning. Just watching the flirting between DeeDee and Logan had filled her with a mixture of envy and jealousy. If only she could meet his eyes that easily and feel the warmth of his masculine charm directed at her! But she couldn't. Jennifer had too much pride to hang on his arm as others did, grateful for whatever crumbs were thrown her way, and she wasn't about to compete with her own sister—Sheila had known so much heartache in her life.

At last, Jennifer's afternoon replacement at the front desk arrived, and she was free to go home. Quickly she shrugged into her suede coat, conscious of DeeDee's giggling voice somewhere in the lobby. Her sixth sense told her that Logan was probably with her. She hurried across the lobby, seeing the airport limousine unloading at the front door. Her heart sank. Glancing over her shoulder, she saw Logan stop with DeeDee and two other people at the front desk. Jennifer stood there, tapping her foot impatiently, nodding and smiling to the new arrivals as they filed through the front door, when one of them stopped suddenly. His face seemed familiar, but she was too preoccupied to really look at him.

"Jennifer?"

She stared numbly into the man's dark eyes before two hands reached out to imprison her shoulders. A black lock of hair fell forward across his forehead.

"Jennifer! I can't believe it's really you!"

"Brad," Jennifer finally whispered incredulously. "What are you doing here?"

"What are *you* doing here?" he asked. His grasp tightened momentarily on her shoulders as if to draw her into his arms, before his expression sobered. "I've been wondering where you were and whether you were all right. And here you are right in front of me—must be fate."

"How did you know I was here?" Her eyes burned with an angry fire at the almost forgotten humiliation she had experienced because of this man.

"I didn't know! I wanted to get away. It was a last-minute decision, and since I couldn't get reservations anywhere in Colorado, I came here," he replied. "Don't look at me like that, Jennifer. I didn't do anything unforgivable."

"I don't want to talk about it." Jennifer twisted out of his arms, glancing up just in time to see Logan walking toward them.

"You're wrong. We've got a lot to talk about," Brad replied firmly.

"Excuse me." Logan glanced politely at Brad before talking to Jennifer. "Your sister wondered if you would pick up the children for her. She can't get away right now."

"Of course," Jennifer nodded, feeling herself pale under his sardonic gaze.

Logan looked expectantly toward Brad, then back to Jennifer, anticipating an introduction that Jennifer was reluctant to make. But one look at his determined expression told her that if she didn't, he would.

"Brad, this is Logan Taylor. He owns the lodge." Jennifer barely suppressed her irritation from creeping into her words. "Bradley Stevenson is a friend of mine from Minneapolis."

Brad accepted Logan's handshake, hiding his impatience with professional politeness.

"Nice to have one of Jenny's friends staying with

us," Logan said smoothly. "How long did you plan to be here?"

"Only three days. I'm booked on a Sunday flight. I hope to see as much of Jennifer as possible while I'm here. Since you're her employer now, I might as well warn you that I'm going to try and persuade her to return with me and take her old job back."

Jennifer's eyes widened with alarm.

"Old job?" Logan asked.

"Yes, Jennifer was my secretary as well as"—Brad hesitated, eyeing her warmly—"other things."

Logan's eyes narrowed as he studied her flushed cheeks and downcast gaze.

"Too bad Jenny didn't tell me you were coming." He didn't hide the disapproval in his voice. "I could've arranged for her to have some free time. But this is the height of the snow season. We really can't spare her."

"I understand," Brad drawled, meeting the challenge of Logan's gaze with his usual self-confidence. His hand reached out for Jennifer's arm and he pulled her possessively to his side. "Now, if you'll excuse us?"

Logan nodded a silent agreement, his penetrating gaze resting briefly on Jennifer before he walked away.

"Let's go somewhere we can talk," Brad suggested the minute Logan was out of earshot.

"I—I can't. I have to pick up the children." Jennifer stalled. "And Sheila won't be home until late tonight, which means I'll have to babysit."

"I'll come over to the house, then."

"No!" Her reply was quick and sharp, but she qualified it in a quieter voice. "We can't really talk with two kids around."

"Tomorrow, then."

"I'll be working."

"Jennifer, I have to get you alone. You aren't going to think up a bunch of excuses to avoid me while I'm here. Just give me a chance to explain," Brad argued. "After that—well, if you don't want to see me, I won't bother you."

"All right," Jennifer sighed. Who would have thought a month ago that she could be so indifferent to Brad today? At this moment she didn't care if she never saw him again. "Tomorrow night the lodge is hosting a New Year's Eve party and I have to attend. I can spend some time with you later in the evening."

"You'll be glad you did." Brad gazed down at her with that big smile that used to win her over so easily.

"I have to go now," she replied, completely unmoved by his charm.

"Till tomorrow," he agreed softly, bending his head to touch his lips to her forehead. They felt cold to her skin, and she barely repressed a shudder as she hurried out the lodge door.

"Going to lunch, Jenny?" the switchboard operator asked.

"Uh-huh," Jennifer confirmed, kneeling down to take out her bag from one of the drawers and discreetly applying a fresh touch of lipstick. "Just a quick bite. I won't be long."

"I bet!" Carol exclaimed with a giggle, looking a little smug.

"What's that supposed to mean?" Jennifer asked indignantly.

"Listen, if I was having lunch with a guy like that, it would take me an hour just to eat the salad!"

"What are you talking about?"

"Before you came on duty this morning, this gorgeous man stopped at the desk and asked what time you went to lunch, and I told him," Carol replied, looking quizzically at Jennifer. "You met him yesterday when he arrived from the airport. I assumed you were having lunch with him—aren't you?"

"No," answered Jennifer, shaking her head. Brad hadn't said anything about lunch.

"You just didn't think you were," the other girl teased. "Boy, you are really lucky having a hottie like that chasing you. He's cuter than that Joe Millionaire."

And just as phony, Jennifer wanted to say. "In his case, hotness really is only skin deep."

"Who cares?" Carol said, rolling her eyes expressively.

"Sooner or later you will, believe me," Jennifer responded.

"Well, speak of the devil—" Carol looked sideways at the man approaching the counter.

"Hey, Jennifer. How about lunch with me before I hit the ski slopes?" Brad suggested. His gaze roved admiringly over Jennifer's gray and black plaid skirt with its matching black jacket.

"Brad, I—"

"I'm sorry, Jenny won't be able to," Logan interrupted. She turned in surprise. With his catlike quietness, she hadn't heard him walk up.

"Why not?" Brad looked at him warily.

"Lodge policy, sorry. Guests and employees aren't allowed to socialize in public," Logan stated firmly. "You two can meet after she's off work."

"What's the harm in two people having lunch together?" Brad's tone was argumentative. "Hey I came all the way from Minneapolis, and I'm leaving in two days!"

"We set aside a table just for the staff. They get prompt service and they're never late. No exceptions." Logan glanced at the growing indignation on Jennifer's face before smiling regretfully at Brad. "It's easier that way."

"And that's your final word?" Brad asked, shoving a clenched fist in the pocket of his blue ski jacket.

"Yes, it is. Now, if you'll excuse me, I have some business to attend to."

With a condescending nod to each of them, Logan returned to the private offices behind the reception area. Jennifer exchanged a puzzled glance with Carol before turning back to Brad.

"Is he usually that obnoxious?" His eyes burned with a black flame as he stared at Jennifer.

"Sometimes," she said, "but that's the policy just the same. It's just as well. I only have time for a quick lunch anyway. I'll see you tonight, Brad."

"Right, and with no interruptions from him!" he snapped as he stalked angrily out of the lobby.

"What was all that about?" Carol whispered as she glanced fearfully toward the offices. "I never heard any objections before about someone on staff eating with a guest. We usually just invite them to the staff table."

"I know." Jennifer's lips were pressed firmly together. "I think I was just made the exception, and I'd like to know why!"

"Are you going to ask him?" Carol breathed in astonishment.

Jennifer hesitated. She had no desire to see Logan alone, but still . . . "If I can," she answered. "But first I'm going to lunch."

Jennifer gazed around the throng of happy vacationers partying away. The live band in the far corner of the room played a dance mix as couples crowded onto the floor, laughing and shouting at one another, singing along with the melody, more or less in tune. It was strictly informal, with dress varying from ski outfits to sexy little dresses and dark suits and ties. Her own dress was white chiffon with a tightly fitted bodice and floating skirt, which gave her a look of ethereal innocence. The jade and diamond pendant on the chain around her neck glittered brightly against the white dress.

The clinking of ice brought Jennifer's attention to the dark-haired man holding out a glass to her. She smiled her thanks to Brad as she accepted the drink. He seemed determined to be as charming and urbane as possible, a model of politeness and solicitude. He'd rarely left her side the entire evening, although she had noticed him looking at the younger women who were there.

There had been several opportunities for them to slip away, but Jennifer was grateful that Brad hadn't wanted to. She needed the noise, needed to take refuge in the noisy party.

Her eyes moved over the crowd, seeking out Logan and finding him with a group around DeeDee. He was listening attentively to her, yet he seemed to be somewhat apart from them. "All wrapped up in himself as usual, Jennifer thought cynically. *That was totally unfair,* she chided herself. What did she expect him to do?

Her eyes misted as she watched her sister make her way toward Logan, touch his arm, and glow at his warm look. Sheila was breathtakingly lovely tonight in a dress of burgundy-red velvet, with her raven hair in sophisticated ringlets atop her head. Their discussion was brief as Sheila nodded at something Logan said before walking away. Jennifer's heart ached when she noted his lingering glance at her sister.

Brad touched her elbow, tearing her attention away from the scene, and suggested that they dance. She let herself be swept into the pulsating rhythm, willing the music to drown out her thoughts. Later, as a dreamy ballad echoed through the room, Jennifer clung tightly to Brad. Her eyes closed, and she let her head rest lightly against his chest. Then Brad's steps stopped suddenly, and Jennifer looked up—at Logan.

"No objection to an employer cutting in, is there?"

Brad consented reluctantly and stepped away. Jennifer stiffened as Logan's hand touched her waist. She held herself apart from him, her hand resting tensely against his shoulder while the other was captured in his firm grip. Her feet became incredibly awkward as she stumbled to follow his simple steps. She found she could look anywhere but into his face.

"If you can't relax, we might as well sit this one out," Logan said sharply.

"Hey, I'm doing my best," Jennifer managed to say, aware that her cheeks were flushed and her heart was beating at an erratic pace.

"I'm beginning to wonder just exactly what your best is." Logan's hand gripped her elbow as he maneuvered her off the floor toward a dark, uninhabited corner of the room.

"Where are we going? Did I break another rule or something?" she asked scathingly, knowing mere words weren't enough to get to him.

"I was under the impression that you wouldn't want him around. Didn't you say he'd made unwelcome advances? Seems like you've forgiven him." Jennifer was surprised at the expression of savage ruthlessness on Logan's face.

"I've forgiven him," she murmured. Of course, she'd forgiven him—because she didn't care anymore. Brad didn't matter to her, but how could she possibly tell Logan that?

"Big of you." Logan studied her for a long moment. "Does that mean you'll be leaving on Sunday?"

"No, it doesn't," Jennifer replied tartly.

"Wouldn't that make the reconciliation complete?"

"There hasn't been one yet. And if there is—" Jennifer paused. Her mind raced over the possibility. Did she dare pretend she had some kind of relationship with Brad? Would it protect her from Logan? One thing was certain: If she didn't end things with Brad, in public, she would have a rock-solid reason for leaving when the time came for her to go. "If there is, I wouldn't leave right away. I'd need time to think it over. And I don't want to leave Sheila with no help."

"Amazing how a woman in love can be so cold-blooded and analytical. Aren't you tempting fate by letting him go back alone?" His eyes raked her body thoroughly, sending a wave of color into her cheeks. "What if he finds some-one else?"

"I'll take my chances," she replied evenly. "Like I said, I need time to think it over."

"You can't be in love with him. There would be nothing to think about. You don't even know what love is." Her heart skipped a beat as Logan's hand forced her chin upward before she could twist away. There was no masking the strong emotions in his eyes. "Go ahead, bring him to heel. But you're not going to marry him!"

"Who gave you the right to—listen, Logan Taylor! I'm not going to let you run my life!" Jennifer exclaimed angrily, even though deep in her heart, she knew he was right.

"You aren't going to marry him," Logan repeated calmly and coldly.

"It's none of your business what I do." Her protest sounded weak and ineffectual, but it didn't matter. Logan wasn't there to hear it. He was already mixing with a group of laughing people on the side of the dance floor.

Silently she watched him, her eyes smarting with unshed tears. She saw him stop beside Sheila and put an arm around her waist to draw her out to the dance floor, a warm smile on his face as he gazed down at her. Jennifer felt as if she were stepping off the lowest rung on the ladder.

"I asked her to dance three times, and she's refused *me* every time." Dirk spoke up from Jennifer's side.

She turned around, startled. Where had he come from? Well, they made a good pair. His bleak, gloomy expression matched hers as they stared at the dancing couple.

"I can't even ask How are you? She gets this chilly expression on her face that says she'd like to turn me into a snowman," Dirk grumbled, running a hand through his dark hair dejectedly.

"Then don't ask," Jennifer sighed. She glanced at him sadly. Somehow Dirk always came out second best, though she sympathized with his frustration at competing with Logan Taylor. "Why don't you go cut in on them?" she suggested softly. "After all, Sheila won't make a scene in the middle of the floor."

It would be a small victory for Dirk, Jennifer thought, but in the end he would feel just as bad when Sheila walked down the aisle to Logan. All the little battles and skirmishes wouldn't change the final outcome, and Logan would be the victor.

Jennifer watched as he handed Sheila over to Dirk, whose eyes gleamed in triumphant hope, but she turned away before Logan's searching eyes could meet hers. Brad would be looking for her by now. There was some comfort in that. Without him around tonight, she would've turned tail and run. Slowly she made her way through the crowd until she saw him chatting with one of the older people in the group. When he finally saw her, his dark eyes sparkled.

"Jennifer." He reached out a hand and pulled her into the circle of his arm. He nuzzled her red-gold hair for a brief moment before excusing himself from the group. "It's almost midnight. Can't we bring in the New Year alone?"

Why not? she thought to herself. The laughter, the music, the noise were all compounding the strain of the evening. She made no protest as Brad led her out of the room, down a vacant hallway.

"Do you have any idea how much I wanted to be alone with you all evening?" Brad murmured, imprisoning her against the wall between his arms.

"Please, Brad, don't," Jennifer protested as he moved in closer.

"I don't blame you for pushing me away." Brad's hand caressed her cheek lightly. "What I did that night really upset you. Give me a chance—just listen for a minute." Jennifer turned her face away from him, fighting the unpleasant memory and the odor of alcohol on his breath now. He removed his hand from her cheek, his pleading eyes searching her face. "I was drunk and angry. I admit that you meant nothing to me then. And I told myself I was glad that you'd gone, that there were plenty more girls where you came from. Then you began to haunt me. No matter what I did, or where I went, I couldn't get you out of my mind. Come back with me."

"Brad, it's over and done with," Jennifer sighed. "There's no way back."

"Don't you see, Jennifer? You were so innocent—that turned me on." His voice was hoarse.

Where had she heard that before? Jennifer thought in defeat.

"I wanted you then, and I want you now."

"You don't love me, Brad," she said calmly. "Be honest with yourself. If you hadn't run into me here by accident, you would've totally forgotten about me in a month."

"That's not true," Brad whispered, gathering her into his arms. "And I can prove it to you."

His lips descended passionately on hers. Indifference would cool his ardor, Jennifer knew, so she remained passive in his arms, unresponsive to his kiss. Distantly she heard the partygoers loudly count down the remaining seconds of the old year before they broke loose in a chorus of jubilant "Happy New Years!" as the band broke into the melancholy strains of "Auld Lang Syne." She closed her eyes tightly to prevent the tears from falling, aware that Brad's mouth had deserted her lips to rain kisses on her neck, but not caring.

Was this a portent of the year to come? she wondered. Trapped in the arms of a man who meant nothing to her, who would never mean anything to her? *"Should auld acquaintance be forgot and never brought to mind?"* The lyrics tore at her heart as Logan's image drifted clearly into her mind. No, she thought wistfully, there was no chance that she would ever forget him.

Her eyes opened to look out through the mist of tears. Slowly her vision cleared, and she became aware of another man in the hallway. Her heart sank as she looked over Brad's shoulder into Logan's glaring eyes. For one brief moment their eyes were locked before he turned and walked stiffly away.

Chapter Eight

It had been almost a month since Brad, after a few more attempts to persuade her, finally realized that Jennifer wasn't interested in him anymore, and flew back to Minneapolis.

Of course, Jennifer had just allowed Sheila and everyone else to believe that she was considering his offer. It was remarkably easy, she discovered, since they all seemed to think it was so romantic that Brad had come all this way just to see her. And it suited her just fine not to mention that he'd had no idea she was even here. It was one way to salvage her pride after she'd gone and fallen irrevocably in love with Logan Taylor.

She had tried desperately to replace that tender emotion with its opposite but only succeeded in generating occasional sparks of anger. The brief flare-ups hadn't amounted to much. Logan seemed to be avoiding her as much as she was avoiding him. That wasn't exactly true. He had been gone for some good reasons. Winter had descended on the mountains with a fury and he was needed at the ranch.

Now that the holiday season had passed, the skiers came in mostly on the weekends. Carol was perfectly capable of handling the switchboard and the front desk duties, with Sheila pitching in when tour groups arrived. Jennifer was back to spending the weekdays at the house and helping out at the lodge on Saturdays and Sundays.

Dependable, determined Dirk was still hanging in there, although he wasn't making much progress. Jennifer wondered how long he would stay.

If by some chance he could succeed with Sheila, though it seemed unlikely, Logan would be free. She just wished there were some way she could help Dirk, but her sister was keeping the poor guy at arm's length.

It was no use Jennifer thought. Not even this morning's window shopping in town had managed to get her mind off the situation. She sighed wearily as she pushed open the lodge door and fixed a cheery smile on her face as she greeted Carol.

"Is Sheila busy?"

"I don't think so." Carol shrugged. "She's back in the office. Go on in."

Jennifer nodded, opening the counter gate and walking down the small hallway behind the reception area. She rapped lightly on the door before opening it and looking in, expecting to see her sister's raven head bent over her desk, but the room was empty. She closed the door quietly and started to return to the reception desk, when she heard Sheila's voice coming from an adjacent office.

"Why do you keep dragging him into our conversations?"

"Because you try so hard to keep him out." That was Logan. Jennifer hadn't realized he was back in town.

"Logan, Dirk means nothing to me!" Sheila said vehemently.

"Then why can't you discuss him rationally? I get the feeling you're protesting too much."

"Don't be ridiculous!"

"I'm not the one who's being ridiculous." Jennifer heard someone get up from a chair, and then footsteps as Logan paused before continuing. "Sheila, don't turn him away if you're not sure."

"Why can't you believe me?" Her sister's voice was strained, as if she was holding back tears.

"I just don't," Logan replied grimly. "You're going to have to prove that he means nothing to you."

"What more can I say? What more can I do?"

"You can stop avoiding him. If he invites you out, go with him. If it's really over, you'll know."

"I couldn't do that."

"Do it for me, Sheila."

"Logan, I . . ."

Whatever statement Sheila was about to make was muffled, and Jennifer knew instinctively it was because Logan had taken her in his arms. She managed to tiptoe back to the front desk, doing her best to swallow her sobs. Somehow she was able to tell Carol that Sheila was busy, and that she was going on home, barely making it out the door before the tears started streaming down her cheeks. She was crying not just for herself, but for Logan as well. He was actually forcing the woman he adored into the company of her former lover, so that when she came to him there would be no ghosts, no regrets.

"Jenny! Jennifer!" a voice called out as she tried to dash past the stocky figure approaching the lodge. His hand caught and held her arm while she wiped desperately at her tears with her free hand.

"Hey, what's this all about?" Dirk brushed a sparkling tear away.

Jennifer shrugged her shoulders and took a deep breath before lifting her head to smile tremulously at him.

"Just being a girl, I guess . . . crying for no reason at all."

"I've seen that look of misery in your eyes before," he said wryly, "when you thought no one noticed." His arm reached out, encircling her shoulders to draw her comfortably against his side. "Come on, tell me all about it."

"There's nothing to tell." Jennifer hoped she sounded convincing.

"Yeah, right." He squeezed her shoulders. "You've been depressed ever since the man from Minnesota left."

"Maybe, maybe not."

"I was just going into the lodge for a sandwich and some soup. If you don't feel like eating, then come and sympathize with me over a cup of coffee," Dirk insisted firmly.

Jennifer glanced reluctantly toward the lodge. Logan was there. Well, so what? Was she going to let him rule her life, dictating where she could go and when?

"Sounds good," she agreed quickly.

He didn't give her an opportunity to change her mind but led her directly into the lodge, through the lobby, and into the café. Once there, he ordered for himself and at the same time asked the waitress to bring Jennifer a small bowl of chili. "To warm her up," he told her in an aside. From there on he took charge of the conversation. His light-hearted banter slowly soothed her jangled nerves until Jennifer was able to chat with some of her usual high spirits.

She was laughing easily over Dirk's account of an oddball art exhibit, when she found herself looking into Logan's narrowed eyes as he gazed at them from the café entrance. Though her heart leaped to her throat, choking her laughter off momentarily, she managed to look back to Dirk, conscious that every step Logan took brought him closer to their table.

They exchanged polite greetings, but Logan declined Dirk's invitation to join them.

"What a coincidence, finding the two of you here together." Logan smiled, but the smile failed to relieve the penetrating harshness of his eyes. "Sheila and I were just discussing the fact that Jenny hadn't had a chance to see the Tetons. I suggested that the four of us go together. How about next week?"

Dirk's expression was as cynical as Jennifer's, though he agreed quickly to the suggestion. Jennifer stared at the table, all too aware of the implications of Logan's plan. Sheila would be in Dirk's company—and under Logan's watchful eye.

"What do you say, Jenny?" Logan's hardening gaze studied her intently.

She longed to tell him off. The last thing she wanted was to spend a day in his company, and he knew it. But even before she began to nod her assent, Jennifer knew she would never say it. Like a lamb being led to slaughter, she bowed her head to fate.

"I'll check the weather channel for a clear day coming up and let you know." His smile was sardonic.

"You don't seem exactly overjoyed." Dirk studied her keenly as her eyes followed the retreating back of Logan Taylor.

What could she say, Jennifer thought—that she didn't like being used as a pawn in one of Logan's calculated moves to capture the queen? No, she couldn't tell Dirk the real reason behind Logan's invitation. He was undoubtedly thrilled at the idea of going somewhere with Sheila.

"That's because he was so damn sure we would say yes," she finally replied.

"Which we did." His expression was thoughtful as he eyed the defiant set of her chin and the rueful gleam in her eyes. "I wonder if you agreed for the same reason as I did?"

She didn't reply, knowing that Dirk would see through any lie.

"I'm sure we'll have a great time," she sighed instead, hoping he wouldn't hear the bitterness and self-pity in her soul.

The brilliance of the morning sun intensified the stark whiteness of the snow as the four walked slowly under the snow-covered archway toward the log chapel. The simple wood cross on the roof peak was edged with snow.

The sight of the humble church increased Jennifer's feeling of infinite sanctity. This little house of God was as inspiring as the glorious mountains that surrounded it.

Logan held the door open as they entered the chapel, crossing the unpretentious wooden floor to the simple log-and-slat pews. No one needed to be reminded that this was a place of worship, as all looked up to the altar. Another simple cross of wood stood silhouetted against the altar window, framing the distant Tetons, their white peaks standing out against the vividly blue sky. An enveloping awe touched Jennifer as she took in the glory of God's own work, majestic and never to be overshadowed by any design of man's.

It was such a powerful image of the mightiness of her Creator that Jennifer's eyes smarted with tears at the holiness of the chapel. All the great cathedrals and palatial temples of worship in the world suddenly seemed to be overstated. Nothing could match the spiritual peace and tranquility she felt within these plain wood walls, or the eternal splendor of God's mountains behind the wooden cross and altar.

Several minutes later, in unbroken silence, Logan, Sheila, Jennifer, and Dirk filed out of the church.

"The Chapel of the Transfiguration," Jennifer whispered reverently, once outside. "Now I understand what it means. . . ."

The unfinished sentence needed no explanation.

"It's so perfect." She searched unsuccessfully for the right words again as she turned toward Logan. "Who? How?"

"A family from California spent several summers here in the nineteen-twenties and they raised the money to build it." He smiled understandingly at her. "It's an Episcopal church, but it's open to all faiths. I couldn't think of a better place to start our tour."

"Neither could I," Jennifer said.

Their short conversation had separated them from Sheila and Dirk, who had already reached the Jeep. It was as if a truce had been called between the warring parties. Everyone had found peace in those few minutes spent inside the chapel.

"Over there is the Maude Noble cabin." Logan gestured toward the building opposite the chapel. "That's where the movement to create the Grand Teton National Park got started. To the north is the Bill Menor cabin. He was the first settler west of the Snake River and operated a ferry here for over twenty-five years. But there's too much to see and do in just one day and the park roads are closed in the winter, so we'll have to stick to the highway running through it."

"I don't mind. There's always another time." A wistfulness colored her words, knowing she wouldn't be there long enough to see the mountains in summer.

"There will be, Jenny."

There was a warm certainty in his voice that made Jennifer raise her head to look at him, but they had already reached their vehicle and Logan was holding the rear door open for her. His gaze was soft as it rested briefly on her face.

Once again they were all back in the Jeep, Sheila safely in front with Logan, Jennifer behind with Dirk. But the strain among the foursome was gone, and Jennifer knew the rest of the trip would be companionable and fun.

Back on the main road, Logan pointed out the wooded mesa called Blacktail Butte, named for the large number of blacktail or mule deer formerly found in the area. They traveled slowly, pausing along the roadside to watch an occasional moose grazing by the Snake River, which coiled between the highway and the mountains. The austere grandeur of the craggy peaks, now decked out in winter splendor, showed in ever-changing views. Wispy trails of blowing snow danced down a slope before fading into stillness where the wind died. The cottonwoods along the riverbank and the aspens on the slopes were dressed in shimmering ice, while the pines wore garlands of snow. The scenes were sometimes ethereal in their beauty, sometimes majestic and imposing, but Jennifer's eyes were always drawn to the towering mountains.

At last Logan pulled to the side of the road and turned off the ignition.

"Snake River overlook," he announced, glancing back at Jennifer before getting out of the Jeep to open her door.

Jennifer stood quietly at his side, expecting Sheila and Dirk to join them. But Logan took her elbow and guided her across the road without waiting for the others. For one unwelcome moment, she was reminded of the real reason for this trip: so Sheila could be with Dirk. Quickly Jennifer shoved the thought aside. It was a perfect day, and she wasn't going to allow anything to spoil it. Still, she couldn't prevent herself from glancing over her shoulder at her sister, who looked like a model in black skiwear. Her black parka, trimmed in white fur with a white hood, framed her own raven black hair beautifully. She sighed inwardly, knowing that her own brown and gold outfit would never make her look as sophisticated as Sheila, not when her button nose practically got lost between her brown eyes.

"There are the Tetons." Logan's voice was quiet as his arm swept out before him.

Jennifer stopped beside him to stare in awe at the magnificent citadels.

"The tall, jagged peak towering over the rest is Grand Teton. The flat-topped one to the north is Mount Moran. Below us is the Snake River. It looks peaceful now, but it can be mean. The Snake twists and turns through Yellowstone Park and back through the Grand Tetons before it gets to Hell's Canyon in Idaho. There's a reason it's called the 'River of No Return' there." She looked where he was pointing, dazzled by the scenery—and him. "Are you impressed, Jenny? I don't believe there's anyplace on earth that matches the Grand Tetons and the Wind River range for this kind of rugged, untouched beauty. There's nothing like it."

She nodded her head in a breathless agreement, casting a shy glance up at Logan. His mouth lifted quickly into that familiar smile.

"Did you know we have a lake named after you here in the park?" he teased.

"After me?"

"Jenny Lake. Actually, it was named for a Shoshone Indian woman."

"Tell me about it," she urged.

"She was the wife of one of the more colorful characters in the Grand Tetons' history, Richard Leigh. He was born in England, though he fought in the U.S.–Mexican War of the eighteen-forties. He came to the Rocky Mountains to live, and later guided a government geological survey team through the Snake River Canyon. So a lake was named after him, Leigh Lake, and one for his wife, Jenny."

"And?" She sensed there was more to the story.

"The entire family was snowbound one winter in a one-room cabin. They contracted smallpox somehow and Jenny was the first to die. With no help and no medicine, Leigh got sick himself. He struggled to save them, but within four days he had lost his wife and all six children. He remarried later and had another family, but years later, he admitted that visiting a place filled with memories of Jenny and their children brought tears to his eyes."

The thought of the long-ago tragedy silenced Jennifer as she gazed back at the mountain range, never changing, never revealing any hint of the many things they had seen.

"Want some cocoa?" Logan offered, uncapping the thermos that had been tucked under one arm.

Jennifer nodded, then glanced around to see Dirk and Sheila standing some distance away, as Dirk gestured toward one of the mountains. Logan's eyes followed Jennifer's. Her face paled when she finally looked back at him, though his expression revealed nothing of the inner jealousy she knew he must feel at the attentive expression on Sheila's face.

"Guess they're discussing the color of the pines or the light," said Logan, his eyes again on Jennifer.

"Maybe so," she agreed, watching him pour the steaming cocoa into a cup and hand it to her.

"Have you decided what you're going to do yet?"

An underlying sharpness edged his voice despite

the casual question. Jennifer's hand trembled for a few seconds.

"You mean about Minneapolis?" She knew very well what he meant, but she wanted time to think about her answer.

"And your Mr. Stevenson."

"He's not 'my' Mr. Stevenson." Her laugh was too nervous to sound genuine.

"I got a different impression. But you're taking a long time making up your mind about his marriage proposal."

"I don't think marriage was part of what he proposed." Jennifer shrugged, a cynical twist in the smile on her lips.

Logan had been staring at the spectacular view as if the idle conversation meant nothing to him, but at her wry statement, he turned his penetrating gaze on her.

"A little affair, huh?" he said sarcastically. "And you're holding out for a ring."

"Maybe." Her eyes strayed to the distant couple, so engrossed in their conversation that they were unaware of anyone else. "Maybe I'm just waiting to see my sister settled, before . . ." Her voice trailed into silence.

"Do you mean that when Sheila marries again, you would actually considering going back to that man?" There was no masking the powerful emotion in Logan's face or voice as he stepped toward her.

She couldn't help noticing, with a sinking heart, that he'd said *when Sheila marries,* not *if.*"

"Don't point fingers, Logan," she said, raising her head defiantly. "You're not immune to the opposite sex. Hey, ten minutes after kissing my sister under the mistletoe, you were trying the same thing on me, remember?"

"Yeah, I remember!" He was clearly angry—and insulted all over again.

Her cup of cocoa was jarred to the ground as he took hold of her shoulders. She stifled a startled cry when he jerked her to his chest, frightened by his sudden show of strength. His gaze left hers to travel over her flushed cheeks, to stop on her parted lips. Her heart hammered wildly against her ribs.

"I think I've proved my point," she managed to say, although her voice was shaky.

His eyes met hers again, the anger gone.

"I think I've learned something, too, Jenny Glenn. You're not totally immune to me either."

"Let me go!" she whispered angrily, averting her eyes before he could see more there than she wanted him to. "I don't want you to touch me!"

"Don't you?" He smiled.

"No! You're impossibly arrogant—and I can't stand you! You could never be faithful to anyone and you know it." Her fear of her own emotions brought her close to tears. "When I think of how Sheila hangs on every word you say . . ."

"You don't know me very well, and your sister doesn't either." Logan's eyes were mocking as he moved away from her. "But you'll change your mind in time."

"That's what you think!" She tried to put as much scorn as she could into her voice. But she only succeeded in feeling childish as Logan's chuckle interrupted her retort. "I'll . . . I'll never think of you the way Sheila does."

No, she thought to herself, somehow her pride

would prevent her love from showing, and protect her from humiliation and embarrassment.

A spark of rekindled anger flared briefly in Logan's brown eyes before it was replaced with amusement.

"Someday you'll regret that big mouth of yours. Don't push me too far. But in the end, Jenny Glenn, you'll give in . . ." He broke off and smiled over Jennifer's shoulder at the approaching couple. "Ready for some sandwiches and cocoa?"

"Good idea." Dirk smiled, his gaze resting affectionately on Sheila, who murmured agreement.

They all tramped through the snow and across the road to the Jeep together. Jennifer wasn't quite sure how Logan managed to settle himself in the backseat with her, opening the picnic basket and passing out the sandwiches, then packing the remnants back in when they were done. With annoying nonchalance he tossed the car keys to Dirk, suggesting he drive the rest of the way.

Despite the breathtaking scenery that rolled by for the rest of the afternoon, Jennifer was miserable. Logan's intimate glances, the touch of his hand on her arm when he wanted to show her something else, only made her nervousness worse. She knew he needed her to distract himself from Sheila and Dirk in the front seat, but she couldn't match his casual, flirtatious manner. There was nothing frivolous about her feelings for him, and her emotions were too overwhelming to take his meaningless attention seriously.

When Dirk parked in front of Sheila's house at last, it was all Jennifer could do to keep from bolting out of the Jeep. She could tell by the gleam of amusement in Logan's eyes that he knew she could hardly wait to get into the house. She finally managed to stammer a good-bye to Dirk and get inside, away from the man she loved.

Chapter Nine

"Good morning, Jenny!" Sheila sang out. Her long blue and lavender robe made it look like she was floating into the kitchen instead of walking.

"Good morning," Jenny replied, sighing as she glanced down at her own robe, a rumpled, discount-store buy that stopped short of her knees. As usual, there was no way she could match Sheila's elegance, especially at this hour in the morning.

"I have a feeling it's going to be a gorgeous day!" her sister exclaimed. The radiant expression on her face was enough to light up the room, Jenny thought, a little sourly.

"Do you realize how long it's been since I went skiing? I think I made it to the slopes once last year." Sheila poured herself a cup of coffee before sitting at the table with Jennifer. "You're really going to enjoy it, Jenny."

"Will you *please* stop calling me Jenny! My name is Jennifer!"

"I . . . didn't realize you were still so touchy about

it," Sheila apologized, taken aback by her sister's unexpected display of temper.

"Well, not really." Jennifer was immediately contrite. "Maybe I got up on the wrong side of the bed this morning."

"Not the first time. Honey, what's been bothering you lately? You just haven't been yourself, not since Brad left. You're so moody. Want to talk about it?" cajoled Sheila. "I heard you tossing and turning all night last night and there's circles under your eyes this morning. I'll admit I've been too busy to spend much time with you. But today— well, I've got the whole day, or at least, most of it."

"Sheila, you are the sweetest sister in the whole world"—Jennifer reached out and squeezed her hand affectionately—"and thanks for putting up with me. It's just that—I have some problems that I've got to work out for myself."

"That's what I'm getting at. Talk them over with me. Between the two of us, we could—"

"No, thanks." Jennifer shook her head sadly.

"Is it Brad?"

"Partly." She ran a hand through her hair, its glossy strands reflecting red in the morning sunlight. "You might as well know I've been considering going back to Minneapolis."

"Jenny—Jennifer," Sheila corrected herself. "You're not going back to work for him?"

"No."

"Then why go? I know you've been unhappy lately, but at first you really seemed to be enjoying yourself here. The children love having you. They'd be lost without you."

"Not for long. It's just that I feel so useless." Jennifer held up a hand to stave off the protest that

Sheila was about to make. "I know I've helped you out, but it's time I went back home. Besides, I'm pretty sure that there's someone else in your life who's going to look after you and the children permanently." Sheila blushed beautifully as Jennifer's morale slipped a notch lower. "And I'm not any good playing the mouse in the corner." She tried to laugh.

"If you're worried about finding a real job, I'm sure Logan could arrange . . ."

"No!" Jennifer interrupted sharply before tempering her voice. "I'm capable of getting a job for myself. But I really think I should go back to Minneapolis. I shouldn't have run away in the first place." Coming to Wyoming had turned out to be the biggest mistake of her life.

"When were you planning on leaving?"

"I hadn't gotten that far." Her mind cried, *Soon, very soon.*

"Well, I hope you stay for a while longer, for personal reasons." Sheila beamed, her brilliant blue eyes revealing her secret happiness.

Jennifer couldn't give an honest reply to that statement, so she made none at all.

"I have a few errands to do in town. Is there anything you need while I'm there?" Jennifer offered instead.

"No, I don't think so. Don't forget we're going skiing this afternoon."

"I won't," Jennifer said quickly, walking out of the kitchen toward the bedrooms to dress.

"I mean it." Sheila followed behind her. "No lame excuses and no cakes in the oven or anything else you mentioned last week whenever Logan made plans for us."

"We can't upset Logan's plans." A teasing smile hid the unhappiness in Jennifer's voice.

"Honestly, Jenny, he planned it just for you. The least you can do is come. I want you to promise you'll be there."

"I will," Jennifer assured her emphatically before disappearing inside her bedroom.

Minutes later, dressed in her russet-brown and gold ski outfit, Jennifer hurried out the door with Sheila's voice calling after her, reminding her to be at the slopes by one o'clock.

She shuffled dejectedly through the snow once out of sight of the house. This last week had been unbearable, with Logan constantly forcing her to join the others. At first, it wasn't so bad. Jennifer even thought that Dirk stood a chance, but it only took one look at Sheila's face when she exchanged glances with Logan to understand the secret intimacy between them. And last night—last night had been the crushing blow.

The children were already in bed when Jennifer attempted to sink into the forgetfulness of sleep, but it was no use. Instead she'd sat alone in the darkened living room, trying to fight off the depression that hung over her head like thunderclouds on the Teton peaks. Then she'd heard the crunching sound of snow as a car halted in front of the house. Although tempted to peek out the window, she'd resisted, not wanting to see what was really happening. Finally the sound of car doors opening and closing, followed by Sheila's laughter, had roused her from the chair.

She would never forget the emotional pain that gripped her when she saw Sheila step into Logan's arms and plant a kiss on his lips before he lovingly walked her to the door, an arm firmly wrapped around her shoulders, hugging her to his side. Jennifer had run swiftly into her bedroom, faking sleep when Sheila glanced in later. And this morning, Sheila practically came right out and announced that she and Logan were getting married.

Jennifer sighed deeply as she stepped off the curb into the street. Simultaneously a horn blared loudly in her ear and a hand jerked her quickly backward as an SUV barreled past just inches away.

"Better watch where you're going," a middle-aged man reprimanded her. "You almost got yourself killed!"

"Th-thank you," Jennifer stammered. "I'm afraid I was daydreaming."

"Daydreaming and walking in traffic don't mix."

"They certainly don't," she agreed shakily. "Thank you again."

The man tipped his Stetson and walked on.

Reaching the shopping center, she glanced at the window displays as she strolled by. The only reason she had come to town was to get away. Oh, she could stop to see if her watch battery had been replaced, maybe splurge on some perfume or make-up, but it was mostly a form of escape. Too bad she couldn't escape this afternoon's skiing somehow, she thought. She increased her pace as she recognized the jeweler's sign just ahead of her.

Jennifer glanced inside the elegant shop. With a tightening throat she saw Logan standing inside, an older well-dressed man hovering beside him with a black velvet ring box in his hand. Logan smiled in approval, taking the box and tucking it into his shirt pocket. When he turned toward the door, Jennifer ducked quickly into an adjoining store, pain constricting her chest until she could hardly breathe.

An engagement ring. *For Sheila.* She should have known.

She watched Logan stride away, then hurried out of the store and into the jeweler's, hesitating just inside the door. The older man who had been with Logan was talking to a young salesclerk.

"I don't know, but diamonds always say 'engagement ring' to me," the younger one was saying.

"But Logan wasn't just settling for something cheaper. That ring cost a small fortune, and the diamonds around it are flawless. He told me it was a tradition in the Taylor family that all prospective brides receive an engagement ring of—"

Jennifer involuntarily let out a low cry at his words, causing the older man to cut off his sentence and turn to her solicitously.

"May I help you with something?" he asked.

"No, no, thank you." And she dashed out of the door.

As Jennifer approached the chairlift, she didn't need a second glance to recognize the man approaching her. Logan wore a bright blue and black jacket and black ski pants. His snow goggles were pushed back from his face, offering her no protection from his angry eyes.

"Where were you? It's half past one." Logan said brusquely.

"Oh, is it that late?" Her own dark-tinted goggles were in place, hiding her misery from his penetrating eyes. "I didn't realize—"

"There are a lot of things you haven't realized

lately." He gripped her arm firmly, pushing her ahead of him, two pairs of skis firmly clamped under his other arm. "I told Sheila not to let you out of her sight today, to drag you here if necessary."

"I promised her I'd come. She knew I would."

"The way you've been dodging us this past week, it wouldn't have surprised me if you hadn't shown up today." He glared at her as they stopped, and dropped the skis on the ground in front of her. "I was just getting ready to look for you, to drag you here myself if I had to."

"And now you're angry because I came and you didn't get that thrill," she lashed out, wishing her sharp words would cut as deep as his.

"I don't know what's eating you." Anger was etched in the line of his jaw and the set of his mouth. "But yes, today is important to me, and I wanted everything to be just right. I thought Sheila's happiness was important to you, too, but I guess that's changed, hasn't it?"

Jennifer wanted to cry. She did want Sheila to be happy, but she couldn't help wishing that her sister wasn't about to be linked in holy matrimony with the man Jennifer loved. Ever since leaving the jewelers', she had been telling herself that she was lucky to find out for sure that Logan and Sheila were going to be married. Now she had an opportunity to put on a convincing show and offer her congratulations to the happy couple. But it wasn't going to be as easy as that. Just seeing Logan brought the aching torment to the surface.

Logan was bending near her feet, shoving her boots into the skis as if they weren't on her feet.

His roughness forced her to grab his shoulder to keep from being thrown off balance into the snow. His muscles tightened at her touch. Instantly she let go as if she had touched a high-voltage wire and were recoiling from the shock.

"Where's Sheila?" Jennifer asked hurriedly as Logan bent to adjust his quick-release bindings.

"I sent them on up to the top"—he paused sarcastically—"when I thought I'd have to go looking for you."

So the foursome was complete once more, Jennifer thought bitterly. And poor Dirk was about to be publicly humiliated.

She avoided Logan's guiding hand as they joined the chairlift line. Minutes later they were swinging toward the top. She glanced bleakly at him out of the corner of her eye. The stocking cap that had been in his pocket completely covered his chestnut brown hair, and the yellow-tinted goggles made his brown eyes look amber. Looking at the grim line of his mouth made Jennifer's heart ache all over again.

Then they were at the top, swinging off the chairs onto their skis, gliding silently across the snow, ignoring the chattering and laughing of the other skiers. They stopped at the edge of the first slope. Jennifer planted her poles in the snow while she adjusted her hat and mittens. She could hardly bear the gnawing tension that grew with each progressive minute of silence.

"Sheila told me you've decided to go back to Minneapolis." There was an indefinable harshness in his calm statement.

"That's right." Jennifer's chin lifted stubbornly.

"You're going to accept Brad's—what should I call it?—proposition." His words cut through her like an icy sword.

The wind whistled out of the leaden clouds above them, picking up the snow at their feet and sending it dancing down the slope.

"Would it do any good to ask you to stay longer?" Logan sighed with exasperated anger. "For Sheila's sake, if nothing else?"

Jennifer's mouth twisted bitterly. It was presumptuous of him to think that all he had to do was ask . . . and all too typical.

"Jenny—" he began. His voice possessed a commandingly tender tone that wrenched at her self-control.

"Don't call me that!" she cried huskily, with tears brimming in her eyes.

Grabbing her poles, she flipped herself expertly around so that she was facing down the slope. Before Logan's outstretched hand could stop her, she was pushing off to race down the ski run.

In seconds she was careening down the hill, the trees blurring into a solid wall on either side and the other skiers becoming faceless objects to be zigzagged around. "Too fast! You're going too fast!" The warning shouts rang in her head. The sound of another pair of skis schussing after her only made her try to go faster.

"Slow down!" Logan ordered as he drew alongside.

For one brief instant, she toyed with the idea of maintaining her breakneck pace. A broken leg, a broken neck—weren't they better than a broken heart? Then she straightened, making her sweeps wider down the run until she turned her skis at right angles and braked to a halt.

"What were you trying to do, kill yourself?" Logan's rage unleashed itself as he stopped in front of her, blocking her way down the mountain.

Her face drained of color while her knees trembled weakly beneath her. The cold air burned her lungs as she gasped for breath.

"You're not going to answer me, as usual," he muttered angrily as Jennifer continued to avoid his face. "If you're not lashing out at me, then you're running away. When are you going to stop fighting me and—"

"Oh, look, there's Sheila and Dirk!" Jennifer exclaimed breathlessly, recognizing her sister's ski outfit.

She waved frantically at them, glad of anything that would distract Logan. At last Sheila spotted them and waved back. Jennifer could sense that Logan gave in with fuming reluctance. His only comment was a biting order to keep their pace down. As Logan and Jennifer neared the other couple, her sister and Dirk set out down the hill, with Sheila darting back and forth in front of the much more cautious Dirk.

In the blink of an eye, the scene changed. There was a spray of snow, a ringing cry, and a cartwheeling figure tumbling in front of Jennifer. Then, almost in slow motion, she saw Dirk rush to help at the same moment that Logan left her side and hurled himself toward both of them.

"Sheila!" The wind dissolved Jennifer's frantic sob.

By the time she reached the group, a ski patrolman had already joined Logan to examine her sister for broken bones while Dirk gently brushed the snow from her face. Jennifer stood silently to one side, watching Logan carefully remove Sheila's skis. Her sister's eyes fluttered open and she moaned softly.

"Looks like it's the right foot," Logan told the man from the ski patrol.

"Okay. I'll go and get the basket sled and radio for an ambulance to meet us at the bottom," he replied before skiing away.

Jennifer felt strangely apart from the scene, as if she were looking into someone else's nightmare. Her anxious eyes fixed on Logan's tight-lipped face as he spoke with Dirk. Stunned, paralyzed by a cold, chilling shock over her sister's accident, she didn't hear what was said. It seemed like an eternity before the ski patrol returned, wrapped her sister in a metallic thermal blanket, and strapped her into the basket sled, but it probably had been only a matter of minutes. Although they were halfway down the mountainside already, they made slow progress to the bottom on their skis. She was half-conscious of Logan by her side; most of her attention focused on Sheila.

Once at the hospital Jennifer still could not shake off her dazed feeling. Dirk was pacing the waiting room floor, and Logan was somewhere in one of the admitting offices, filling out an endless medical form. And she was sitting on the green tweed couch, a cup of vending-machine coffee still clutched tightly in her hands. Logan had given it to her shortly after they had wheeled Sheila in, ordered her to drink some and waited long enough to see that she did, and then left. The rest of the coffee had been cold for a while. A hand touched her shoulder and she jumped.

"You didn't finish it," Logan said softly, removing the cup from her hands and placing it on the table. "Are you all right?"

Jennifer shook her head numbly.

"How is Sheila?" she asked.

"They've taken her up to X-ray," Logan told her, his eyes following Dirk's nervous pacing. "She put a ski pole through her foot. The doctor thinks she's probably broken a bone as well."

A man wearing pale green scrubs walked into the room, and a woman in white appeared at his side, glancing at the people in the waiting room before she spoke. Jennifer caught the muffled words "sister" and "fiancé" as the man nodded his head and turned to them.

"Good to see you, Logan." The man reached out and shook Logan's hand affably. "You must be Sheila's sister," he said to Jennifer, then turned to the impatient Dirk. "Mr. Hamilton, I'm Dr. March."

Jennifer tried to concentrate when he began to explain Sheila's condition. But the only words that penetrated were "puncture" and "a fracture of the tarsal bone in her foot."

"She's under mild sedation now, but you can see her for a few minutes," he finished calmly.

Jennifer clutched Logan's hand tightly as he helped her from the couch and led her down a hallway. She stared down at her sister silently, hardly recognizing the pale face surrounded by a cloud of black hair. Then her eyelids fluttered open, revealing the familiar, brilliant blue eyes. Jennifer smiled down at this fragile china doll who'd always seemed so indestructible . . . until today.

"Hello," Sheila said thickly. "I really did it good this time, huh?"

"You sure did," Logan smiled, filling in the silence when Jennifer was only able to nod. "We can't stay long. Dirk's outside waiting to see you."

"The kids?" Sheila raised her head weakly from her pillow. "Do they know?"

"Don't worry about them," Logan assured her. "And we'll come back to see you later when you're not so groggy."

Logan had already guided her to the doorway when Jennifer finally found her voice and managed a tremulous good-bye to her sister. He led her back into the waiting room, set her on the couch, and told her to wait for him.

With Logan gone, Jennifer fought to get a grip. She knew the strain of this last month had been hard on her, but now Sheila would need her more than ever, and so would the children. She had to get control of herself before she saw Eric and Cindy, and make sure that she didn't communicate her nervousness to them. They would need a lot of loving reassurance that their mother was going to be okay, and plenty of extra attention.

If only she could seem as calm as Logan, she thought, watching him come confidently toward her. She managed a brief but composed smile as she met his questioning glance.

"Ready to go?" he asked.

Jennifer nodded. Once outside the hospital, Logan reached over and removed the knit cap from her head. The sudden coolness of the brisk afternoon air was a refreshing balm to her tense nerves.

"What did you do that for?" Jennifer asked, automatically shaking her head, enjoying the feel of the cool wind playing through her red-gold hair.

"To perk you up. Just let that fear and tension blow away. It'll do you good." Logan smiled. Instantly Jennifer was captured by the comforting warmth of his gaze.

Sheila. She had to remember her sister and not let her personal feelings interfere. Not now, though, later, when she was alone, she told herself.

Although they drove to Sheila's house without exchanging a word, it was nothing like the cocoon of silence that had surrounded Jennifer after the accident. This silence was companionable, and she drew strength from it. When Logan slowed the car to a stop, Jennifer turned and began to offer her thanks.

"Want me to come with you while you tell the kids?" Logan interrupted before she could finish.

"Would you?" Her smile was shaky with relief. For all her hard-won composure, Jennifer really didn't want to face Eric and Cindy alone.

"Of course. I planned to all along." His teasing smile made her heart do flip-flops as he opened the car door and stepped outside. She did the same.

They had barely gotten inside the front door when the children rushed at them, followed by their babysitter.

"Where have you been?" Cindy asked nervously.

"Where's Mom?" Eric's voice expressed the alarm that Cindy had tried to hide.

As calmly and as patiently as she could, Jennifer explained what had happened. She understood the panic-stricken looks. Mothers were supposed to be invulnerable to accidents, injuries—all the things they guarded their children from. But somehow, with Logan's steadying presence, Eric and Cindy managed to accept it and—Jennifer said a silent prayer of gratitude—even to see the humor in it, thanks to him. Before Jennifer knew what was happening, they talked him into staying for supper after he took the sitter home.

A smile of pleasure played on Jennifer's lips as she realized that it hadn't taken much coaxing on their part to get him to agree. Of course, it was for the children's sake, she reminded herself. But still, it didn't hurt too much to indulge in a little wishful thinking. When she glanced at the clock, Jennifer was surprised to see how late it was. She excused herself quickly and hurried into the kitchen, planning a special meal—and not just to boost the children's spirits, either.

When Jennifer called them in to supper, it was with pride, knowing that the meal of seasoned pork chops, wild rice with mushrooms, mesclun salad, and an old-fashioned pineapple upside-down cake for dessert, was just plain delicious—and even healthy.

There was so much laughter and chatter at the table that evening, Jennifer found it difficult to remember that Sheila was lying in a hospital bed. But her sister wouldn't have wanted her absence to spoil their evening together. To Jennifer, seated across the table from Logan, watching his smiling face as he listened to a long explanation from Eric on the things that were wrong with school, this was a stolen hour, one she could cherish and dream about—she and Logan seated at a table with two sweet kids. Maybe someday . . .

His eyes locked with hers. There was such an intense intimacy in his gaze that she felt he had somehow read her mind and knew what her imagination had conjured up. She managed to break the spell and cover up her embarrassment with a flurry of activity, gathering plates and passing out the dessert.

"I forgot to tell you, Jenny," Logan said with a mock seriousness. "We got roped into a game of Chinese checkers."

"Girlth againth the boyth," Cindy said quickly.

"How did we manage to do that?" Jennifer laughed.

"It was easy," said Eric. "I dared him."

"And I double-dared him," Cindy joined in.

"So you see"—Logan tilted his head in resignation—"What could I do?"

"Exactly!" Eric agreed enthusiastically.

"Hmm. What would happen if I double-dared all of you to do the dishes?" Jennifer wanted to laugh at the horrified looks on Eric's and Cindy's faces, but she kept a straight face.

"It doesn't work for that," Eric gulped.

"I think it works for stacking dishes," Logan stated. "Otherwise Jenny might not think that double-dare was any good for Chinese checkers."

With a speed previously unheard of when it came to household chores, the two children had the dishes scraped and stacked and the board and marbles ready on the kitchen table.

After two games, with each side winning one, Jennifer looked up to the kitchen clock and announced that it was bedtime. The grumblings and pleadings were swept aside when Logan announced that if they were ready for bed in ten minutes, he'd read them a story.

Standing over the kitchen sink, her hands immersed in dishwater, Jennifer listened to the rhythmic sound of Logan's voice as he read to the two drowsy children in the other room. As she dried the last pan with a fresh dishtowel, an overwhelming tiredness engulfed her. This cozy evening would never be repeated in the future, and the thought drained what happiness she had felt. The almost sinful guilt of wanting what belonged to her sister rested heavily on her shoulders. She should be the one lying in that hospital bed, not Sheila. If only the accident had happened to her! Two lonely tears rolled slowly down her cheeks.

"It's been a long day for you, hasn't it, Jenny Glenn?" Logan stood by the counter staring down at her, his gaze so tender and compassionate that the two tears Jennifer had wiped away so quickly were instantly replaced by two more.

If he hadn't spoken in that gentle, caressing tone, she might have been able to resist him when he drew her into his arms. Instead Jennifer went meekly, letting him hold her close, nestling against his chest. Although she wanted to cry buckets of tears, the ache was too deep and painful. She stilled the wild racing of her heart, forbidding herself to enjoy the possessive touch of his hand on her head or the rock-hardness of his muscles. But in her imagination she felt the erratic beat of his heart match hers. Then her hand brushed a small shape—the ring box, where he had first put it, in his shirt pocket. She slowly disengaged herself from his embrace, shivering slightly, and not only because she had left the warmth of his arms.

"Going to see Sheila tonight?" She hoped her trembling voice didn't betray her mixed emotions.

"It's already after visiting hours, but I'll try to stop in for a few minutes," Logan replied, studying her intently as he spoke.

"I shouldn't have let the children talk you into staying."

"They didn't," Logan corrected her. He stepped toward her, but halted when Jennifer moved involuntarily away. "You need a good night's rest."

Thanks for telling me how great I look Jennifer wanted to say before chiding herself for self-pitying thought.

"I'll pick you up in the morning around nine-thirty. We can be at the hospital when the doctor makes his rounds."

Jennifer nodded. As if she had a choice. But she would be ready.

"Call me tonight if you need anything." His tone was almost stern. "I'll be staying at my mother's. Her number's on speed dial."

She agreed, assuring him that there would be no need for her to call, that everything was fine. Logan left, almost reluctantly, Jennifer thought, then dismissed that idea. Most likely he could hardly wait to get to the hospital.

Dressing for bed, Jennifer felt wide awake, but the tension, anxiety, and strain of the day had tired her more than she realized. Within minutes after her head touched the pillow, she was asleep.

Chapter Ten

Mrs. Taylor, Logan's mother, was in the waiting room when Logan and Jennifer left Sheila the next morning. Her sister had been in high spirits, laughing at her accident and generally assuring the doctor that she was much better. There had been no ring on her finger, which made Jennifer think that Logan wanted to wait until she was out of the hospital, and the ring could be presented with a little more ceremony. She was glad she hadn't had to make small talk with her sister, except to answer questions about the children. Jennifer hated the jealousy that consumed her whenever she watched Logan and Sheila together. Her surprise at seeing Logan's mother was quickly hidden. After all, Sheila would be her daughter-in-law someday.

"There's something I want to talk over with you, Jenny," said Logan, ushering her over to a chair next to his mother. "I discussed it with Mom last night, and she's all for it, so I brought her along for moral support."

Jennifer frowned. "What is it?"

Logan took a deep breath and glanced almost apprehensively at his mother before he began.

"Dr. March said that he would be releasing Sheila tomorrow. She'll probably be in a lot of pain the first few days, and taking care of the kids won't be easy." Logan paused, examining Jennifer's face for her reaction. "I suggested that Cindy and Eric stay with the Jeffries for a week."

"Sounds like a good idea." Jennifer was puzzled by his hesitation.

"That's not all. I have to go back to the ranch to attend to a few things personally. Sheila's going to worry about the lodge, because she won't be able to work for at least a week. If she stays in town, she'll be tempted to go in to work. I want her to rest up at the ranch for a week."

"I see." Jennifer hesitated. She could tell there was more to it than that. "I don't know why she wouldn't agree. I could work at the lodge in her place."

"No." His mouth tightened at her suggestion. "Mom can take care of things there. She ran it for years, and she'd enjoy taking over for a week. No, you'll come to the ranch with Sheila."

"What?" Jennifer stared first at Logan, then at his mother. He couldn't possibly mean it.

"It's the only thing to do, dear," Mrs. Taylor spoke up. "And it would work out well for everyone."

"I don't think so." Jennifer twisted her hands together nervously. "Sheila can stay at the house. I can look after her there and make sure she doesn't limp over to the lodge."

"It wouldn't work," Logan said sharply. "You know how headstrong she is. She'd talk you into taking her there for a change of scene or something like that. No, the solution is the ranch."

"I won't go!" Jennifer declared, almost defiantly.

"Oh, yes you will." Logan reached out and captured her wrist, pulling her closer to him. "You can't say no. She's your sister, and right now she needs you. So go home, pack clothes for both of you, and I'll pick you up tomorrow morning at eleven o'clock sharp. Got that?"

"Logan don't order her around like that," his mother said softly.

Her wrist was released, and Logan walked arrogantly away as Jennifer turned toward Mrs. Taylor.

"Guess I'll have to apologize for my son," Mrs. Taylor said ruefully. "He's been moody lately. I'm sure he didn't mean to get on your case like that, but he knows Sheila pretty well."

"I don't see why it's so important . . ." Jennifer stopped before the sobbing in her heart moved to her voice.

"Jenny . . ." Mrs. Taylor hesitated. "Our ranch is beautiful—and peaceful. It would be the perfect place for your sister to rest and relax. And I think you'd like our home very much."

"I'm sure I would," Jennifer agreed, not wanting to be rude to Logan's mother but still baffled by his behavior.

"Please come with your sister. I'm sure she wouldn't understand if you don't."

Jennifer's eyes flashed at Amanda Taylor, sensing that perhaps she had guessed Jennifer's true feelings toward Logan. But the twinkling brown eyes smiled innocently back at her.

"Okay. Tell Logan I'll be ready at eleven. But I

have a lot to do between now and then." She realized her voice was slightly edgy, but Jennifer had just lost another battle with Logan Taylor. Somehow, during the week ahead, she had to find a way to prevent the final humiliation of Logan's discovering her love for him.

Jennifer added another log to the fire blazing cheerfully in the fireplace. Mrs. Taylor was right; she had fallen in love with the ranch at first sight. It nestled snugly on the lee side of a mountain, a sturdy row of pines sheltering the buildings from the winter winds. The rustic barns, stables, and outbuildings were surrounded by a picturesque split-rail fence.

But it was the house that had called to her, as if saying, "This is home." It wasn't rambling and grand, or white and elegant. Its two-story roof was steeply pitched to shed the heavy snows, and there was a wide screened porch on the side to watch the evening sunset. The walls were native wood, strong and thick and sheltering. Perhaps it was the way the windows reflected the sun's golden light that had given Jennifer such an overwhelming feeling of welcome.

Logan had explained, once he'd brought them inside the house, that the upstairs was closed off in the winter, as well as the dining room and parlor, to conserve heat. But Jennifer hadn't minded, not when she had the cozy living room with the large stone fireplace to sit in front of all day. They took their meals in the kitchen, except for Sheila, who was restricted to the large master bedroom the first two days. Logan had put a day bed in the bedroom so that Sheila wouldn't have to risk bumping her foot by sharing the big double bed with her sister. Logan slept in the little room off the kitchen that had once been used by a housekeeper.

All in all, it wasn't as difficult as Jennifer thought it would be. Logan was gone from dawn to dusk. The evenings he spent in the house, sharing a meal with Jennifer at the kitchen table—potentially an intimate experience except for his indifference. But it wasn't really indifference—more like a total lack of interest. And that, Jennifer found, was something she could bear. After dinner, Logan went in to see Sheila while Jennifer occupied herself with dishes and, later, television. They were almost like two strangers sharing the same roof.

But Jennifer found a way to dull the pain of being so near to him, yet emotionally far away. She could take care of his home, cook his meals, including breakfast, and do all the little things that a wife would do. There were times, especially when Logan was with Sheila, that the old jealousy and longing would surface, but she managed to remain composed when his brown eyes met hers. She even was happy when she was with Sheila.

The big Black Forest cuckoo clock sounded twice, and she straightened up from her kneeling place by the fire, smoothing her blue jeans as she rose. Through the open doorway to the bedroom, Jennifer could hear her sister talking on the phone with Dirk, who called at least twice a day. Sheila didn't seem to mind, accepting his attention with a calmness that surprised Jennifer.

She sighed heavily before making her way into

the kitchen. Baking a cake for dessert that night would at least keep her busy. The sound of footsteps in the snow followed by the banging of the back door stopped her. Logan was standing outside with something large and black cradled in his arms.

"Get me some of those big towels out of the linen closet," he said briskly as she opened the door and let him in.

One look at the inert baby calf sent Jennifer scurrying to carry out his order. He had the calf by the fireplace when she returned. Taking one of the towels from her hand, he began rubbing the black fur roughly.

"What happened?" Jennifer asked as she kneeled beside him.

"He was born out of season. His mother just abandoned him," Logan replied. "Warm some milk up—and there are bottles in the lower right-hand cupboard."

In minutes she had the milk heated, and poured in a bottle, capped with a black nursing nipple she found in one of the drawers. She dipped a clean dish towel in the milk and brought that in as well. As weak as the calf was, it just might take a little persuasion to start him nursing. Logan's glance of appreciation let her know that her years on her parents' farm hadn't been a total loss.

He signaled her to go ahead with the feeding while he continued to massage the calf to get the circulation going in its nearly frozen body. Jennifer had to force its mouth open, letting the milk-soaked dish towel trickle its life-giving fluid down its throat. At last its feeble suckings allowed her to switch to the bottle. Between the warmth of the fire, Logan's rubbing, and the warm milk now in its stomach, the little black calf began to show signs of life, weakly butting its head forward in a pathetic effort to get more milk out of the bottle.

At this small but promising attempt, Jennifer glanced at Logan. His smile of shared triumph stopped her heartbeat for a second before it took off again at a hammering pace.

"I didn't think he'd make it," Logan said with a doubtful but happy smile. "How the coyotes missed him I'll never know."

"I'm glad they did," Jennifer said softly, lowering her gaze to the little black head that was now resting comfortably on her knees, its hunger satisfied. "Will he make it now?"

"He has a good chance. We'll let him sleep here by the fire and feed him again later. How about some coffee for us?"

"Of course." Jennifer rose quickly before the magic of his smile captured her again.

When she returned to the room with the coffee, she found Logan gone. The muffled voices in the bedroom seemed to chide her for those few minutes alone with him. She placed his cup on the table and curled up on the floor by the fireplace. Logan returned to find her fondling the calf's black head as it looked around with some confusion from the towels swaddling its spindly body. He smiled down at them both, and Jennifer suddenly wanted to flee, to escape the magnetic virility that attracted her so. But she merely sat gazing into the flames, forcing herself not to react to his presence.

"I was just telling Sheila that tomorrow afternoon might be a good time for you to take a ride around the ranch," said Logan, breaking the silence that had begun to weigh on Jennifer.

"Thank you, but I think I'll pass," she replied in a tightly controlled voice.

"Hey, I've got a gentle horse that would suit you perfectly." She could tell he was smiling, but she didn't turn to meet his eyes. "And I'll be there to make sure that she doesn't run away with you."

"Oh, I can ride quite well, even though I'm probably a little rusty. I just don't like the idea of leaving Sheila alone."

"She won't be alone," Logan said quietly. "Dirk will be here."

Although he spoke calmly enough, Jennifer couldn't stop herself from studying his expression, knowing how possessive he was. She couldn't imagine him allowing Sheila to be all alone with Dirk.

As if he could read her thoughts, he added, "They have some things to discuss . . . in private."

"Oh." An utterly inadequate reply considering that Sheila was undoubtedly going to tell Dirk that she'd decided to marry Logan. Yet another reason why the ring still wasn't on her finger. She should have realized that her sister was too thoughtful to wear it. "In that case," Jennifer said hesitantly, "I'll be happy to go with you tomorrow."

"Well, then I'd better get back to work." And he was gone.

The following afternoon Logan was happy to help Jennifer get accustomed to riding again, and she gradually relaxed and enjoyed herself. The air was brisk and invigorating, and the sun's rays cast a patchwork quilt of light from the partly cloudy sky. Logan was polite and friendly, showing her all over the ranch, explaining, when she questioned him about the picturesque but impractical split-rail fence, that it was necessitated by the few inches of sandy soil that covered the solid rock below.

As they cantered back to within sight of the house, Dirk's car was just pulling away. Jennifer looked sideways at the thoughtful expression on Logan's face, struck by the ruggedness of his pro-file under the Stetson. The virile good looks were still there, along with the engaging crinkles around his eyes, but the Levi's, the sheepskin jacket, and the classic rancher's hat added a steely strength to his appearance. She realized with startling clarity that that strength would always be there.

One of the foreman's sons took their horses when they dismounted by the big barn. Logan smiled easily at Jennifer, nodding for her to walk ahead of him to the house.

Sheila's face was radiantly happy as Logan and Jennifer walked in the front door to find her com-fortably settled on the luxurious leather sofa. Her blue eyes shone up at them.

"Well?" Logan asked, an expectant lightness in his tone.

"Excuse me," Jennifer said quickly. "I'll go and put some coffee on."

Sheila didn't seem to notice her sister walking out of the room. "I didn't think it would be so easy," she was saying to Logan. "He didn't even blink an eye when I explained. He said he under-stood and if I would be happy—"

The connecting kitchen door swung shut on

Sheila's words as Jennifer's stomach twisted into a knot. Poor, dependable Dirk, she thought, managing to spare a little pity for him rather than wasting it all on herself.

Jennifer kept busy in the kitchen for the rest of the afternoon, grateful to be preparing supper. By the time the food was ready to be served, she had a violent headache, probably from suppressed emotions. One look at her pinched, pale face made both Logan and Sheila insist that she lie down and rest. Bitter tears filled her eyes at the knowledge that they would be happy to have the evening to themselves, without her to get in the way.

Jennifer dozed fitfully in the darkened bedroom. The muted voices from the living room awoke her now and then, but never all the way.

The glowing numerals on the nightstand clock said *10:45* when Jennifer woke again. The house seemed silent except for the steady breathing from Sheila's bed. Jennifer lay there quietly, wide awake, the headache replaced by an emotional emptiness. At last, she crept slowly out of the day bed and threw on her short robe. She had only nibbled at the evening meal and could definitely use some hot tea and buttered toast.

She tiptoed through the living room into the kitchen, flicking on only the low overhead light above the stove. As she filled the kettle with cold tap water, she wished she could sneak away somehow into the night and not have to face Logan and Sheila in the morning. Absently Jennifer placed the kettle on the burner and turned on the flame beneath it, trying to decide whether cowardice or courage was telling her to stay. She felt as if all her willpower had been drained away, that even the simplest decision was more than her mind could handle.

As her toast popped out of the toaster, she thought about the incident that had made her run out here from Minneapolis. That embarrassing night with Brad seemed insignificant now when compared with the destructive force of her one-sided love for Logan. The kettle whistled loudly in the silent kitchen, and she quickly took it off the burner. Just as Jennifer began pouring the hot water over the teabag in her cup, a voice spoke from the darkness.

"I thought you were asleep."

The dim light above the stove revealed Logan standing beside the table, clad only in Levi's. The bareness of his chest with its V of curly brown hair made Jennifer uncomfortably conscious of her short robe and the threadbare pajamas underneath it. Her heart thudded so loudly, she was sure Logan could hear it even from where he was standing.

"I was hungry. . . . I was making tea and toast." She could hardly breathe.

"Watch what you're doing!" Logan exclaimed sharply as her hand trembled in an effort to pick up her cup, sloshing the hot liquid over the side and onto the back of her hand. With a barely stifled cry, Jennifer set it down.

"Are you all right? Let me see your hand," he demanded, at her side almost before the cup touched the counter.

She tried to pull away, but she was not fast enough. Her whole body felt as if it were on fire from his touch as he examined her hand. When he met her gaze, his breathing was nearly as ragged as hers.

"Jenny," he whispered. His hand brushed the red-gold bangs away from her forehead, then stroked her hair. "Jenny," he whispered again as he drew her into his arms.

Her lips trembled beneath his as he slowly melted what little resistance she had. She was clinging to him weakly, her arms around his neck, as her senses reeled under the ardent desire in his kiss. Jennifer reveled in the pressure of his naked chest against her body as he crushed her more tightly in his embrace, moaning softly when Logan's mouth left her lips and buried itself in the creamy smoothness of her neck, sending fresh waves of passion through her.

Her mind tried to argue with her body, commanding it to stop responding to him. But she knew she was his to possess, that nothing mattered but his lips on hers and the feel of his hands as they roughly caressed her shoulders and back.

"Oh, Jenny," he groaned, raining kisses on her face and lips. "I want you. Now. Here."

She stiffened in his arms, a chill creeping through her body with deadly swiftness. *Don't be a fool,* her heart cried. *He doesn't love you. He's engaged to your sister. . . .*

"Logan—stop, please," she sobbed, pushing ineffectually against his chest. "Don't!"

"Don't fight me, Jenny Glenn," Logan protested softly, seeking her mouth again, only to have her twist away from him.

Her hands doubled up into fists, and she began beating his chest, humiliated tears streaming down her cheeks.

"What's the matter with you?" A frown creased his forehead as he stared down at the tears on her face and the fists now imprisoned in his hands. "What did I do?"

"You let me go!" she sobbed angrily, wishing she didn't feel so small glaring up at him. "I hate you!"

"Are you crazy?" he shouted.

"Not anymore!" Jenny screamed back, finally managing to free her hands from his grip. As he took a step toward her, she added in a trembling voice, "Don't you touch me! Don't you ever touch me again!"

She cringed at the look on his face at her words and stumbled backward against the counter as he walked menacingly forward.

"I'll touch you any damned time I please!"

His hand reached out, grasping the sleek material of her robe. She felt it tear in his hands as he pulled her to him. Then his lips were ravaging her mouth with passionate thoroughness. Her fingernails dug into his shoulders, and a drop of red flowed as she dragged them across his chest. But it was as if Logan felt nothing, only the desire to possess her with or without her consent. Jennifer clawed at him, her love mixed with hate. When she couldn't summon the strength to take another breath, he pushed her away from him in disgust.

"Get out of here!" His chest was rising and falling rapidly. The low, raw tone of his voice reduced her to a sobbing, trembling nothing. Somehow she managed to stagger from the kitchen, all too conscious of the steely hardness of his eyes as he watched her leave.

* * *

"Jennifer! What are you doing?" Sheila cried, hobbling into the bedroom on her crutches to see her sister tossing clothes into the suitcase.

"What does it look like? I'm leaving," she replied.

"Leaving? What do you mean, leaving? Where? How?"

"How?" Jennifer glanced up at her sister's startled blue eyes. "I've got two feet that are going to carry me and my suitcase out that door, into the Jeep, and to the airport. I'm booked on a flight to Minneapolis." That was a lie, but Sheila didn't have to have all the details.

"Does Logan know this?" Sheila questioned after a horrified gasp.

"No. You can tell him if you want to. I don't need his permission to leave," Jennifer replied sarcastically. After last night, she didn't owe him a thing. Sheila continued to stare at her in disbelief. "I think I hear someone knocking at the door, Sheila. Why don't you go and answer it?"

Seconds later, Dirk entered the room.

"What's this all about, Jenny?" he demanded.

Jennifer snapped her suitcase shut before turning toward him defiantly.

"I'm leaving, that's what it's all about! Are you going to stop me?" A sob choked her throat. She didn't know what she would do if Dirk tried to stand in her way.

"You sure this is what you really want to do?" he asked quietly, walking over to stand beside her, taking in the eyes swollen from crying herself to sleep, and the dark smudges beneath them that told him sleep had been a long time coming.

"Yes." Her voice was lower than a whisper as her chin trembled traitorously.

"I'll drive you to the airport, then," he said grimly.

"Dirk!" Sheila cried. "You can't! Jennifer, you can't leave like this. What about your clothes, your things at the house?"

"Throw it all in a big box and ship it to me." Jennifer put on her coat, handed her suitcase to Dirk, and took a deep breath before turning toward her sister to kiss her cheek lightly. "I'll write you and tell you all about it . . . as soon as I can."

She followed Dirk out the door to his car, ignoring Sheila's confused protests. She was grateful that he sensed she didn't want to talk, that she couldn't talk without breaking down. Last night, when she'd finally stumbled into her bedroom, she knew that she couldn't stay, that she couldn't possibly face Logan ever again after what had happened. There was some comfort in knowing that he hadn't guessed she loved him.

In Logan's opinion, she must have acted like a tease. Because there was no doubt that she had responded wholeheartedly to his first kiss. It was just that he said he wanted her, not needed or loved her, but wanted her, casually, as if she were some dumb girl he'd picked up in a bar, that he could have and forget. She loved him, Jennifer thought, she loved him so much, but she would never allow him to use her in that way.

"What did he do to you?"

Jennifer started at his question. The silence had gone on for so long that she had only been conscious of the miles she was putting between herself and Logan. She'd completely forgotten that she wasn't the only person in the car.

"I can guess," Dirk said flatly, "so you might as well tell me what happened."

"Please, Dirk, I don't want to talk about it," she protested weakly, staring through the windshield at the town spreading out before them.

"You don't have to hide the fact that you've fallen in love with Logan, you know. It's pretty obvious."

"It's no big deal."

"If it was no big deal, you wouldn't be running away." He maneuvered the car slowly through the town traffic.

"It sounds too silly to put into words," she said uneasily.

"Try me."

"He kissed me. And then I got angry, and he got angry. When he grabbed hold of my arm, he was a little rough. Don't tell Sheila, please," she begged, her eyes clouding with tears.

"Sheila? What does it matter if Sheila knows?" Dirk glanced at her with a frown.

"She might get the wrong idea." As Dirk continued to eye her with that puzzled expression, Jennifer exclaimed in exasperation, "You know very well that Logan and Sheila are engaged. I know she told you yesterday."

There was a stifled exclamation from Dirk as he pulled the car to a stop in front of the airport and turned to stare at her.

"And just how do you know they're engaged?"

"I'm not deaf and blind," she retorted angrily. "Besides, I saw Logan in the jewelery store when he bought the ring, and I heard Sheila telling Logan yesterday how well you took the news."

"You *saw* Logan buy the ring?" He stared at her thoughtfully.

"Yes," Jennifer said in irritation. "I don't have to have everything spelled out for me in black and white."

"I see that," Dirk mocked. "Well, here you are at the airport. Are you leaving or not?"

"Yes, of course." She was startled by his abrupt questions.

"Let's skip the long good-byes, okay? Unless you need some help with the suitcase, I'll just say so long here." Dirk smiled sympathetically.

"Okay. That's fine with me." Now that it was time to get out of the car, Jennifer wasn't so sure she wanted to go. She reached over and kissed him lightly on the cheek. "I wish you the best of everything, Dirk."

"You, too, Jenny. Bye."

She waved bravely as the car pulled away. The wind whipped and whistled around her, tugging her coat as if taunting her and making fun of the tears that trembled in her eyes. Jennifer had never felt so alone in her life. Resolutely she turned to enter the airport, only to discover once inside that the only flight out of Jackson wasn't until after four that afternoon. Five hours to wait! Why hadn't she called to get the schedules? In her desperate rush to get away from Logan, it just hadn't occurred to her to check departure times.

Resigning herself to a long wait, Jennifer bought her ticket. She wandered through the concourse for half an hour before finally stopping to gaze out the window at the empty runway. She felt like the hare, running, then waiting, running and waiting, as the tortoise was slowly winning the race. A draft suddenly blew around her legs, and she looked around to find its source. In petrified stillness, she watched Logan walk through the door and stride toward her, anger and irritation in every movement of his body.

"Didn't waste much time getting out, did you?" he growled when he finally stopped in front of her.

"Who told you I was gone?" she asked bitterly, turning away to stare out the window again.

"Dirk called me soon after Sheila got one of the ranch hands to bring me back to the house. He told me some wild story about my, uh, engagement to Sheila. Would you like to explain that to me?" Logan asked, making an effort to control his temper.

"Explain?" Jennifer said incredulously. "What is there to explain? You haven't given her the ring yet—at least I didn't see it on her finger this morning—but I know you're going to marry her."

He scowled at her for a minute, his eyes searching hers intently.

"I'm not going to marry Sheila." He shook his head as he spoke, a gleam appearing in his eyes. His hand went into his shirt pocket and took out the small black velvet box. He handed it to her.

Puzzled, Jennifer just stared at him. A dimple appeared briefly in one cheek as Logan watched her hesitantly flip open the lid and stare at the jade ring. The deep green gem was surrounded by a circlet of diamonds that blazed in the morning light.

"I don't understand," she mumbled, gazing bewilderedly into his mocking eyes. Her hands began to shake when Logan took back the box.

"It's very simple, Jenny Glenn. Sheila is going to

marry Dirk. There was never even the slightest chance that it would be any other way," he finished calmly.

"But the jeweler . . . called it an engagement ring." Jennifer struggled to get the words out.

"It is."

Jennifer covered her mouth with her hand. Her mind was jumping to conclusions that couldn't possibly be true.

"But that conversation yesterday between Sheila and Dirk . . . she said he took the news so easily," she persisted.

"The news was that Sheila wants to keep managing the hotel, unless Dirk wins the lottery," Logan explained. "Now, aren't you going to ask who the ring is for?"

"It's jade," she said as he removed it from its box.

"Yes, it is." At her gasp of surprise, he smiled broadly. "A beautiful stone, don't you think?"

"It matches my necklace," Jennifer said breathlessly, her eyes beginning to glow. "So it isn't costume jewelry."

"Um, I lied."

"Logan . . ."

"All Taylor wives wear jade rings. I'm surprised you didn't notice my mother's. Until Christmas, my mother thought the jade necklace would be my gift to Sheila," Logan said. "Read the engraving." He handed the ring to Jennifer so that she could see the inscription inside the wide gold band.

" 'Equal Rights.' What does it mean?" she asked cautiously.

"Just that. 'Equal rights' is the state motto of Wyoming. Because we gave women the right to vote fifty years before the rest of the country. I told you we respected women. And I respect and love you."

"Are you asking me to marry you? Logan, I couldn't stand it if this was all a joke." Her voice broke as she gazed into his eyes, trying to find the answer.

"I'm asking you to admit once and for all that you love me," he said earnestly, his hands resting gently on her shoulders. "I want to hear you say that."

"I love you, Logan," she whispered. "I love you so much I could die."

"I was almost sure of that last night," Logan smiled, pulling her close. "What happened, anyway? One minute you were kissing me so completely that I thought you were handing me your heart, and the next minute you were spitting at me like a cat!"

"I thought . . ." Jennifer blushed, hiding her face from his eyes. "I thought you only wanted me. That's what you said," she cried as he groaned and crushed her tighter against him.

"Yes, I do want you—because I love you. Because I've been crazy about you from the moment you stepped off that plane. But you put up a wall so high I thought I'd never get over it, around it, through it—never mind. It was worth it all just to hold you like this." He spoke with feeling, lifting her chin up so that he could look into her face as she heard his words.

"Oh, Logan, I was so stupid." The corners of her mouth drooped sadly. "I thought—I thought you couldn't be trusted. And I was sure you were in love with Sheila—"

"There's never been anyone else for me but

you, darling Jenny," said Logan, kissing her so thoroughly that when he was done, there was only blissful wonder on her face. "Soon to be Jenny Glenn Taylor."

Jennifer gazed at him, knowing she could never express the joy in her heart. Instead she whispered as she raised her lips to his, "How soon?"

"Before next Christmas."

STRANGE
BEDFELLOW

Chapter One

The air was clear and the moon over Rhode Island was new, but there was a tangle of cobwebs in her mind. Dina Chandler couldn't seem to think her way out of the confusion. She shut her ears to the voices quietly celebrating in other parts of the house and stared out the window.

A shudder passed through her. It couldn't have been from the night's chill, since the house was comfortably heated. Her arms crossed in front of her, hugging her middle. Perhaps it was the cold weight of the precious metal around her finger.

Dina turned from the window. Her restless gaze swept the library, noting all that was familiar. Interrupting the dark, richly paneled sides of the room was a wall of bookshelves, floor to ceiling. A myriad of deeply toned bindings formed rows of muted rainbows. A sofa covered in antique velvet faced the fireplace, flanked by two chairs upholstered in a complementing patterned fabric. In a corner of the room stood a mahogany desk, its top neat and orderly.

The door to the library opened, and Dina turned. Her hair shimmered in the dim light, a paler gold than the ring on her finger. A pang of regret raced through her that her solitude had been broken, followed by a twinge of remorse that she had felt so much need to be alone.

Closing the door, Chet Stanton walked toward her, smiling despite the faintly puzzled gleam in his eyes.

"So this is where you are," he murmured, an unspoken question behind the indulgent tone.

"Yes," Dina nodded, unaware of the sigh in her voice, or how forced her smile looked.

As he came closer, her gaze made a detached inspection of him. Like hers, his coloring was fair. His sandy blond hair fell rakishly across his forehead, always seeming to invite fingers to push it back in place. His eyes were a smokey blue, nothing like the brilliant shade of hers.

At thirty-six, he was twelve years her senior, a contemporary of Blake's, but there was a boyish air about him that was an integral part of his charm. In it. it was with Blake that Dina had first met Chet. he cobwebs spun around that thought to block it out. Lean and strong, Chet was only a few inches taller than she was in her heels.

He stopped in front of her, his intent gaze studying her expressionless face. Dina was unconscious of how well she masked her inner turmoil. As his hands settled lightly on her shoulders, she remained passive under his touch.

"What are you doing in here?" Chet cocked his head slightly to the side, his gaze still probing.

"I was thinking."

"That's forbidden." His hands slid around her, and Dina yielded to his undemanding embrace, uncrossing her arms to spread them across his chest.

Why not? His shoulder had become a familiar resting place for her head, used often in the past two and a half years. Her eyes closed at the feathery caress of his lips over her temple and cheek.

"You should be in the living room, noisily celebrating with the others," he told her in mock reproof.

Dina laughed softly in her throat. "They're not 'noisily' celebrating. They don't 'noisily' do anything, whether it's rejoice or grieve."

"Perhaps not," he conceded. "But even a restrained celebration has to have the engaged couple there, namely you and me. Not just me alone."

"I know," she sighed.

His shoulder wasn't as comfortable as it had seemed. Dina turned out of his unresisting embrace, nerves stretching taut again from her sense of unease and confusion. Her troubled gaze searched the night's darkness beyond the windowpanes, as if expecting to find the answer there.

With her back turned to him, she felt Chet resting his hands on either side of her neck, where the contracted cords were hard bands of tension.

"Relax, honey. Don't let yourself get all worked up again." His strong fingers began to gently knead the coiled muscles in her neck and shoulders.

"I can't help it." A frown puckered her forehead despite the pleasant massage. "I just don't know if I'm doing the right thing."

"Of course you are."

"Am I?" A corner of her mouth lifted in a half smile, self-mocking and skeptical. "I don't know how I let you talk me into this engagement."

"Me? Talk *you* into it?" Chet laughed, his warm breath fanning the silver-blond strands of her hair. "You make it sound as if I twisted your arm, and I'd never do that. You're much too beautiful to risk damaging."

"You know what they say about flattery."

"It got me you."

"And I know I agreed to this engagement," she admitted.

"After some hesitation," added Chet, continuing the slow and relaxing massage of her shoulders and neck.

"I wasn't sure. And I still don't know if I'm sure."

"I didn't rush you into a decision. I gave you all the time you wanted because I understand why you felt you needed it," he reasoned. "And there won't be any marriage until you set the date. Our agreement isn't much more than a trial engagement."

"I know." Her voice was flat. Dina didn't find the necessary reassurance in his words.

"Look"—Chet turned her to face him—"I was Blake's best friend."

Yes, Dina thought. He had been Blake's right arm; now he was hers. Always there, ready to support her decision, coaxing a smile when her spirits were low and the will to go on had faded.

"So I know what kind of man your husband was," he continued. "I'm not trying to take his place. As a matter of fact, I don't want to take his place any more than I want you to take his ring from your finger."

His remark drew her gaze to the intertwining

gold band and diamond solitaire on the third finger of her left hand. The interlocking rings had been joined by a third, a diamond floret designed to complement the first pair, Chet's engagement ring to her.

He curved a finger under her chin to lift it. "I'm hoping that with a little more patience and persistence you can find some room in your heart to care for me."

"I do, Chet," Dina said. "Without you, I don't know how I would have made it through those months when Blake was missing—when we didn't know if he was alive or dead. And when we were notified that he'd been kil—"

The rest of her words were silenced by his firm kiss. Then he gathered her into his arms to hold her close, molding her slender curves to his lean, muscular body.

His mouth was near her temple, moving against her silken hair as he spoke. "That's in the past. You have to forget it."

"I can't." There was a negative movement of her head against his. "I keep remembering the way I argued with Blake before he left on that South American trip," she sighed. "He wanted me to go to the airport with him, but I refused." Another sigh came from her lips, tinged with anger and regret. "Our quarrels were always over petty things, things that seem so stupid now."

Chet lifted his head to gaze at the rueful light in her eyes. "Well, I like strong-minded women."

His teasing words provoked the smile he wanted. "I suppose I have to admit to being that, don't I?"

A fire smoldered in his look, burning away the teasing light. "And I love you for being strong,

Dina." His hand slid to the small of her back. "And I love you for being all woman."

Then his mouth was seeking hers again in a kiss that was warm and passionate. She submitted to his ardor, gradually responding in kind, reveling in the gentle caress that was not quite intimate. Chet never demanded more from her than she was willing to give. His understanding restraint endeared him to her, making her heart swell with quiet happiness.

When he lifted his head, Dina nestled into the crook of his arm, resting her cheek against his shoulder, smiling with tender pleasure. That lock of hair, the color of sun-bleached sand, was across his forehead. She gave in to the impulse to brush it back with the rest, knowing it would spring forward the instant it was done. Which it did.

"Feel better?" His fingers returned the caress by tracing the curve of her cheekbone.

"Mmm."

"What were you thinking about when I came in?" Her hand slid to his shirt, smoothing the collar.

"I don't know. I guess I was wishing."

"Wishing what?"

Dina paused. She didn't know what she had been wishing. Finally she said, "That we hadn't told the others about our engagement, that we'd kept it to ourselves for a while. I wish we weren't having this engagement party."

"It's just family and friends. There's been no official announcement made," Chet reminded her.

"I know." She usually had no difficulty in expressing herself, but the uncertainty of her own thoughts made it impossible.

Something was bothering her, but she didn't

know what it was. It wasn't as if she hadn't waited long enough before deciding to marry again. It had been two and a half years since Blake had disappeared, and a little more than a year since the South American authorities had notified her that they had found the plane wreckage but no survivors.

And it wasn't as if she didn't love Chet, although not in the same tumultuous way she had loved Blake. This was a quieter and gentler emotion, and probably deeper.

"Dina"—his smile was infinitely patient—"we couldn't keep our engagement from our family and friends. They need time, too, to get adjusted to the idea that you soon won't be Mrs. Blake Chandler."

"That's true," Dina acknowledged. It was not an idea that she could get used to overnight.

The door to the library opened, and an older woman dressed in black stood there. An indulgent smile curved her mouth as she saw the embracing pair. Dina stiffened for an instant in Chet's arms, then forced herself to relax.

"We've been wondering where the two of you went," the woman chided them. "It's time you came back to the party."

"We'll be there in a minute, Mrs. Chandler," Dina replied.

Blake's mother was the epitome of a society woman, belonging to all the right clubs and fundraising organizations for charity. Her role in life had always been the traditional one, centered in her home and family. With both husband and son dead, Norma Chandler clung to Dina as her family and to her home as security.

"If you don't, I'm afraid the party will move in here, and there's hardly enough room for them all." A hand touched the strands of pearls at her throat, the gesture indicating such a thing could never happen at one of her parties. The pearl-gray shade of her elegantly coiffed hair blended with the jewelry she wore.

"We'll be there in a minute, Mrs. Chandler," Chet added his promise to Dina's. With a nod the woman closed the door, and Chet glanced at Dina. "Do you suppose you'll be able to persuade her not to wear black to our wedding?"

"I doubt it." She moved out of his arms, a faintly cynical smile curving her lips. "Norma Chandler likes the idea of being a tragic figure."

A few weeks after Dina's marriage to Blake, Kyle Chandler, his father, had died unexpectedly of a heart attack, and Norma Chandler had bought an entire wardrobe of black. She'd barely been out of mourning when they got the news that Blake's plane had gone down over the jungle and was missing. Instantly Mrs. Chandler began dressing in black, not even waiting for the notification that came a year ago declaring her son legally dead.

"She approves of our marriage. You know that, don't you?" Chet asked.

"Yes, she approves," Dina agreed, "for the sake of the company." And for the fact that there would only be one Chandler widow instead of two—but Dina didn't say that, knowing it would sound petty when her mother-in-law had been almost smothering in her love toward her.

"Mrs. Chandler still doesn't believe you're capable of running the company after all this time,"

Chet concluded from her response. He shook his head wryly.

"I couldn't do it without you." Dina stated it as a fact, not an expression of gratitude.

"I'm with you." He curved an arm around her waist as she started to leave the room. "So you won't have to worry about that."

As Chet reached forward to open the door for her, Dina was reminded of that frozen instant when Norma Chandler had opened the door seconds ago. She recalled the numerous times Mrs. Chandler had opened the library door to find Dina sitting on Blake's lap, locked in one of his crushing and possessive embraces. This time it had been Chet's arms that held her instead of Blake's. She wondered if her mother-in-law was even aware of the vast differences between the two men.

In the past months, after the uncertainty of Blake's fate had been settled and there had been time to reflect, Dina had tried to imagine what the past two and a half years might have been like if Blake had lived. Their brief marriage had been stormy, promising many more years of the same, always with the possibility that one battle could have ended the union permanently.

Chet, on the other hand, was always predictable, and the time Dina spent with him was always pleasant. With his support, she had discovered skills and a potential she hadn't known she possessed. Her intelligence had been channeled into constructive work and acquiring knowledge, instead of being sharpened for warring exchanges with Blake.

Her personality had matured in a hurry, owing to the circumstances of Blake's disappearance. She had become a confident and self-assured woman, and she gave all the credit for the change to Chet.

Some of her misgivings vanished as she walked out with him to rejoin the party in the main area of the house. There was no reason not to enjoy the engagement party, none whatsoever.

The instant they returned to the spacious living room, they were engulfed by the gathering of well-wishers. Everyone seemed at home amid the antique furniture that abounded in the room: beautiful Victorian pieces enhanced by paintings and art objects. The atmosphere decreed formality and sedate behavior.

"I see you found the two of them, Norma," Sam Lavecek announced belatedly. His voice had a tendency to boom, and it drew unnecessary attention to their absence from the party. "Off by yourselves, huh?" He winked with faint suggestiveness at Dina. "Reminds me of the times you and Blake were always slipping away to cuddle in some corner." He glanced down at the brandy in his hand. "I miss that boy." It was an absent comment, his thoughts spoken aloud.

An awkward tension charged the moment. Chet, with his usual diplomacy, smoothed it over. "We all miss him, Sam," he asserted quietly, his arm curving protectively around Dina's shoulders.

"What?" Sam Lavecek's initial reaction was blankness, as if unaware that he had said out loud what was on his mind. He flushed uncomfortably. "Of course we do, but it can't stop us from wishing you happiness," he insisted, and lifted his glass, calling the others to a toast. "To Dina and Chet, and their future together."

Dina maintained her smiling facade, but it was

an odd feeling to have the celebrants of their engagement party consist of Blake's family and friends. Without family herself, her parents having been killed in an automobile crash the year before she met Blake, there had been no close relatives of her own to invite. Her Newport friends, she'd met through Blake. Chet's family lived in Florida.

When Norma Chandler had asked to give them an engagement party, it had been a difficult offer to reject. Dina had chosen not to, finding it the easiest and quickest means to inform all of the Chandler relatives and friends of her decision to accept Chet's proposal. She wasn't blind to her mother-in-law's motives. Norma Chandler wanted to remain close to her. All her instincts were maternal, and Dina was the only one left to mother.

But the engagement party had proved to be more of a trial than Dina had thought. The announcement had made her uneasy and restless, though none of the celebrants could see that. She was too good at concealing her feelings. When the party ended, no one was the wiser. Not even Chet suspected that she was still bedeviled by doubts when he kissed her good night. It was something Dina knew she would have to work out alone.

Over the weekend, the news of their engagement filtered into the main office of the Chandler hotel chain in Newport. Dina was sure she'd spent most of the morning confirming the rumors that she was engaged to Chet.

She didn't think there was anyone in the building who hadn't stopped at her office to extend congratulations and questioning looks.

A mountain of work covered the massive walnut desk—letters to be answered, reports to be read, and memos to be e-mailed. With her elbows on the desktop, Dina rested her forehead on her hands, rubbing the dull throb in its center. Her pale blond hair had grown long enough to be pulled to the nape of her neck in a chignon, the style adding a few years to her relatively youthful appearance.

Her office clothes were conservative as well. Today she wore a long-sleeved blouse of cream yellow with a wine-colored skirt, not too short, though she had great legs.

The intercom buzzed, and Dina lifted her head, reaching over to press the button. "Yes?"

"Harry Landers is here to see you, Mrs. Chandler," was the reply from her secretary, Amy Wentworth—about the only one of the executive staff younger than Dina.

"Send him in."

Dina picked up her reading glasses, which were lying on a stack of papers she had been reading, and put them on. She could see to read without them, but after hours of reading and computer work, the eyestrain became too much. Lately she had taken to wearing them almost constantly at the office to avoid the headaches that accompanied the strain, and subconsciously because they added a businesslike air to her appearance.

There was a wry twist of her mouth as the doorknob to her office turned, an inner acknowledgment that she'd been wrong in thinking everyone had been in to offer congratulations. Harry Landers hadn't, and the omission was about to be corrected. As the door opened, her mouth finished its curve into a polite smile of greeting. "Good morning, Harry."

The brawny white-haired man who entered grinned. "Good morning, Mrs. Chandler." Only Chet used her first name at the office, and then only when they were alone. "I just heard that you and Chet are getting married. Congratulations," he offered predictably.

"Thank you," she nodded for what seemed like the hundredth time that morning.

There was no silent, unasked question in the look he gave her. "I'm really glad for you, Mrs. Chandler. I know there are some people here who think you're somehow being unfaithful to Blake's memory by marrying again. Personally, I think it speaks well of your marriage to him."

"You do?" Her voice was briskly cool; she disliked discussing her private life, although her curiosity was rising as she tried to follow his logic.

"Yes—I mean, obviously your relationship with Blake was happy or you wouldn't want to marry again," he reasoned.

"I see." Her smile was tight, lacking warmth. "Blake and I did have a good marriage." Whether they did, she couldn't say. It had been too brief. "And I know Chet and I will, too."

"When is the wedding?"

"We haven't set the date yet."

"Be sure to send me an invitation."

"We will." Dina's hopes for a quiet wedding and no reception were vanishing under the rush of requests to attend. A good old-fashioned elopement was beginning to sound very tempting.

"At least you won't have to concern yourself with

the company after you're married," Harry Landers observed with a benign smile.

"I beg your pardon?" Dina was instantly alert and on the defensive, no longer mouthing the polite words she had repeated all morning.

"After you're married, you can quit. Chet will make a good president," he replied.

Dina's voice was quiet. "My marriage to Chet won't affect the company. It will continue to be run by both of us with myself as president," she stated, not wanting to remember that the work had been done by Blake alone. Rigid with suppressed anger, she turned to the papers on her desk. "I don't see the monthly report from the Florida hotel. Has it come in?"

"I don't believe so." Her abrupt change of subject warned the man he was treading on forbidden ground. He looked at her warily.

"Frank Miller is the manager there, isn't he?"

"Yes."

"Call him and find out where the report is. I want it on my desk by four this afternoon even if he has to fax it," she ordered. "Or tell him to e-mail it as an attachment."

"I'll get on it right away, Mrs. Chandler."

When the door closed behind him, Dina rose from her office chair and walked to the window. Aftershocks of resentment were still trembling through her. Almost since Blake's disappearance, she had run the company with Chet's help; but her competence still didn't seem to register with some of the executives.

It hadn't been by design but from necessity that she had taken over. When Blake disappeared over South America, the company had been in trouble, though it had operated smoothly for a while; then it began to flounder helplessly.

The key members of the executive board, those who might have been tapped to take over, had resigned to take positions with more solid companies, like rats deserting a sinking ship. That was when Dina had been forced to step in.

It hadn't been easy. The odds were stacked against her because she was young, female, and without much business experience. Exerting her authority had been the most difficult part. Most of the staff were old enough to be her parents, and some, like Harry Landers, were old enough to be her grandparents.

Dina had learned the hard way, by trial and many errors. Her worries, her fears about Blake, she kept to herself. Very early she discovered that a man who offered her a shoulder to cry on might also be interested in a whole lot more.

More and more in those early days, she began turning to Chet for his unselfish and undemanding support. Not once did he make a move on her, not until several months after Blake's death had been confirmed. She trusted him implicitly, and he had never given her a reason to doubt him.

But Harry Landers had just put a question in her mind—one Dina didn't like facing, but there seemed to be no avoiding it.

Shaking her head, Dina walked back to her desk. She picked up the telephone receiver and hesitated, staring at the numbers on the keypad. There was a quick knock on her office door, followed by the click of the latch as it was opened without waiting for her permission to enter. Replacing the receiver, Dina turned to the door as Chet appeared.

"You'll never guess what I just heard," he whispered with exaggerated secrecy.

"What is it?" Dina grew tense.

"Chet Stanton is going to marry Mrs. Chandler."

What she'd expected him to say, Dina had no idea. But his answer made her laugh with a mixture of amusement and relief, some of her tension dissolving.

"You've heard that rumor, too, have you?"

"Are you kidding?" He grinned in a boyish way that made her heart warm to him all the more. "I've been trying to get to my office since nine o'clock this morning and haven't made it yet. I keep getting stopped along the way."

"As bad as that?" Dina smiled.

"The hallway is dangerous."

She knew the feeling. "We should have called everybody together at nine, made the announcement, then gone to work. We would have had a much more productive morning."

"Oh, well," he said, walking over to kiss her lightly on the cheek.

Dina removed her glasses and made a show of concentrating on them as she placed them on the desktop. "Now that everyone knows, they're all waiting for me to hand in my resignation and name you as the CEO of Chandler Hotels." Without seeming to, she watched Chet's reaction closely.

"I hope you set them straight about that," he replied without hesitation. "We make an excellent team. And there's no reason to break up a winning combination in the company just because we're getting married."

"That's what I thought," she agreed.

Taking her by the shoulders, Chet turned her to face him. "Have I told you this morning how beautiful you are?"

"No." She smiled and dimpled slightly as she answered him in the same serious tone that he had used. "But you can tell me now."

"You're very beautiful, honey."

With the slightest pressure, he drew her to him. As his mouth lightly took possession of hers, the intercom buzzed. Dina moved out of his arms with a rueful smile of apology.

She pressed the button. "Yes, Amy?"

"Jacob Stone on line one," came the reply.

"Thank you." Dina broke the connection and glanced at Chet with a resigned shrug of her shoulders.

"Jake Stone," he repeated. "He's the Chandler family attorney, right?"

"Yes," she nodded, reaching for the phone. "Probably something to do with Blake's estate."

"That's my exit cue." And Chet started for the door.

"Dinner tonight at eight?" Dina questioned.

"Sounds like a plan," he agreed with a wink.

"Call Mrs. Chandler and tell her I've invited you." She picked up the receiver, her finger hovering above the blinking button on line one.

"Consider it done."

Dina watched him leave. Just for a few minutes, Harry Landers had made her suspect that Chet might be marrying her in order to rise in the company. But his instant and casual rejection of the idea of becoming CEO had erased that. Her trust in him was well founded.

She pushed the button. "Hello, Mr. Stone. Dina Chandler speaking."

"Ah, Mrs. Chandler. How are you?" came the gravelly voice in answer.

"Just fine, thank you."

Chapter Two

By the end of the week, the excitement generated by the news of their engagement had died down and life settled into a routine again. The invisible pressure the news had evoked eased as well.

Yet on Saturday morning Dina awoke with the sun, unable to go back to sleep. Finally she stopped trying, got up and dressed. The other members of the household, Blake's mother and their housekeeper, Deirdre, were still asleep.

Dina hurriedly tidied the room, unfolding the blue satin coverlet from the foot of the four-poster bed and smoothing it over the mattress. Deirdre was such a perfectionist that she would probably do it over again. Fluffing the satin pillow shams, Dina placed them at the head of the bed.

The clothes she had worn last night were lying on the blue and gold brocade cushion of the love seat. Dina hung them up in the large closet. The scarf she folded and carried to its drawer.

Inside, the gilt edge of a picture frame gleamed

under the lingerie and accessories. It lay face down, concealing the photograph of Blake. Until Chet had given her an engagement ring, that picture had been on her bedside table. Now it was relegated to a dresser drawer, a photograph of the past that had nothing to do with the present. Dina closed the drawer and glanced around the room. Everything seemed to be in order.

After Blake's disappearance two and a half years ago, it had seemed impractical for both Dina and Blake's mother to keep separate households, especially when the days began to stretch into weeks and months. In the end, Dina sublet their apartment in town to move to the suburbs with his mother.

She'd thought it would ease her loneliness and give her a chance to talk, but Dina had spent a lot of time consoling her mother-in-law, and kept her own feelings private.

Still, it was a reasonable arrangement, a place to sleep and eat, with all the housekeeping and meals taken care of. With most of her time and energy concentrated on keeping the company going, the arrangement had become a definite asset.

Now, as she tiptoed out of the house into the dawn, Dina wished for the privacy of her own home, where she could go into the kitchen and fix an early breakfast without feeling like she was invading someone else's turf. And Deirdre was jealously possessive about her kitchen.

Closing the door, she listened for the click of the lock. When she heard it, she turned to the steps leading to the driveway and the white Porsche convertible parked there. Inside the house the phone rang, loud in the morning silence.

Dina stopped and began rummaging through

her oversize purse for the house key. It was seldom used since there was always someone to let her in. Before she found it, the phone had stopped ringing. She waited several seconds to see if it would start ringing again. Someone in the house must have answered it, she decided.

Skimming down the steps, she hurried to the Porsche, folding the top down before climbing in and starting the engine. With doughnuts and coffee to go from a local shop, she drove through the quiet streets.

There was a salty tang to the breeze ruffling her hair. Dina shook her head to let it have its way with the silken gold strands. Her blue eyes narrowed as she turned the sports car away from the street that would take her to the office building and headed toward the solitude of the beach.

Sitting on a huge piece of driftwood, Dina watched the sun rise higher on Rhode Island Sound, the water shimmering and sparkling as the waves lapped the long strand of ocean beach.

The doughnut crumbs had been tossed to the seagulls, still swooping and soaring nearby in case she offered more. It was peaceful and quiet with only her and a surf fisherman in the distance. She thought of many things as she sat, but couldn't remember a single one when she rose to leave.

It was nine o'clock, the time she usually arrived at the office for a half-day's work, minimum. But there wasn't anything that she absolutely had to do today, she thought.

Returning to her Porsche, parked off the road near the beach, she rummaged through her purse for her cell phone and dialed the office number. It was answered on the second ring.

"Amy? It's me." She covered the small mouthpiece for a moment to shut out the whine of the semi going by. "I won't be in this morning, but there's some correspondence on my computer you can print out."

"I've already started it," her young secretary answered.

"Thanks. You can leave it on my desk for my signature. Then you can call it a day. All right?"

"Great, thank you, Mrs. Chandler." Amy Wentworth was obviously delighted.

"See you Monday," Dina said, and hung up.

She headed for the marina where Blake's sailboat was docked and parked the car by the small shed that served as an office. A man sat in a chair out front.

Balanced was a better word, since the chair was tilted back, supported by only the two rear legs. The man's arms were folded in front of him, and a faded captain's hat was pulled over his face, permitting only a glimpse of his double chin and graying stubble.

Dina hopped out of the Porsche, smiling at the man. He hadn't changed a bit in almost three years. "Good morning, Cap'n Tate."

She waited for his slow, drawling New England voice to return the greeting. He was a character and he enjoyed being one.

The chair came down with a thump as a large hand pushed the hat back on top of his head. Gray eyes stared at her blankly for a minute before recognition flickered in them.

"How do, Miz Chandler." He rose lumberingly

to his feet, pulling his faded trousers up to cover his paunch, which only emphasized it.

"It's been so long since I've seen you. How have you been?"

"I'm fine, Miz Chandler; thanks for asking." The owner of the marina smiled and succeeded in extending the smile to his jowled cheeks. "I s'pose you're here to get the *Starfish* cleaned out. Your attorney told me you was goin' to rent it out."

"Yes, I know." Her smile faded slightly. Getting rid of the boat seemed to be like closing the final chapter of her life with Blake. "But it's pointless to keep the boat dry-docked forever."

"She's a damn fine boat," he insisted, puffing a little as he stepped inside the shed door and reached for a key. "Never know, someday you might want it yourself."

Dina laughed, a little huskily. "You know I'm no sailor, Cap'n Tate. I can't make it out of the harbor without getting seasick, unless I take Dramamine."

"Then you sleep the whole time." He guffawed and started coughing. "I never will forget that time Blake came carrying you off the boat sound asleep. He told me aft'wards that you didn't wake up till the next morning."

"That was the last time he even suggested I go sailing with him." She took the key he handed her, feeling a poignant rush of memories and trying to push them back.

"D'ya want some help movin' any of that stuff?" he offered.

"No, thank you." She couldn't imagine the two of them in the small cabin, not with Cap'n Tate's big gut. "I can manage."

"Just give a holler if you need anything," he said,

nodding his grizzled head. "You know where she's docked."

"I do." With a wave of her hand, Dina started down the long stretch of dock.

Masts stood in broken lines along the pier, sails furled, the hulls motionless in the quiet water. Her steps were directed by memory along the boards. Although she rarely went with Blake after her first two disastrous attempts at sailing, Dina had often come to the marina to wait for his return. But Blake wouldn't be coming back anymore.

The bold letters of the boat's name, *Starfish*, stood out clearly against the white hull. Dina paused, feeling the tightness in her throat. Then, scolding herself, she stepped aboard. The wooden deck was dull, no longer gleaming and polished as Blake had kept it.

It didn't do any good to tell herself she shouldn't have waited so long to do something about the boat. There had been so many other decisions to make and demands on her time, and so many legal entanglements surrounding Blake's disappearance. Since his estate wasn't settled, the boat couldn't be sold until the court decreed the dispensation of his property.

The *Starfish* had been dry-docked since his disappearance, everything aboard exactly the way he had left it after his last sail. Dina unlocked the cabin to go below. The time had come to pack away all his things. Jake Stone, the family attorney, had decided the boat should be leased, even if it couldn't be sold yet, to eliminate the maintenance costs.

Dina knew that she could have arranged for someone else to clear away his things and clean up the boat. That was what she planned to do when the attorney called to tell her he had the court's permission to lease the boat. But she was here now and the task lay ahead of her.

Opening drawers and doors, she realized that the galley was fully stocked. The canned delicacies in the cupboards would have brought a smile of delight to any gourmet, but Blake had always been very particular about his food and the way it was prepared. Sighing, Dina wondered how many of the cans were still good. What a waste it would be to throw them out.

Picking up a can, she quickly set it down. First, she needed to get a general idea of what had to be done. She continued her methodical examination of the cabin's contents. The clean, if now musty, clothes brought a smile to her lips. Funny how a person's memory of little things could dim over a few years.

A glance at his clothes brought so much back. Blake had been kind of fussy about his clothes. Even the several pairs of Levi's kept aboard the boat were creased and pressed. A thin coating of dust couldn't hide the snow white of his sneakers.

Dina couldn't remember a time when she had seen him dressed in a way that could be described as carelessly casual. Blake had been used to good things all his life—a beautiful home, excellent food, vintage wines, and good clothes. Spoiled? A little arrogant? Perhaps, Dina conceded. He had been something of a playboy when she had met him, with devastating charm when he wanted to turn it on. Brilliantly intelligent and ultraorganized, he had been exciting and difficult to live with.

Not at all like Chet, she concluded again. But

what was the point in comparing the two? Blake's smooth sophistication to Chet's easygoing nature? With a shrug of confusion, she turned away from the clothes, shutting her mind to the unanswerable questions.

For the better part of the day she worked aboard the boat, first packing and then carrying Blake's belongings to the Porsche, where she stuffed them in every conceivable corner of the small sports car. Then she began cleaning away the years of dust and salt spray, airing the mattresses and cushions, and polishing the interior woodwork.

Dirty and sweaty and physically exhausted, she returned the key to the marina operator. Yet the laborious job had left her with an oddly refreshed feeling. Lately all her energy had been expended mentally. The hard work felt good, even if her muscles would be stiff and sore tomorrow.

She was humming to herself as the white Porsche rounded the corner onto the street where she lived with her mother-in-law. Ahead was the Chandler home, an imposing brick structure that towered two and a half stories into the air. It was set back from the road by a formal lawn dotted with perfectly shaped trees and well-cut shrubs and a scattering of flower beds. The many windows and double entrance doors were a pristine shade of ivory. At the sight of the half-dozen cars parked in the driveway, Dina frowned and slowed down, eventually forced to park some distance from the entrance.

She wondered if she'd forgotten a dinner party. The cars resembled those belonging to close family friends. One, the silver-gray Cadillac, was Chet's. She glanced at her watch. He'd said he would stop around seven for a drink before taking her out to dinner, but it was barely five o'clock.

Her mouth formed a tight line. She'd hoped for a luxurious soak in a tub full of scented bubbles for an hour, but obviously that wasn't going to happen. And why hadn't Mrs. Chandler mentioned she would be entertaining this evening? It wasn't like her.

Puzzled, Dina raised the convertible top and rolled up the windows. This didn't seem to be the time to transport stuff from the car into the house, so she climbed out of the car, her handbag slung over her shoulder, and locked the doors.

Happy voices were talking all over each other from the living room as she entered the house. The double doors of carved oak leading into the room were closed, concealing the unexpected guests. The foyer, with its richly grained oak woodwork and pale yellow walls, was empty. The wide staircase rising to the second floor beckoned, the sunlight on its treads showing her the path, the carved oak balustrade catching the reflected light. She hesitated, then decided to freshen up and change before anyone noticed that she had returned.

But as she started to cross the foyer for the stairs leading to the second floor, one of the double doors opened. Her eyes widened as Chet slipped out, his handsome features strained and tense.

"Where have you been?" There was a hint of desperation in his voice.

If it weren't for the joyful tone of the voices in the other room, Dina might have thought that something terrible had happened, judging by Chet's expression.

"At the marina," she answered.

"The marina?" he repeated in disbelief. Again there was that strangled tightness in his voice. "What were you doing there, for heaven's sake?"

"The *Starfish*—the boat's been leased. I was getting it cleaned up." The explanation was made while Dina wondered what on earth Chet was so worked up about.

"Of all the times—"

Dina broke in sharply. "What's going on?" His attitude was too confusing when she couldn't fathom the reason for it.

"Look, there's something I have to tell you." Chet's gray-blue gaze darted over her face as if trying to judge something from her expression. "But I don't know how to say it."

"What is it?" she demanded impatiently. His tension was becoming contagious.

He took her by the shoulders, his expression deadly serious as he gazed intently into her eyes. Her muscles were becoming sore and they protested at the tightness of his hold.

"It's this . . ." he began earnestly.

Then a low, very male voice interrupted. "Chet seems to think you're going to go into a state of shock when you find out I'm alive."

The floor rocked beneath her feet. Dina managed a half turn on her treacherously unsteady footing, magnetically drawn to the voice. The whole floor seemed to give way when she saw its owner, yet she remained upright, supported mostly by Chet.

There was a dreamlike unreality to the moment.

What a cruel joke. Someone was standing in the doorway of the living room pretending to be Blake, mimicking his voice.

She stared wordlessly at the tall figure framed by the living room doors. The chiseled features certainly resembled him—the wide forehead, the carved cheek and jaw, the strong chin and classically straight nose.

Yet there were differences, too. The sun had tanned this man's face deeply, making it leathery and tough, giving a hardness to features that had once been suavely handsome. The eyes were the same dark brown as Blake's, but they wore a narrowed, hooded look and seemed to pierce her soul.

His hair was the same deep shade of brown, but was much longer than Blake had ever worn it, giving the impression of being rumpled instead of smoothly in place. As tall as Blake, this man was more muscular, and more developed without appearing heavier.

The differences registered with computer swiftness, her brain working while the rest of her was reeling from the similarities.

But Dina didn't trust her eyes. What finally convinced her was Chet's odd behavior before this man appeared, his innate kindness, which never would have permitted a cruel joke like this to be played on her, and whatever he was going to tell before they were interrupted.

Blake was *alive*. And he was standing in the doorway. She swayed forward, but her feet wouldn't move. Chet's hands tightened, and she turned her stunned gaze to him. The confirmation was there in his watchful face.

"It's true," she breathed, neither a statement nor a question.

Chet nodded, a silent warning in his eyes. It was then that Dina felt the cold weight of his engagement ring around her finger, and the blood drained from her face. Her hands reached out to cling to Chet's arms, suddenly and desperately needing even more support to remain upright.

"Looks like Chet was right," that familiar, lazy voice drawled. "My return is more of a shock to you than I thought it would be," Blake observed. He directed his next words over his shoulder without releasing Dina from his level gaze. "She needs some hot, sweet coffee, laced with a stiff shot of brandy."

"Exactly," Chet agreed, and curved a bracing arm around her waist. "Let's find you a place to sit down, Dina." Numbly she accepted his help, aware of his gaze flicking to Blake. "Seeing you standing in the doorway was like seeing a ghost. I told you we were all convinced you were dead."

"Not me," Mrs. Chandler contradicted him, moving to stand beside her son. "I always knew somehow that he was still alive somewhere out there, despite what everyone said."

Fleetingly, Dina was aware of the untruthfulness in her mother-in-law's assertion. The thought had barely formed when she realized there were others in the living room. She recognized the faces of close family friends, gathered to celebrate Blake's return. They had been watching the reunion between husband and wife—or rather, the lack of it.

In that paralyzing second, Dina realized she had not so much as touched Blake, let alone joyously flung herself into his arms. Her one swaying attempt had been accidentally checked by Chet's steadying hold. It would seem staged and faked if she did so now.

Equally startling was the discovery that she would

have to fake it because, although the man in front of her was obviously Blake Chandler, he didn't seem at all like the man she had married. She felt as if she was looking at a total stranger. He knew what she was thinking and feeling; she could see it in the coolness of his expression, aloof and chilling.

As she and Chet approached the doorway, Blake stepped to one side, giving them room. He smiled down at his mother, his expression revealing nothing to the others.

"If you were so sure I was alive, Mother, why are you wearing black?" he chided her.

Color rose in Norma Chandler's cheeks. "For your father, Blake," she responded, never at a loss for an explanation.

Everyone was still standing, watching, as Chet guided Dina to the sofa. After she was seated, he automatically sat down beside her. Blake had followed them into the room.

Every nerve in Dina's body was aware of his presence, although she wasn't able to lift her gaze to him. Guilt consumed her ability to respond spontaneously, and it didn't help when Blake sat down in the armchair nearest her end of the couch.

The housekeeper appeared, setting a china cup and saucer on the glass-topped table in front of the sofa. "Here's your coffee, just the way Mr. Blake ordered it."

"Thank you, Deirdre," she murmured. She reached for the china cup filled with steaming dark liquid, but her hands were shaking too much for her to hold on to it.

Out of the corner of her eye, she caught a suggestion of movement from Blake, as if he was about to lean forward to help her. Chet's hand was already there, lifting the cup to carry it to her lips. It was purely an automatic reaction on Chet's part. He had become used to doing things for her in the past two and a half years, just as Dina had become used to having him do them.

Instinctively, she knew he hadn't told Blake of their engagement, and she doubted if anyone else had. But Chet's solicitous concern was telling its own story. And behind that facade of lazy interest, Blake was absorbing every damning detail. Without knowing it, Chet was making matters worse.

Sipping the hot and sweetly potent brew eased the constriction strangling her voice, and she found the strength to raise her hesitant gaze to Blake's.

"How . . ." she began self-consciously. "I mean when . . ."

"I walked out of the jungle two weeks ago." He anticipated her question and answered it.

"Two weeks ago?" That was before she had agreed to marry Chet. "Why didn't you let . . . someone know?"

"It was difficult to convince the authorities that I was who I claimed to be. They believed I was dead." There was a slashing line to his mouth, a cynical smile. "I guess Lazarus didn't have it any easier back in biblical times."

"Are you sure I can't fix you a drink, Mr. Blake?" the housekeeper asked. "A martini?"

"Nothing, thanks."

Dina frowned. In the past Blake always had two, if not three martinis before dinner. There were more than just surface changes in him during the past two and a half years. Unconsciously she covered her left hand with her right, hiding not only the wedding rings Blake had given her but Chet's engagement ring as well.

"The instant they believed Blake's story," his mother said, "he caught the first plane out to come home." She beamed at him adoringly, like the doting mother that she was.

"You should have called." Dina couldn't help saying it. Forewarned, she might have been better prepared for the new Blake Chandler.

"I did."

Dina suddenly remembered the telephone ringing at dawn when she left the house. Seconds. She had missed knowing about his return by seconds.

"I'd switched off my extension," Norma Chandler said, "and Deirdre was wearing her earplugs. Did you hear it, Dina?"

"No. No, I'd already left," answered Dina.

"When Blake didn't get any answer here," Chet continued the story, "he called me. And I was so shocked I didn't think to call your cell phone."

"Chet was as stunned as you were, Dina." Blake smiled, but Dina suspected that she was the only one who noticed the lack of amusement in his voice. She knew her gaze wavered under the keenness of his.

"I came over right away to let you and Mrs. Chandler know," Chet finished.

"Where were you, Dina?" Sam Lavecek grumped. He was Blake's godfather and an old friend of both Blake's parents. Over the years he had become like an uncle to Blake, later extending the relationship to Dina. "Chet was worried about you. Played hooky from the office, did you?"

"I was at the marina," she answered, and turned

to Blake. "The *Starfish* has been leased to a couple who plan to sail to Florida for the winter. I spent the day cleaning it up and moving out all of your things."

"Too bad!" Sam Lavecek sympathized, slapping the arm of his chair. "You always did love going out on that boat. Now, the day you come home, it's being turned over to someone else."

"It's only a boat, Sam." There was an enigmatic darkness in Blake's eyes that made his true thoughts impossible to see.

To Dina, in her hypersensitive state, he seemed to be implying something else. Perhaps he didn't object to his boat being loaned to someone else—as long as his wife wasn't. Her apprehension mounted.

"You're right!" the older man agreed with another emphatic slap of his hand on the armchair. "It's only a boat. And what's that compared to having you back? It's a miracle! A miracle!"

The statement brought a flurry of questions for Blake to answer about the crash and the months that followed. Dina listened silently. Each word that came from his mouth made him seem more and more a stranger.

The small chartered plane had developed engine trouble and crashed in the teeming jungle. When Blake came to, the other four people aboard were dead and he was trapped in the twisted wreckage with a broken leg and a few broken ribs. He had suffered a deep gash on his forehead and a few cuts and bruises. Dina's gaze found the scar that had made a permanent line on his forehead.

Blake didn't go into too much detail about how he'd clawed his way out of the plane the following day, but Dina had a vivid imagination. He must have endured agony fighting to struggle free with his injuries, letting the wreckage become a coffin for the mangled bodies of the others. Not knowing when or even if he'd be rescued, Blake had been forced to set his own leg.

That was something Dina could not visualize him doing. In the past, if Blake thought something required a professional's skill or experience, he'd always hired one. So for Blake to set his own broken bone, regardless of the dire circumstances, seemed completely out of character, something the man she'd known never would have done.

When the emergency rations stowed on the plane ran out, Blake had foraged for his food, eating fruits and whatever wild animals he could trap, catch, or kill. And this was supposed to be the same Blake Chandler who had considered hunting a disgusting, bloodthirsty sport and who preferred gourmet cuisine.

Blake, who despised flies and mosquitoes, talked matter-of-factly of the insects that swarmed in the jungle, flying, crawling, biting, stinging until he no longer noticed them. The heat and humidity of the jungle rotted his shoes and clothes, forcing him to improvise using the skins of the animals he killed. Blake, always so well groomed—it was hard to believe.

As he began his tale of the many months it took him to walk out of the jungle, Dina realized that Blake had left Rhode Island a civilized man and come back half wild. She stared at him with seeing eyes.

Leaning back in his chair, he looked indolent and relaxed, yet Dina sensed that his muscles were like coiled springs, ready to react with the swiftness of a predatory animal. His senses, his nerves were alert to everything going on around him. Nothing escaped the notice of that hooded, dark gaze. From the lurking depths of those hard brown eyes, Blake seemed to be viewing them all with cynical amusement, as if the so-called dangers and problems of their comfortable world were nothing at all compared to the battle of survival he had fought and won.

"There's something I don't understand," Sam Lavecek commented, frowning when Blake fell silent. "Why did the authorities tell us you were dead after they'd found the wreckage? Didn't they discover there was a body missing?" he asked bluntly.

"I don't think so," Blake answered calmly.

"Did you bury their bodies, Blake?" his mother asked. "Is that why they didn't find them?"

"No, I didn't." The cynical amusement that Dina suspected he felt was there, glittering through the indulgent look he gave his mother. "It would have taken a bulldozer to carve out a grave in that tangled mess of brush, trees, and roots. I had no choice but to leave them in the plane. Unfortunately, the jungle is filled with scavengers."

Dina blanched. He sounded so cold and insensitive, but Blake had been a passionately vital and volatile man, quick to fly into a temper and quick to love.

What had he become? Had the savagery of his life in the past two and a half years changed him forever? But he was still her husband, and Dina shuddered at what the answers to those questions might be.

Distantly she heard the housekeeper enter the

room. "What time would you like dinner served this evening, Mrs. Chandler?"

There was hesitation before Norma Chandler replied, "In about an hour, Deirdre. That's all right for everyone, isn't it?" and received a murmur of agreement.

From the sofa cushions beside her, Chet asked quietly, "That'll give you enough time to freshen up before dinner, won't it, Dina?"

She clutched at the tactful out he'd just given her. "Yes, it will." She wanted desperately to be alone for a few minutes, to sort through her jumbled thoughts, afraid she was overreacting. Rising, she spoke to no one in particular. "Please excuse me. I won't be long."

Dina had the disquieting sensation of Blake's eyes following her as she walked from the room. But he made no attempt to stop her, or offer to come with her to share a few minutes alone, much to her relief.

Chapter Three

The brief shower had washed away the last lingering traces of unreality. Wrapping the sash to her royal blue robe around her middle, Dina walked through the open doorway of the private bath to her bedroom. She moved to the closet to choose something to wear to dinner, all the while trying to assure herself that she was making mountains out of molehills where Blake was concerned.

There was a click, and she turned as the door opened and Blake walked in. Her mouth opened to order the intruder out, then closed. He was her husband. How could she order him out of her bedroom?

His gaze swept the room, located her, and stopped, fixing her with a predatory stare. Her fingers clasped the folds of her robe at the throat, and Dina was suddenly conscious of her own nakedness beneath the luxurious robe. Blood pounded in her head, signaling some kind of danger. Vulnerable and alone, she was wary of him.

The new suit and tie he wore gave him the look of a *GQ* model, but she wasn't taken in by the veneer of refinement. It didn't conceal the latent power of that muscled physique or soften the rough edges of his sun-hardened features. Blake closed the door, not releasing her from his pinning gaze, and her breath just about stopped.

"I went through hell to get back to you, Dina, yet you can't seem to walk across a room to meet me." The accusation was made in a smooth tone filled with sardonic amusement.

His words prodded her into movement. Too much time had gone by since his disappearance for her to rush into his arms. Her steps were slow, her back rigid as she approached him. Even if she wanted to, she doubted if she could overcome her reserve—or her fear. Stopping in front of him, she searched her mind for welcoming words that would sound sincere.

"I'm glad you came back safely," was all she could manage to say.

Blake was waiting . . . for her kiss. The muscles in her stomach contracted sharply with the realization. After a second's hesitation, she forced herself on tiptoe to press her lips briefly against his mouth. His large hands spanned the back of her waist, their imprint burning through the robe onto her bare skin. His light touch didn't seem at all familiar. It was almost alien.

At her first attempt to end the kiss, he held her tighter, his fingers raking into her silver-gold hair to bring her lips to his again. Her slender curves were pressed against the hard contours of his body. Her heartbeat skittered madly, then accelerated in alarm.

The hungry demand of his bruising mouth asked more than Dina could give to a man who seemed more of a stranger than anything else. She struggled to free herself of his iron hold and was surprised when Blake let her twist away.

Her breathing was rapid and uneven as she avoided his eyes. "I have to get dressed." She pretended that was her reason for rejecting his embrace. "The others are waiting downstairs."

Those fathomless eyes seemed to be boring holes into her. Dina could feel them even as she turned away to retrace her steps to the closet and her much-needed clothes. Her knees felt wobbly.

"You mean *Chet* is waiting," Blake corrected her with deadly softness.

Her blood ran cold. "Of course. Isn't Chet there with the others?" She pretended not to understand his meaning and immediately regretted not taking advantage of the opening he had given her to tell him about Chet.

"I've had two and a half years of forced celibacy, Dina. How about you?" The dry contempt in his question spun her around, blue fires of indignation flashing in her eyes, but Blake didn't give her a chance to defend herself. "How long was it after I disappeared before Chet moved in?"

"He did not move in!"

With the swiftness of a swooping hawk, he seized her left hand. His powerful grip was too much for the slender bones of her fingers, drawing a gasp of pain from her.

His mouth was a thin line as he lifted her hand. "Don't you call it moving in when another man's ring is next to the ones I put on your finger? Did you think I wouldn't see it?" His eyes blazed. "I saw the looks you two exchanged and the way the others watched the three of us." He released her hand in a violent gesture of disgust. Dina rubbed her fingers and cradled them in her right hand. "And neither of you had the guts to tell me!"

"We didn't have a chance," she responded defensively, her temper flaring from the flame of his. "What was I supposed to say when I saw you standing in the doorway, a husband I thought was dead? 'Honey, I'm so glad you're alive. Oh, by the way, I'm engaged to another man.' I didn't know what to say or do!"

He gave her a long, hard look. His anger was so tightly controlled that it almost frightened her.

"Some homecoming," Blake declared in a contemptuous voice. "My wife wishes I were still dead!"

"I don't wish that," she denied.

"This engagement—" he began, bitter sarcasm coating his words.

"Don't start," Dina protested. "Chet and I have been engaged for barely a week. At the time that he proposed to me, I thought you were dead and I was free to accept."

"Now you know differently. I'm alive. You're my wife, not my widow. You're still married to me." The way he said it, his cold, concise tone made it sound like a life sentence.

Dina was trembling and she didn't know why. "I'm aware of that, Blake." Her voice was taut to keep out the tremors. "But this isn't the time to discuss the situation. Your mother is waiting, and I still have to get dressed."

For a few harrowing seconds, she thought he was going to argue. "Yes," he agreed slowly, "this isn't the time."

She heard the door being yanked open and flinched as it was slammed shut. If this was a new beginning for their marriage, it was off to a rotten start. They had argued before he'd disappeared, and now war had nearly been declared. Dina shuddered and walked to the closet again.

Her arrival downstairs coincided with Deirdre's announcement that dinner was served. Blake was there to escort her into the formal dining room. A chandelier of cut crystal and polished brass hung above the table, glittering down on the Irish linen tablecloth set with his mother's best silver and china. An elaborate floral arrangement sat in the center of the buffet, not too near the table, so its scent wouldn't interfere with the aroma of the food. Blake was being warmly welcomed home, by everyone but her, and Dina was painfully conscious of the fact.

As they all took their chairs around the long dining table, the tension in the air was almost electric. Yet Dina seemed to be the only one who noticed it. Blake sat at the head of the table, the place of honor, with his mother at the opposite end and Chet seated on her right. Dina sat on Blake's left.

Ever since she'd come down, Blake had kept her at his side, as if showing everyone that she was his and effectively separating her from Chet. On the surface, he seemed to be all smiles, at times giving her glimpses of his former devastating charm. But there was still anger smoldering in his eyes whenever his gaze was directed to her.

When everyone was seated, the housekeeper came in carrying a tureen of soup. "I fixed your favorite, Mr. Blake," she announced, a beaming smile on her square-jawed face. "Cream of asparagus."

"Bless you, Deirdre." He smiled broadly. "Now that's the way to welcome a man home!"

The sharp side of his double-edged remark sliced at Dina. She paled but otherwise gave no sign of being upset.

The meal was an epicurean's delight, from the soup to the lobster thermidor to the ambrosia of fresh fruit. Blake made all the right comments and compliments, but Dina noticed he didn't seem to savor the various dishes the way he had in the past. She had the impression that fancy food almost disgusted him now.

Coffee was served in the living room so Deirdre could clear away the dishes. Again Blake kept Dina beside him. Chet was on the far side of the room. As she glanced his way, he looked up, smokey blue eyes meeting the clear blue of hers. He murmured a quick excuse to the older woman who had him cornered—a Mrs. Burnside, an old school friend of Norma Chandler—and made his way toward her.

Through the cover of her lashes, Dina dared a glance at Blake and saw the faint narrowing of his gaze as his rival approached. The smile on Chet's face was strained when he stopped in front of them. Dina guessed he was trying to find a way to tell Blake of their engagement, and she wished there was a way to let him know that Blake was aware of it.

"You know it seems like old times, Blake," Chet began, forcing a camaraderie into his voice, "coming over to your house for dinner and seeing you and . . ." His gaze slid nervously to Dina.

"Chet," Blake interrupted calmly, "Dina told me about your engagement."

The room grew so quiet that a feather could have been heard dropping on the carpet. All eyes were focused on the trio, as if a brilliant spotlight were shining on them. She discovered that, like everyone else, she was holding her breath. After the savage anger Blake had displayed upstairs, she wasn't sure what might happen next.

"I'm glad you know. I . . ." Chet lowered his gaze, searching for words.

Blake filled in the moment's pause. "No hard feelings, pal. You've always been a good friend and I'd like it to continue that way." Dina started to sigh with relief. "After all, what are friends for?"

No one except Dina seemed to pay any attention to the tone of the last comment. Chet was too busy shaking the hand Blake offered in friendship. The others were murmuring among themselves about the moment they had been awaiting all day.

"Naturally the engagement is broken," Blake said with a smile that contrasted with the serious look in his eyes.

"Naturally," Chet agreed with an answering smile.

And Dina felt a rush of anger that she could be set aside just like that, as if she had no say in the matter. She hadn't even been consulted by either man.

Immediately she berated herself. It was what she wanted. Blake was alive and she was married to him. She didn't want to divorce him to marry Chet, so why was she fussing? It had to do with her pride—and her ego, she decided.

After the confrontation over the engagement, the party became anticlimactic. There was a steady trickle of departures among the guests. One minute she was saying good-bye to Mrs. Burnside and the next she was alone in the foyer with Blake, his eyes watching her in that steady, measured way she found so unnerving.

"That's the last of them," he announced.

Dina glanced around. "Where's your mother?"

"In the living room, helping Deirdre clean up."

"I'll give them a hand." She started to turn away.

But Blake caught her arm. "There's no need." He released it as quickly as he had captured it. "They can handle it by themselves."

Dina didn't protest. The day had been too long, and she felt exhausted by physical and mental stress. What she really wanted was a long night of deep, dreamless sleep. She started for the stairs, only half aware that Blake was following.

"You didn't return Chet's ring," he reminded her in a flat tone.

Raising her left hand, she glanced at the flower-like circlet of diamonds. "No, I . . . must have forgotten." She was too tired at this point to care about such a small detail.

When she started to lower her hand, Blake seized it and pulled off the ring from her finger before she could stop him. He tossed it carelessly onto the polished mahogany table standing against the foyer wall.

"You shouldn't leave valuable things lying around!" Dina instantly retrieved it, clutching it in her hand as she frowned at him—Blake, who insisted there was a place for everything and everything in its place.

"Valuable to whom?" he asked with cool arrogance.

Her fingers tightened around the ring. "I'll keep it in my room until I can give it back to him." She waited for him to challenge her decision. When he didn't, she walked to the stairs.

"He'll be over tomorrow," Blake said, speaking from directly behind her. "You can give it to him then."

"What time is he coming?" Dina climbed the stairs, knowing she didn't want to return the ring when Blake was around, but he wasn't leaving her much choice.

"At ten for Sunday brunch."

At the head of the stairs, Dina turned. Her bedroom was the first door on the right. She walked to it, only to have Blake's arm reach around her to open the door. She stopped abruptly as he pushed it open, her look bewildered.

"What are you doing?" She frowned.

"I'm going to bed." He eyed her coolly. "Where did you think I was going to sleep?"

She looked away, her gaze darting madly around. She was thrown into a trembling state of confusion by his taunting question. "I didn't think about it." She faltered. "I guess I've gotten used to sleeping alone."

His hand was at the small of her back, firmly directing her into the room. "I hope you don't expect that to continue."

"I . . ." Oh, yes, she did, Dina realized with a start. "I think it might be better . . . for a while." She stopped in the center of the room and turned to face him as he closed the door.

"You do?" Inscrutable brown eyes met her wavering look, his carved features expressionless.

"Yes."

Her nervousness only intensified as she watched

Blake peel off his jacket and tie and begin unbuttoning his shirt.

She tried to reason with him, her voice quivering. "Blake, it's been two and a half years."

"Tell me about it," he said dryly.

Her throat tightened, making her voice small. "I don't know you anymore. You're a stranger to me."

"That can be changed."

"You aren't even trying to understand, Blake." Dina fought for self-control. "I can't just hop into bed with—"

"Your husband?" he finished the sentence, and gave her a searing look. "Who else would you choose?"

The shirt was coming off, exposing a bare chest and shoulders tanned as darkly as his face. The result heightened Dina's impression of a primitive male, powerful and dangerous, sinewy muscles rippling in the artificial light.

Her senses reacted with alarm as she felt the force of his earthy, sensual attraction. In an attempt to break the magic of its spell, she turned away, walking quickly to her dresser to place Chet's ring in her jewelry box.

"No one. That isn't what I meant." She stayed at the dresser, her hands flattened on its top. He came up behind her, and she lifted her gaze. In the dressing table mirror her wary eyes saw his reflection join with hers. "You've become bitter, Blake, and cynical," she said accusingly. "I can imagine what you've gone through. . . ."

"Can you?" There was a faint curl of his lip. "Can you imagine how many nights I held on to my sanity by clinging to the vision of a blue-eyed woman with corn-silk hair?"

His fingers twined themselves through the flowing strands of her pale gold hair, and Dina closed her eyes at the savage note in his voice.

"Roughly nine hundred and twenty-two nights. And when I finally see her again, she's clinging to the arm of my best friend. Is it any wonder that I'm bitter, when I've been waiting all this time for her lips to kiss away the pain? Did you even miss me, Dina?" He twisted her around to face him. "Did you grieve?"

Her eyes smarted with tears that she refused to cry. "When you first disappeared, I was nearly beside myself with fear. But your mother was even more distraught—losing her husband, then possibly you. I had to spend most of my time comforting her. Then the company started to fall apart and Chet insisted I take over before it failed. So I was plunged headfirst into another world. During the day I was too busy to think about myself, and at night your mother was depending on me to be her strength. The only moments I had alone were in this room. And sometimes I took sleeping pills so I would get enough rest to struggle through another day. I didn't have time to grieve."

He was unmoved by her words, his dark eyes flat and cold. "But you had time for Chet," he said with icy calm.

Dina winced as the point of his arrow found its target. "Blake, he was your closest friend and he kept in touch with your mother and me. And, there was the company connection. He was always there, encouraging me and offering me a shoulder to lean on in the odd moments that I needed it, without asking for anything in return," she explained, refusing to sound guilty. "It grew from there after you were reported killed. I needed him."

"And I need you—now." He drew her inside the steel circle of his arms, flattening her against his chest.

The hard feel of his bare chest rocked her senses. The warmth of his breath wafted over her face, the musky scent of him enveloping her. She pushed at his arms, straining to break out of his hold.

"You haven't listened to a word I've said!" she stormed angrily, inwardly battling against his physical arousal of her senses. "You've changed. I've changed. We need time to adjust!"

"Adjust to what?" Blake snapped. "The differences between a man and a woman? Those are differences we could explore all night long." The zipper of her dress was instantly undone. "Starting now."

"Stop it!" She struggled to keep him from sliding the dress off her shoulders. "You're making me feel like an animal!"

"You are. So am I." The words were said in a cold, insensitive tone. "Put on this earth to sleep, eat, and breed, to live and die. I learned in the jungle that that's the essence of our existence."

Hysterical laughter gurgled in her throat. "Oh, right." Dina choked on the sound. " 'You Tarzan, me Jane,' is that it?"

"Eliminate the social conventions and all the stupid games and that's what it comes down to."

"No, our minds are more fully developed. We have feelings, emotions," she protested. "We . . ."

Her dress was stripped off despite her efforts. "Shut up!" He growled the order against her mouth and smothered the sounds when she refused to obey.

Leaning and twisting backward, Dina tried to escape the domination of his kiss, but his hands used the attempt to mold her lower body more fully to his length, her hips pressed to oak-solid thighs. The silk of her slip was a second skin, concealing and revealing, while callused fingers moved roughly around, exploring at will.

Beneath her own hands she felt the flexing of his muscles, smooth as hammered steel, powerfully sensual. He was stealing her strength by degrees, slowly and steadily wearing her down.

With a determined effort, she broke out of his arms. Gasping for air, she backed away from him, quivering. Blake swayed toward her, then stopped. A second later she realized why, as her retreat was stopped short by a wall. A cornered animal, she stared at the man who held her at bay.

She lifted her head, summoning all her pride to beg, "Don't do this, Blake."

Slow, silent strides carried him to her, and she didn't attempt to flee. There was no mercy in his eyes, and she refused to cower. Her resistance became passive as he undressed, her eyes tightly closed.

"Don't play innocent, Dina," Blake taunted. "My memory wasn't damaged. I remember what a passionate lover you are."

Dina paled as she remembered, too. A flicker of the old, searing fire licked through her veins as he drew her to him and her bare curves came in contact with his nude body. The tiny flame couldn't catch hold, not when the hands fanning it were callused and rough instead of the smooth, manicured hands that had once brought it to a full blaze.

"Don't destroy our marriage," she whispered, trying not to notice the burnished bronze of his muscular chest. "I want to love you again, Blake."

With a muffled curse, he buried his face in her hair. "Damn you! Why didn't you say that when I came home?" he muttered in a rasping sound that suggested pain. "Why did you have to wait until now?"

"Would it have mattered?" Dina held back a sob.

"It might have then." Effortlessly he swung her off her feet into his arms, his jaw set in a ruthless line. "I couldn't care less now. You're mine and I want you."

The overhead light was switched off, throwing the room into darkness. As if guided by animal instinct, Blake carried her to the bed. Without bothering to pull down the covers, he set her down on the bed and towered beside it.

"Blake." There was an unspoken plea in the way she spoke his name, a last attempt to make him understand her unwillingness.

"No," he answered, and the mattress sagged under his weight. "Don't ask me to wait." His low voice was commanding near her ear, his breath stirring her hair. "It's been too long."

And we both have changed too much, Dina thought, stiffening at the moist touch of his mouth along her neck. As his hand slid over her ribs to cup her breast, she remembered the first time he'd caressed her like that and introduced her to a thousand erotic joys. Blake's caressing hands roamed over her with intimate familiarity, and she felt her body responding, reluctantly at first. A series of long, drugging kisses soon made her mind blank to all but the demands of her flesh.

Her own instincts took over, reigning supreme. She gloried in the feel of his sensual lips and the brush of the soft, curling hairs on his chest, hardening her nipples.

The rapid throb of her pulse was in tempo with his, building to a climax. And the heady male scent of him, heightened by sweat and his rising body heat, served to stimulate all her senses until she was filled with nothing but him.

For a time she reached heights she had thought she would never see again. Unerringly, Blake found all the places that brought her the ultimate pleasure, waiting for his own until she moaned his name in final surrender.

Chapter Four

Dina lay in bed, the covers pulled up to her neck, but she knew the blankets couldn't warm the chill. Her passion spent, she felt cold and empty inside as she stared upward into the darkness of the room.

Physically, her desires had been satisfied by Blake's skilled knowledge, but she had not been lifted to the rapturous heights of a spiritual union. That only happened when there was love involved. Tonight it had been merely a mutual satisfaction of sexual needs. And that special something that was missing eliminated the warm afterglow Dina had hoped to feel once more.

Blake was beside her, their bodies not touching. An arm was flung on the pillow above his head. She could hear the steady sound of his breathing, but doubted that he was asleep. Her sideways glance found his carved profile in the dim light. There seemed to be a grim line to his mouth, as if he was experiencing the same reaction.

As if feeling her look and hearing her question,

he said in a low, flat voice, "There's one argument you didn't make, Dina. If you had, it might have prevented this disillusionment."

"What is it?" she asked in a tight voice, longing to know what it was so she could keep this from happening again.

"The real thing can't match two and a half years of expectations."

No, she agreed silently, *not when there are no words of love exchanged, no mating of our hearts or coming together of souls.* It had been an act of lust, born out of anger and frustration.

"Passion never can, Blake," she murmured.

He tossed aside the blanket draped across his waist and swung his feet to the floor. Her head turned on the pillow to stare at him in the darkness.

"Where are you going?" she asked softly, yearning for Blake to hold her in his arms.

There was a faint sheen to his sun-browned skin in the shadowy light. She could make out the breadth of his shoulders and the back muscles tapering to his waist. His steps were soundless, silent animal strides.

"You know what? Civilization has its drawbacks. For one thing the mattresses are too soft." His tone was cynical. "I'm used to firm beds. That's what comes from sleeping in trees and on hard ground."

She lost him in the darkness and propped herself up on an elbow, keeping the covers tightly around her. "Where are you going?"

"To find a spare blanket and a hard floor." There was the click of the door being opened. "You have part of your wish, Dina," he added caustically. "The bed's yours. You can sleep alone."

As the door closed, a convulsive shudder ran

through her. She turned her face into the pillow, curling her body into a tight ball of pain. With eyes squeezed shut, she lay there, waiting for the forgetfulness of sleep.

A hand gently but persistently shook her shoulder. "Mrs. Blake? Wake up, please." Dina stirred, lashes fluttering as she tried to figure out whether or not she was imagining the voice. "Wake up, Mrs. Blake!"

But she wasn't imagining the hand on her arm. Her head throbbed dully as she opened her eyes and rolled over, dragging the covers with her. Her sleepy gaze focused on the agitated expression of the housekeeper hovering above her.

Dina became conscious of several things at once: the rumpled pillow beside her where Blake had been, her own nakedness beneath the covers, and the clothes scattered around the room—hers and Blake's.

"What is it, Deirdre?" she questioned, trying to maintain her composure despite the surge of embarrassment.

The older woman bit her lip as if uncertain how to reply. "It's Mr. Blake."

The anxious look on the housekeeper's face brought an instant reaction as Dina propped herself up on her elbows, concern chasing away the remnants of sleep. "Blake? What's wrong? Has something happened to him?"

"No, it's . . . it's just that he's sleeping downstairs—on the floor in the library." A dull red was creeping up her neck into her cheeks. "And he isn't wearing any . . . any pajamas."

Dina swallowed back a smile, her relief lost in

amusement. Poor Deirdre Schneider, she thought, never married in her life, or anything close to it, and probably shocked to her prim core when she found Blake sleeping in the library, buck naked.

"I see." She nodded and tried to keep her face straight.

"Mr. Stanton will be arriving in just more than an hour." The woman was trying desperately to avoid looking at the bareness of Dina's shoulders. "I thought you should be the one to . . . to wake up Mr. Blake."

"I will," said Dina, and started to rise, then decided against adding to the housekeeper's embarrassment. "My robe—it's at the foot of the bed—thanks, Deirdre."

After handing the robe to her, the housekeeper turned discreetly away while Dina slipped into it. "Mrs. Chandler kept a few things around for Mr. Blake," she informed Dina. "There are pajamas and a man's robe. I put them in the empty closet."

"I'll take them to him." Dina tied the sash of her robe. "And, Deirdre, tomorrow I think you'd better make arrangements with Mrs. Chandler to buy a bed with an extra-firm mattress, one that's as hard as a rock."

"I will," Deirdre promised as if taking an oath. "Sorry to have awakened you, Mrs. Blake."

"That's all right, Deirdre," Dina answered, smiling.

With a self-conscious nod, the housekeeper left the room. Dina put on her slippers and walked to the small closet Deirdre had indicated. It was used mostly for storage. Amid the few boxes and garment bags hung three shirts and a brown suit. On the two inside door hooks were the silk pajamas and matching dressing robe in a muted shade of cranberry. Leaving the pajamas, Dina took the robe.

Downstairs, her hand hesitated on the knob of the library door. Tension hammered in her temples, and her stomach was twisted into knots. Steeling herself to ignore the attack of nervousness, she opened the door quietly and walked in. Her gaze was directed first to the floor and its open area around the fireplace.

"Deirdre sent in the reserves, I see," Blake's low voice mocked from the side of the room.

Dina turned in its direction and saw him standing near the solid wall of shelves filled with books. A dark green blanket was wrapped around his waist, his naked torso gleaming in that deep shade of tan. His thick brown hair was finger-combed into a semblance of order, but it was still unruly. Dina's pulse fluctuated in alarm; her head lifted as if scenting danger. He looked irresistibly male—proud and savage.

"Did you hear her come in?" She realized it was a foolish question after she had asked it. Those long months in the jungle had to have sharpened his senses, making them more acute.

"Yes, but I decided to pretend I was still asleep rather than shock her," he admitted with a wink. "I thought she would scamper up the stairs to inform you or my mother of my lewd behavior."

Behind his veiled look Dina felt the dark intensity of his gaze scanning her face—searching for something, but she didn't know what. It made her uncomfortable, and she wished she had dressed before coming down.

"I brought you a robe." She held it out to him, aware of her faint trembling though it wasn't visible.

"Deirdre's suggestion? She must have been more shocked than I thought." But Blake made no move toward it, forcing Dina to walk to him as he hitched up his improvised sarong.

"She isn't used to finding naked men sleeping on the library floor," she said, defending the housekeeper's reaction as Blake reached down to unwrap the blanket from around his waist. Self-consciously she averted her eyes, her color mounting as if a stranger were undressing in front of her, instead of her husband.

There was a rustle of silk, then, "Okay. It's safe to look now," Blake taunted, his mouth curving in ungentle mockery.

She flashed him an angry look for drawing attention to her sudden burst of modesty and turned away. The vein in her neck pulsed with a nervousness that she wasn't able to control. His hand touched her shoulder, and she flinched from the searing contact.

"For God's sake, Dina, I'm not going to rape you!" he cursed beneath his breath. "Damn it, can't I even touch my wife?"

Her blue eyes were wide and wary as she looked over her shoulder at his fiercely burning gaze. "I don't feel like your wife, Blake," she said tightly. "I don't feel as if I'm married to you."

Immediately the fires were banked in his eyes, that freezing control that was so unlike him coming into play. "You are married to me," he stated, and walked by her to the door. Opening it, he called, "Deirdre! Bring some coffee into the library for my *wife* and me."

"Chet is coming and I still have to dress," Dina reminded him, not wanting to spend one more minute alone with him.

"He isn't due for an hour," Blake said, dismissing her protest.

An awkward silence fell, broken by the sound of brisk footsteps in the foyer signaling the housekeeper's approach. Seconds later she entered the library with a coffeepot and two china cups on the tray she carried. A pink tint still flushed her cheeks as Deirdre steadfastly avoided looking directly at Blake.

"Where would you like the tray?" she asked Dina.

"The table by the sofa will be fine."

Despite his casual reply, Dina knew he was aware of the housekeeper's every movement. After setting the tray on the table at the opposite end of the sofa from where Blake stood, Deirdre straightened up.

"Will there be anything else?" Again her query was directed to Dina.

It was Blake who answered. "Thank you. That will be all," he said. "Please close the door on your way out, Deirdre."

"Yes, sir." Her cheeks were crimson now.

As Deirdre made a hasty exit, firmly closing the door, Blake walked to the tray. Lifting the coffeepot, he filled the two cups and offered one to Dina.

"Black, as I remember, with no sugar," he said quietly.

"Yes, thank you." Dina took the cup and saucer from his hand.

Scalding steam rose from the brown liquid, and Blake let his cup sit. A wry smile crooked his mouth.

"I'd forgotten how good real coffee tastes."

Dina felt as edgy as a cat. She couldn't help retorting, "I thought you hadn't forgotten anything."

"Not the important things, I haven't," Blake replied, levelly meeting her irritated glance.

With a broken sigh, she wandered to the library window overlooking the expansive front lawn of the house and its long driveway. She was caught by the memory of the last time she had stared out the window in troubled silence. It seemed like an eternity ago.

"What are you thinking about?" Blake was close, only a few feet behind her.

"I was remembering the last time I stood at this window." She sipped the hot coffee.

"When was that?" He seemed only idly curious.

Dina felt his gaze roaming her shapely length as surely as if he touched her, and answered bluntly, "The night of my engagement party to Chet."

"Forget about him." The command was crisp and impatient, as Dina guessed it would be.

"It isn't that easy," she muttered tightly.

The cup nearly slipped from her fingers as she felt the rasping brush of his fingers against her hair. Her throat constricted, shutting off her voice and her breath.

"Have I told you I like your hair this long?" His low voice was a caress running down her spine.

He lifted aside the molten gold of her hair, pushing it away from her neck. The warmth of his breath against her skin warned her an instant before he pressed a kiss in back of her ear.

His unerring mouth sought and found the ultrasensitive and vulnerable spot at the nape of her neck. Her heart felt as though it had been knocked sideways, and Blake took full advantage of her vulnerability.

The cup rattled in its saucer, but she managed to hold on to it. His arms wound around her waist to mold her back to his muscular length. For a magic second she was transported back to another time. Then a roughened hand slid under the overlapping fold of her robe to encircle the swell of her breast, teasing one nipple, and the embrace felt suddenly strange.

"Blake, no!" Weakly she tugged at his wrist, no match for his strength.

She gasped as his sensual mouth moved upward to her ear again and desire licked through her veins at the touch of his tongue. He hadn't lost one iota of his sexual expertise. Just being held by him was a dizzying sensation.

"Do you remember the way we used to make love in the mornings?" Blake murmured against her temple.

"Yes," she moaned, the memory all too vivid.

The cup disappeared from her hand, carried away by a swift movement of Blake's hand. It took only the slightest pressure to turn her around. She was drawn to his side, his muscular silk-covered thigh insinuating itself between her legs as she was arched against him. She lifted her head, braced to resist his irresistible kisses, her fingers curled into the muscular flesh of his shoulders.

There was the tantalizing touch of his lips against hers. "After last night, I thought I had you out of my system," he said against them, "but I want you more than before."

A half sob came from her throat at the absence of any mention of love. But in the next second she didn't care, as his mouth closed over hers with sweet pressure. There was no plundering demand, only a sensual coaxing to respond.

Her lips parted willingly to the mastery of his exploration. The dream world of sensation seemed almost enough. She slid her fingers through the springy thickness of his hair, the scent of him earthy and clean.

As if tired of bending his head to reach her lips, Blake tightened his arm around her waist to lift her straight up, bringing her to eye level. His mouth moved downward to explore the pulsing vein in her neck. "Did Chet ever make you feel like this?"

Was this a macho attempt to erase the memory of another man's kisses from her mind? She pushed out of his hold, staring at him with wounded pride.

"Did he?" Blake repeated, a faintly ragged edge to his breathing.

"You'll never know," she answered in a choked voice. "Maybe he made me feel better."

He took a threatening step toward her, his features dark with rage. There was nowhere for Dina to retreat. She had to stand her ground, despite her shakiness. Just then there was a knock at the door. Blake stopped.

"Who is it?" he demanded angrily.

The door opened and Chet walked in. "I'm a little early, but Deirdre said you were in here having coffee. She's going to bring me a cup." He stopped, noticing Dina's rumpled robe and Blake's sullen look. "Mind if I join you?" The question was as awkward as the moment.

"Of course not." Dina was quick to reply.

"Morning, Chet," Blake said casually. "Speak of the devil, Dina and I were just talking about you."

"Something good, I hope," Chet said jokingly.

"Yes." Blake's dark gaze swung to Dina, a considering grimness in their depths. "Yes, it was." But he didn't explain what it had been.

She took a deep breath and decided to make a fast exit. Any excuse to leave.

"If you two don't mind, I'll let you have coffee alone," she said.

"I hope you aren't going on my account," Chet said, frowning.

"No," Dina assured him, avoiding Blake's mocking look. "I was going upstairs anyway to dress before brunch. I'll be right down."

As Dina left, she met Deirdre bringing the extra cup for Chet. The housekeeper's embarrassment was under control now, and she was her usual composed self.

Once she was dressed, Dina slipped Chet's ring into the pocket of her skirt. At some point during the day she hoped to have the chance to return it to him while they were alone. But it was late afternoon before the opportunity presented itself.

The media had learned of Blake's return, and the house was in a state of siege for most of the day. Either the doorbell or the telephone seemed to be ringing constantly. Blake had to grant a few interviews to obtain any peace, but his answers were concise, without elaboration, downplaying his ordeal. As his wife, Dina was forced to be at his side, while Chet took on the role of press secretary and spokesman for the Chandler company to the horde of TV reporters camped out with video and sound equipment on the front lawn.

Finally, at four o'clock, the siege seemed to be over, and a blessed quietness began to settle over the house. Blake agreed to one last interview, if it could be conducted over the phone. Dina noticed Chet slip away to the library and excused herself, knowing she might not get another chance to speak to him alone.

As she stepped inside the library, she saw him pouring whiskey from a crystal decanter over ice cubes in a short glass. The engagement ring seemed to be burning a circle in her pocket.

"Hello, Chet. Is there any cognac?" She quietly closed the door, shutting out Blake's voice coming from the living room.

Chet's sandy blond head lifted, his surprised look melting into a smile when he saw her. "Of course." He reached for another glass and a different decanter. Pouring, he remarked, "It's been quite a day."

"Yes, it has." Dina walked over to take the glass from his hand.

Ice clinked as Chet lifted his glass to take a quick swallow of whiskey. "A reporter that I know from one of the local papers called and got me out of bed this morning. He'd heard that there was some kind of a shake-up in the Chandler hotel chain and he wanted to know what it was. I pleaded ignorance. But that's why I rushed over here so early—to warn Blake that the onslaught was coming. I knew it was only a matter of time before they found out."

"Yes." She nodded, glad there had been no announcement of their engagement in the newspaper or the reporters would have turned Blake's return into a circus.

"Blake really knows how to handle himself with the press," Chet stated with undisguised admiration. "They treated him like he was Indiana Jones."

Dina sipped at her drink. "He's almost that arrogant."

"Hey, he's a local hero. And it'll be great publicity for the hotels," he added.

"Yes." She was beginning to feel like a puppet whose strings were being pulled to nod agreement with everything Chet said—when it really wasn't what she wanted to talk about at all.

"I imagine somebody in the company let it slip about Blake." He stared thoughtfully at the whiskey in his glass. "I called all the honchos yesterday to let them know he was back. That's probably how the word got out."

"Probably," Dina agreed, and promptly changed the subject. "Chet, I've been wanting to see you today, alone"—she reached in her pocket to take out the circlet of diamonds—"to return this to you."

He took it from her outstretched hand, looking uncomfortable. His thumb rubbed it between his fingers as he stared at it, not meeting the sapphire brightness of her gaze.

"I don't want you to get the idea that I was deserting you yesterday." His voice was uncertain, almost apologetic. "But I know how you felt about Blake and I didn't want to stand in the way of your happiness."

With that quiet explanation for calling off their engagement, Chet lifted his head to gaze at her earnestly, a troubled look in his eyes. Affection rushed through Dina at his unselfishness. He always put her needs first and foremost, unlike Blake.

"I understand, Chet."

His relief showed in his smile. "You must be really glad to have him back."

"I . . ." She started to reply almost automatically, but she stopped herself. Among other things, Chet was her best friend, as well as Blake's. She could speak her mind with him. "He's changed, Chet."

He hesitated for a second before answering, as if her response had caught him off guard and he wanted to word his reply carefully.

"Considering all Blake's been through, it's bound to have affected him," he offered.

"I know, but . . ." She sighed, frustrated because she couldn't find the words to explain exactly what she meant.

"Hey, come on, now," Chet said, setting his glass down and grasping her gently by the shoulders, his head bent down to look into her apprehensive face. "When two people care as much about each other as you and Blake do, they can work out their differences. It just won't happen overnight," he reasoned. "Now, what do you say? How about a little smile? You know it's true that nothing is ever as bad as it seems."

Reluctantly almost, her lips curved at his coaxing words. His steadying influence was having its effect on her again.

"That's my girl!" he grinned.

"Oh, Chet," Dina declared with a laughing sigh, and wrapped her arms lightly around him, taking care not to spill her drink. She hugged him fondly. "What would I do without you?"

"I hope we never find out," he remarked, and affectionately kissed the tip of her nose.

The knob turned, and Blake pushed open the library door. At the sight of Dina in Chet's arms, he froze, and she paled as she saw his lips thin into an angry line.

But the violence of his emotion wasn't detectable in his casual tone. "Is this a private party or can anyone join?"

His question broke the spell holding Dina motionless. She withdrew her arms from around Chet to hold her glass of cognac in both hands. Chet turned to greet him, unaware of the heightening tension in the air.

"Now that you're here, Blake, we can drink a toast to the last of the newspaper reporters," he announced cheerily, not displaying any self-consciousness about the interrupted embrace.

"For a while anyway," Blake agreed, his gaze swinging to Dina. "What are you drinking?"

"Cognac." There would be no explosion now, Dina realized. Blake would wait until they were alone.

"I'll have the same."

It was late in the evening before Chet left. Each minute that dragged by honed Dina's nerves to a razor-thin edge. By the time he had left, she could no longer stand the suspense of waiting for the confrontation with Blake.

With the sound of Chet's car revving in the driveway, Dina paused in the foyer to challenge Blake. "Aren't you going to say it?"

He didn't pretend ignorance of her question, his gaze hard and unrelenting. "Stay away from him."

All the blame for the innocent encounter was placed on her, and she reacted with indignant outrage. "Chet's not—"

"I know him well enough to be sure he'll stay off my turf. Unless you encourage him."

"So I'm supposed to avoid him, is that it?" she snapped.

"Whatever relationship you had with him in my absence is finished," Blake declared coldly. "From now on he's simply an acquaintance of mine. That's all he is to you."

"That's impossible!" How dare he suggest that she dismiss Chet from her life. "I can't forget everything he's done for me. You should be grateful that—"

Suddenly the breath was knocked out of her by the hard contact with the solid wall of his chest. He pulled her close for a hot, unexpected kiss, a kiss that seared his brand of possession on her and burned away any memory of another's mouth.

Dina was released with equal force. Shaken and unnerved, she retreated a step. With the back of her hand she tried to rub away the imprint of his mouth.

"You—" she began with helpless rage.

"Don't push me, Dina!" Blake warned.

They glared at each other in furious silence. Dina had no idea how long the battle of wills would have continued if his mother hadn't entered the foyer seconds later.

"Deirdre just told me you'd asked her to bring some blankets to the library, Blake." Norma Chandler wore a worried frown. "You aren't going to sleep here again tonight, are you?"

"Yes, I am," he responded decisively.

"But it's so uncivilized," she protested.

"Maybe," Blake conceded, meeting Dina's look for an instant. "But it beats not sleeping."

"I suppose so." His mother sighed. "Good night, dear."

"Good night," he replied, and coldly arched an eyebrow at Dina. "Good night."

Chapter Five

The library door stood open when Dina came down the stairs the next morning. She smoothed a nervous hand over her cream linen skirt and walked to the dining room, where breakfast coffee and juice were already on the table. But there was no sign of Blake. Dina helped herself to juice and coffee and sat down.

"Isn't Blake having breakfast this morning?" she asked the housekeeper when she appeared.

"No, ma'am," Deirdre replied. "He already left. Said he was meeting Jake Stone for breakfast and going to the office from there. Didn't he tell you?"

"Oh, I believe he did," Dina lied, and forced a smile. "I must've forgotten."

"Mrs. Chandler was so upset about it," the woman remarked with a knowing nod.

Dina frowned. "Because Blake is meeting the attorney?"

"No, because he's going into the office. Mrs.

Chandler thought he should wait a few days. I mean, he just came back and all, and right away he's going to work," Deirdre explained.

"He probably wants to check things for himself." There was a smug feeling of satisfaction in knowing that he would find the entire operation running smoothly, and that a great deal of the credit was hers.

"What'll you have this morning, Mrs. Blake? Would you like an omelet?"

"Just juice and coffee, Deirdre, thank you." She wanted to be at the office when Blake arrived, if only to see his face when he realized how capably she had managed in his absence.

"Okay," the housekeeper said cheerfully.

The morning traffic seemed heavier than usual, and Dina was delayed. Still, she arrived at the office building on time. As she stepped out of the elevator, she remembered that Chet had already notified the various executives of Blake's return, relieved that she was spared that task. She would have time to go over her notes for the department meeting this afternoon and get through most of the Monday morning routine before Blake arrived.

She breezed down the corridor to her office, waving greetings and good mornings to colleagues along the way. She didn't want to stop and chat with anyone and waste precious time. She felt positively buoyant as she entered her secretary's office.

"Good morning, Amy," she said cheerfully.

"Good morning, Mrs. Chandler." The young woman beamed back a smile. "You're in a good mood today."

"Yes, I sure am," Dina agreed. Her secretary was sorting the morning mail, and she walked to her desk to see if there was anything she had to deal with before Blake arrived.

"Is that because Mr. Chandler came back?" Amy Wentworth asked eagerly. Dina smiled politely as her secretary continued, "All of us here are so happy he's alive. He looks great. And so tan," she added somewhat irrelevantly.

Dina nodded and looked over the girl's shoulder. "Anything special in the mail this morning?"

"Not yet," her secretary replied, returning her attention to the stack of letters.

"Any calls?"

"Only one. Mr. Van Patten."

"Did he leave a message?" Dina asked, glad that nothing needed her immediate attention.

"Oh, no," Amy hastened to explain. "Mr. Chandler took the call."

"Mr. Chandler?" she repeated. "Do you mean Blake is already here?"

"Yes, he's in there." Amy motioned toward Dina's private office. "I'm sure he won't mind if you go right on in, Mrs. Chandler."

For several seconds Dina was too stunned to speak. It was *her* office, her pride protested. And *her* secretary was grandly giving her permission to enter it. Blake had moved in and managed to convey the impression that she had moved out.

Her blue eyes darkened with rage. Turning on her heel, she walked to the private office. She didn't bother to knock, simply pushed the door open and walked in. Blake was seated behind the massive walnut desk—*her* desk! He glanced up when she entered. The arrogantly inquiring lift of his eyebrow lit the fuse of her temper.

"What are you doing here?" she demanded.

"I was about to ask you the same question," countered Blake with infuriating calm.

"It happens to be *my* office, and that's *my* secretary outside!" Dina retorted. Her flashing eyes saw the papers in his hands, and she recognized the notes as the ones she planned to go over for the departmental meeting that afternoon. "And those are *my* notes!"

He leaned back in the swivel chair, viewing her tirade without much emotion. "I was under the impression that all of this"—he waved his hand in an encompassing gesture—"belonged to the company."

"I happen to be in charge of the company," she reminded him.

"You *were* in charge of the company," Blake corrected her. "I'm taking over now."

She was trembling violently now, her anger almost uncontrollable. She fought to keep her voice low and not reveal how much he had angered her.

"You're taking over," she repeated. "Just like that!" She snapped her fingers.

"Your job is done." Blake shrugged and fingered the papers on the desk. "And excellently, from all that I've seen this morning."

It was the compliment she'd hoped for, but not delivered the way she had intended it to be.

"And what am I supposed to do?" she demanded.

"Go home. Go back to being my wife." His sun-roughened features wore a frown, as if not understanding why she was so upset.

"Did you fall into a time warp in the jungle?" challenged Dina. "I can't twiddle my thumbs all day until you come home. Deirdre does all the cooking and the cleaning. It's your mother's house, Blake. There's nothing for me to do there."

"Then start looking for an apartment for us. Or better yet, a house of our own," he suggested. "That's what you wanted before, a place of our own that you could decorate the way you wanted to."

A part of her wanted it still, but it wasn't the motivating force in her life. "That was before, Blake," she argued. "I've changed. If we did have a house and the decorating was all done the way I wanted it, what would I do then? Sit around and embroider the guest towels? No, I enjoy my work here. It's demanding and fulfilling."

He was sitting in the chair, watching her with narrowed eyes. "What you're saying is you enjoy the power that goes along with it."

"That's right. I enjoy the power," Dina admitted without hesitation, a hint of defiance in her voice. "I enjoy the challenge and the responsibility, too. Men don't have a monopoly on running things."

"What are you suggesting, Dina? That we reverse roles and I turn into a house husband? Get my kicks decorating, cleaning, and entertaining? What a thrill."

"No, I'm not suggesting that." Confusion was tearing at her. She didn't know what the solution was.

"Maybe you'd like me to take another flight to South America and not come back this time."

"No, I wouldn't—and stop twisting my words!"

Hot tears flooded her eyes as the emotional turmoil inside her became too much to control. She turned sharply away, blinking frantically at the tears, trying to force them back before he saw them.

There was a warning squeak of the swivel chair as Blake rose and approached her. Her lungs were bursting, but she was afraid to take a breath for fear it would sound like a sob.

"Is this the way you handle a business disagreement?" he said impatiently.

Aware that he towered beside her, Dina kept her face averted so he wouldn't see that she was about to cry. "I don't know what you mean," she lied.

His thumb and fingers touched her chin and turned it around so he could see her face. "Do you usually indulge in a female display of tears when you don't get your own way?"

The threatening tears blurred her vision. Dina could barely see his face. "No," she retorted, pushing at the hand that held her chin. "Do you always make it personal when someone doesn't agree with you wholeheartedly?"

She heard his impatient sigh; then his fingers curved to the back of her neck, forcing her head against his chest. An arm encircled her to draw her close. His embrace was strong and warm, but Dina forced herself to remain indifferent to Blake's attempt to comfort her. She felt the pressure of his chin resting atop her head.

"Would you mind telling me what the hell I'm supposed to do about this?" Blake muttered.

She wiped away her tears with shaking fingers and sniffed, "I don't know."

"Here." He reached into his jacket pocket to

hand her his handkerchief. There was a light rap on the door, and Blake stiffened. "Who is it?" he snapped, but the door was already opening.

Self-consciously Dina tried to twist out of his arms, but they tightened around her protectively. She submitted to his hold, her back to the door.

"Sorry," she heard Chet apologize with chagrin. "I guess I've gotten used to walking in unannounced."

He must have made a move to leave, because Blake said, "It's all right. Come on in, Chet." He let her go. "You'll have to excuse Dina. She still gets emotional once in a while about my return," he said, briskly explaining away her tears and the handkerchief she was using to wipe away their traces.

"That's understandable," said Chet, "Just wanted to let you know that everyone's waiting in the conference room."

His statement got Dina's attention, and she frowned. "There isn't any meeting scheduled on my agenda this morning."

"I called it," Blake announced smoothly, his bland gaze meeting her sharp look. Then he shifted his attention to Chet. "Tell them I'll be there in a few minutes."

"I will." And Chet left.

At the click of the closing door, Dina turned to Blake, furious now. "You weren't going to tell me about the meeting, were you?" she accused him.

Blake walked to the desk and began leafing through the papers on top of it. "Well, no. I didn't see the need to tell you at first. But you should attend—"

"You didn't see the need?" Dina sputtered.

"To be truthful, Dina"—he turned to look at

her, his bluntly chiseled features seeming to be carved out of teakwood—"I wasn't sure that you would come into the office today."

"Why not?" She stared at him in confusion and disbelief.

"I guess I thought you'd be glad, if not grateful, to turn over the company to me again. I mean, you were an interim president. Do you really want so much responsibility? I thought you would be happy to take some time off, discover other interests—"

"You obviously don't know me very well," Dina retorted.

"So I'm beginning to discover," Blake responded grimly.

"What now?" she challenged him.

"No man should have to compete with his wife for a job, and I have no intention of doing so with you," he stated.

"Why not?" Dina argued. "If I'm equally competent—"

"But you aren't," Blake interrupted, his eyes turning cold.

"I am." She'd proven that many times over.

He ignored the assertion. "Don't forget that our age difference gives me fourteen more years of experience in the business than you. Compared to mine, your qualifications are negligible. I've got a few years to catch up on, I'll admit, but I'm prepared to work like a dog to do it."

His logic deflated her pride. He made her seem like a child who was protesting because a toy was taken away. Contrary to what he obviously thought, Dina had learned how to disguise her feelings, and now she used the skill to her advantage.

"You're probably right," she said stiffly. "I'd forgotten that Chet actually ran the company. I was too busy having my nails done and my hair highlighted."

"Yeah, right." Blake dismissed the statement with a contemptuous jeer. "Chet is incapable of making an important decision."

Her eyes widened at the accusation. "How can you say that? He's been so loyal to you all these years, your best friend."

The angry flick of his gaze mocked her reference to Chet's loyalty, but he made no mention of Chet's engagement to her when he spoke. "Just because he's been my friend doesn't mean I'm blind to his faults."

Dina didn't pursue the topic. It was dangerous ground, likely to move the conversation to highly personal issues. At the moment, she wanted to keep it on business.

"None of that really matters. It still comes down to the same thing—I'm out and you're in."

Blake raked a hand through his hair, rumpling it into sexy disorder. "What am I supposed to do, Dina?" he demanded impatiently.

"That's up to you." She shrugged, feigning indifference when she only wanted to yell and scream about how incredibly unfair this was. "If you don't object to my borrowing *your* secretary, a formal letter of resignation will be on *your* desk when you return from your meeting."

"No, I don't object." But Blake bristled at her cutting sarcasm. As she turned on her heel to leave, he covered the distance between them with long strides, grabbing at her elbow to spin her around. "What do you expect me to do?" His eyes were ablaze with anger.

"I don't know—"

He got to the point. "Do you want me to offer you an executive position? Is that it?"

Excited hope leaped into her expression. After Blake had put it into words, she realized that that was exactly what she wanted—to still have a part in running the company, to be involved in its operation.

"I can't do it, Dina!" Blake snapped.

Crushed, she demanded in a thin voice, "Why?"

"I can't just give you someone else's job. It smacks of nepotism and it implies that I don't approve of the people you hired to fill key positions. The logical deduction would be that I believed you'd done an inadequate job of running the company in my absence." His expression was hard and grim.

"That settles it, then, doesn't it?" Her chin quivered, belying the challenge in her voice.

His teeth were gritted, a muscle leaping in his jaw. "If you weren't my wife . . ." he began, about to offer another explanation of why his hands were tied in this matter.

"No problem, Blake." Dina pulled her arm free before his grip could tighten. She didn't expect it to last long, but he made no attempt to recapture her.

"That's where you're wrong." He clipped out the words with biting precision.

Inwardly quaking under his piercing look, Dina turned away rather than admit his power to intimidate her. "I don't think so," she said quietly. "And my resignation will be on your desk within an hour." She walked to the door.

"Dina." The stern tone of his voice stopped her from leaving.

She didn't remove her hand from the doorknob or turn to face him. "What?"

"Maybe I can keep you on as a consultant." The stiffness of his words took away from the conciliatory gesture.

"I don't want any favors! And certainly not from the great Blake Chandler!" Dina yanked open the door. It closed on a few well-chosen curses from Blake.

When Dina turned away from the door, she looked into the curious eyes of the secretary, Amy Wentworth. Dina knew that the walls of the private office were thick, but she doubted they were thick enough to muffle the sound of loud, arguing voices. She wondered how much of the aftereffect of her quarrel with Blake was apparent in her face. She did her damnedest to seem in command of herself as she walked to Amy's desk.

"Please put aside whatever you're doing, Amy," she ordered, trying to ignore the girl's wide-eyed look.

"But . . ." The young secretary glanced hesitantly toward the inner office, as if uncertain whether to obey Dina or Blake.

Dina didn't give her a chance to put her doubts into words. "I want you to type a letter of resignation—for me. Just keep it simple and direct. Effective immediately."

"Yes, Mrs. Chandler," Amy murmured, and immediately opened a new document on her computer.

The connecting office door was pulled open, and Dina glanced over her shoulder to see Blake stride through. She could tell he had himself under rigid control, but it was like seeing a predatory animal in chains. The minute the shackles were removed, he would pounce on his prey and tear it apart. And she was his prey.

Yet, even knowing she was being stalked, she was mesmerized by the dangerous look in his gaze. She waited, motionless, as he walked toward her, the force of his dark vitality vibrating over her nerve ends, making them tingle in sharp awareness.

"Dina, I . . ." Blake never got the rest of his sentence out.

Chet, who had a way of being in the right place at the wrong time, entered the room through the door to the outer corridor. "Oh, you're on your way," he concluded at the sight of Blake. "I was just coming to see how much longer you'd be." He switched his attention to Dina and couldn't help noticing the lines of stress on her face.

"Yes, I'm on my way," Blake agreed crisply, and looked back at her. "I want you to attend the meeting, Dina." The veiled harshness in his gaze dared her to defy him.

But Dina felt safe with others around. "No. It's better for everyone to realize that you're in charge now and not confuse them by having a former head of the company present." She saw his mouth tighten at her response, and he turned away in a gesture of dismissal.

"Dina has a good point," Chet said tactfully, but a glare from Blake made him waver. "Of course, unless you think it's wiser to—"

"Let's go," Blake snapped.

He strode from the room with Chet in his wake,

leaving Dina feeling drained and colorless. Her nerves seemed to be delicate filaments, capable of snapping at the slightest pressure. When the brief letter of resignation was printed out, her hand trembled as she signed it.

"You can put that on Mr. Chandler's desk," she said, and returned it to Amy.

"It was nice working for you, Mrs. Chandler," the young secretary offered as Dina turned to go, the words spoken in all sincerity.

"Thank you, Amy." Dina smiled mistily, then hurried from the room.

Leaving the building, she walked to her car. She knew there was no way she could return to the house and listen to Mrs. Chandler's happy chatter about Blake's return. With the top down on the white Porsche, she removed the scarf from her hair and tucked it in the glove compartment.

With no destination in mind, she climbed into the car and took off, the wind whipping at her hair, which glittered in the morning air as she drove around and through the back streets, the main streets, and the side streets of Newport.

Half the time she was too blinded by tears to know where she was. She didn't notice the row of palatial mansions on Bellevue Avenue or the crowds gathered on the wharf for the America's Cup trials.

She didn't know who she was, what she was, or why she was. Since Blake's return, she was no longer Dina Chandler. She was once again Mrs. Blake Chandler, lost in her husband's identity. She was no longer a businesswoman, and she didn't feel like a wife, since she had a stranger for a husband. As to the reason why, she was in total confusion.

It was sheer luck that she glanced at the instrument panel and noticed she was nearly out of gas. Necessity forced her to set aside the bewildering questions until she was at a gas station and waiting in line for a full-service pump.

Dina rummaged in her purse for her cell phone and speed-dialed the number of the one person who had already seen her through so much emotional turmoil.

The impersonal voice of a receptionist answered, and Dina requested in an unsteady voice, "Chet Stanton, please."

"Who's calling, please?"

Dina hesitated a fraction of a second before answering, "A friend."

There was a moment when Dina thought the receptionist was going to demand a more specific answer than that; then she heard the call being put through. "Chet Stanton speaking," his familiar voice came on the line.

"Chet, this is Dina," she rushed.

"Oh." He sounded surprised and guarded. "Hello."

She could guess the one reason why he would respond that way. "Are you alone?"

"No."

Which meant that Blake must be in his office. Dina wasn't sure how she knew it was Blake and not someone else, but she was positive she was right.

"Chet, I have to talk to you. I have to see you," she declared in a burst of despair. Glancing at her wristwatch, she didn't give him a chance to reply. "Can you meet me for lunch? I know it's short notice. . ."

She heard the deep breath he took before he answered, "I'm sorry, I can't."

"I have to see you," she repeated. "What about later?"

"Let me think." Chet began to enter into the spirit of the thing, however uncertainly. "Why don't we get together for a drink? Say, around five-thirty?"

It was so long to wait, she thought desperately, but realized it was the best he could offer. "Okay," she said, and named the first trendy bar that came to mind. The Krokodile Klub was overpriced, but at least she wouldn't have to rub elbows with beer-bellied guys in flannel shirts.

"I'll meet you there," Chet promised.

"And, Chet"—Dina hesitated—"please don't say anything to Blake about meeting me. I don't want him to know. He wouldn't understand."

There was a long pause before he finally said, "No, I won't. See you then."

Turning off the phone, Dina saw the gas station attendant wave her up to the pump.

"Cash or credit, miss?" he asked, looking at her curiously. "Hey, are you all right?"

She glimpsed her reflection in her rearview mirror and understood his reason for asking. Her hair was windblown and tangled, and her nose was red. Tears had streaked her mascara to make smudgy lines around her eyes. She looked like an out-of-luck hooker, despite the expensive clothes she wore.

"I'm fine," she lied. "Allergies."

She found a tissue in her bag and wiped the dark smudges from beneath her eyes. A brush took the tangles out of her silky gold hair before she tied the scarf around it.

Get a grip, she told herself silently.

She paid and drove away, wondering what on earth she was going to do for the rest of the day.

Chapter Six

Typically, the Krokodile Klub was dimly lit. What a ridiculous name for a bar, Dina thought glumly. The slithering crocodile printed on her drink napkin wasn't even cute. She looked around. The dark wood paneling was oppressive, as was the beamed low ceiling.

Tucked away in an obscure corner, Dina had a total view of the room and the entrance door. A drink was in front of her, untouched, the ice melting. Five more minutes, her watch indicated, but the wait already seemed interminable.

An hour earlier she had phoned Mrs. Chandler to tell her she would be late, without explaining why or where she was. Blake would be angry, she realized. *Let him,* was her inward response. The consequences of her meeting with Chet—well, she would think about later.

Brilliant sunlight flashed into the room as the door was opened. Dina glanced up, holding her breath and hoping that this time it might be Chet. But a glimpse of the tall figure that entered made her heart stop beating, if only for a second or two.

Once inside, Blake paused, letting his eyes adjust to the gloom. There was nowhere Dina could run without attracting his attention. She tried to make herself small, hoping he wouldn't see her in this dim corner. Dina felt rather than saw his gaze fasten on her just before his purposeful strides carried him to her table.

When he stopped beside her, Dina couldn't look up. Her teeth were so tightly clenched they hurt. She curled her hands around the drink she hadn't touched since it had been set before her. Despite the simmering resentment she felt, there was a sense of inevitability, too. Blake didn't speak, waiting for Dina to acknowledge him first.

"Imagine seeing you here," she offered in a bitter tone of mock surprise, not letting her gaze lift from the glass cupped in her hands. "Small world, isn't it?"

"It's quite a coincidence," he agreed.

There was a bright glitter in her blue eyes when she finally looked at him. His craggy features were in the shadows, making his expression impossible to see. The inescapable maleness of his presence began to make itself felt despite her attempt to ignore it.

"How did you know I was here?" she demanded, knowing there was only one answer he could give.

And Blake gave it. "Chet told me."

"Why?" The simple word came out unknowingly, directed at the absent friend who had betrayed her trust.

"Because I asked him."

"He promised he wouldn't tell you!" Her voice was choked, overcome by the discovery that she was lost and completely alone in her confusion.

"So I gathered," Blake said dryly.

Dina drew in a shaky breath. "Why did he have to tell you?"

"I am your husband, Dina, despite how often you try to forget it. Don't I have some right to at least know where you are?"

His voice was as smooth as polished steel, outwardly calm and firm. She noticed his large hands had clenched into fists at his side, revealing the control he was exercising over his anger. He was filled with a rage that his wife had arranged to meet another man. Dina was frightened, but it was fear that prompted the courage to challenge him.

"You were in Chet's office when I called, weren't you?" she said accusingly.

"Yes, and I could tell by the guilty look on his face that he was talking to you. After that, it didn't take much to find out what was going on."

"Who did you think I would turn to? I needed him." Dina changed it to present tense. "I need Chet."

Like the sudden uncoiling of a spring, Blake leaned down, spreading his hands across the tabletop, arms rigid. In the flickering candlelight his features seemed ruthless and dangerously compelling.

"When are you going to get it through your head that you've never needed him?" he demanded.

Her heart was pounding out a message of fear. "I really don't know you," she breathed in panic. "You frighten me, Blake."

"That makes two of us, because I'm scared as hell of myself!" He straightened abruptly, issuing an impatient "Let's get out of here before I do something I'll regret."

Throwing caution away, Dina protested, "I don't want to go anywhere with you."

"I'm aware of that!" His hand grasped her arm to haul her to her feet, overpowering her weak resistance. Once she was upright, his fingers remained clamped around her arm to keep her pressed to his side. "Is the drink paid for?" Blake reminded her of the untouched contents of the glass on the table.

As always when she came in physical contact with him, she seemed to lose the ability to think coherently. His muscular body was like living steel, and the softness of her shape had to yield. Everything was suddenly reduced to an elemental level. Not until Blake had put the question to her a second time did Dina take in what he had asked.

She managed a trembling, "No, it isn't. And I don't want it."

Releasing her, Blake took a money clip from his pocket and peeled off a bill, tossing it on the table. Then the steel band of his arm circled her waist to guide her out, oblivious to the curious stares.

In towering silence he walked her to the white Porsche, its top still down. He opened the door and pushed her behind the wheel. Then, slamming the door shut, he leaned on the frame, an unrelenting grimness to his mouth.

"My car is going to be glued to your bumper, following you every inch of the way. So don't take any detours on the route home, Dina," he warned.

Before Dina could make any kind of retort, he

walked to his car, parked in the next row of the lot. Starting the car, she gunned the motor as if she were accelerating for a race, a pointless gesture of defiance.

True to his word, his car was behind hers all the way, an ominous presence she couldn't shake even if she had tried—which she didn't. Stopping in the driveway of his mother's house—their house—Dina hurried from her car, anxious to get inside.

Halfway to the door Blake caught up with her, a hand firmly clasping her elbow to slow her down.

"This little episode isn't over yet," he stated in an undertone. "We'll talk about it later."

Dina swallowed the impulse to challenge him. It was better to keep silent with safety so near. Together they entered the house, both concealing the state of war between them.

Mrs. Chandler appeared in the living room doorway, wearing a black chiffon dress. Her elegantly coiffed silver hair was freshly styled, thanks to an afternoon at her favorite salon. She smiled brightly at them, unaware of the crackling tension.

"You're both home—how wonderful!" she exclaimed, assuming her cultured tone. "I was about to tell Deirdre to delay dinner for an hour. I'm so glad it won't be necessary. I know how much you detest overcooked meat, Blake."

"You always did like your beef very rare, didn't you, Blake?" Dina followed up on the comment, her gaze glittering at his face with diamond sharpness. "I think your appetite for raw flesh is positively barbaric."

"I love it. Just poke it through the bars at feeding time," he countered.

Mrs. Chandler seemed impervious to the barbed exchange as she waved them imperiously into the living room. "Come along. Let's have a drink and you can tell me about your first day back at the office, Blake." She rattled on, covering their tight-lipped silence.

It was an ordeal getting through dinner and making the necessary small talk to hide the fact, that there was anything wrong. It was even worse afterward, when the three of them sat around with their coffee in the living room. Each tick of the clock was like the swing of a pendulum, bringing the moment nearer when Blake's threatened discussion would take place.

The phone rang and the housekeeper answered it in the other room. She appeared in the living room seconds later to announce, "It's for you, Mr. Blake. A Mr. Carl Landstrom."

"I'll take it in the library, Deirdre," he responded.

Dina waited several seconds after the library door had closed before turning to Mrs. Chandler. "It's a business call." Carl Landstrom was head of the accounting department, and Dina knew that he would never call after office hours unless it was something important. "Blake is probably going to be on the phone for a while," she explained, a fact she was going to use to make her escape and avoid his private talk. "Would you tell him that I went up to bed? I'm exhausted."

"Of course, dear." The older woman smiled, then sighed with rich contentment. "It's good to have him back, isn't it?"

It was a rhetorical question, and Dina didn't offer a reply as she bent to kiss her mother-in-law's smooth cheek. "Good night, Mrs. Chandler."

"Good night."

Upstairs, Dina undressed and took a quick shower. Toweling herself dry, she wrapped the royal blue robe around her and removed the shower cap from her head, shaking her hair loose. She wanted to be in bed with the lights off before Blake hung up. With luck, he wouldn't bother her. She knew she was merely postponing the discussion, but for the moment that was enough.

Her nightgown was lying neatly at the foot of the bed as she entered the bedroom that adjoined the private bath, her hairbrush in hand. A few brisk strokes to unsnarl the damp curls at the ends of her hair was all it needed, she decided, and sat on the edge of the bed to do it.

The mattress didn't give beneath her weight. It seemed as solid as a wooden table. Dina sat motionless for a moment, then realized that the new mattress and box spring for Blake had arrived and hers had been removed.

She sprang from the bed as if hot coals lay beneath it. No, her heart cried, she couldn't sleep with him—not after that last humiliating experience; not with his anger simmering so close to the surface because of today.

The door opened and Blake walked in, and she burst out in panic. "I'm not going to sleep with you!" she cried.

A brow flicked upward. "At the moment, sleep is the last thing on my mind."

"Why are you here?" She couldn't even think beyond the previous moment.

"To finish our discussion." Blake walked to the chair against the wall and motioned toward the matching one. "Sit down."

"No," Dina refused, too agitated to stay in one place even though he sat down, seemingly relaxed, while she paced restlessly.

"I want to know why you were meeting Chet." His hooded gaze watched her intently, like an animal watching its trapped prey expend its nervous energy before moving in for the kill.

"It was perfectly innocent," she began in self-defense, then abruptly changed her tactics. "It's really none of your business."

"If that's true—that it was innocent," Blake said, deliberately using her words, "then there's no reason not to tell me."

"What you can't seem to understand, or refuse to understand, is that I need Chet," she said. "I need his comfort and understanding, his gentleness. I don't get that from you!"

"If you'd open your eyes, you'd see you're not getting it from him, either," Blake retorted.

"Don't I?" Her sarcastic response was riddled with disbelief.

"Chet only says what he thinks you want to hear. He's incapable of original thought."

"I'd hate to have you for a friend, Blake," she declared tightly, "if this is the way you talk about people when they aren't around, cutting them into little pieces."

"I've known Chet much longer than you have. He can't survive on his own in this business. When I disappeared, he transferred his allegiance to you. Dina, for all his charm," Blake continued his cold dissection, "he lived on your strength. He persuaded you to take charge of the company because he knew he was incapable of heading up a major corporation."

"You don't know what you're saying," Dina breathed, walking away from his harsh explanation.

"Oh, Dina," he said wearily, "can't you see that you've been supporting him through all this, not the other way around?"

"No!" She shook her head in vigorous denial.

"I should have stayed away for a couple more months. Maybe by then the rose-colored glasses would have come off and you would have found out how heavily he leans on you."

Pausing in her restless pacing, Dina pressed her hands over her ears to shut out his hateful words. "How can you say those things about Chet and still call him your friend?"

"I know his flaws. He's my friend anyway," Blake responded evenly. "Yet you were going to marry him without acknowledging that he had any."

"Yes. Yes, I was going to marry him!" Dina cried, pulling her hands away from her ears and turning to confront him.

"But when I came back, he dropped you so fast it made your head swim. Admit it." Blake sat unmoving in the chair.

"He wanted me to be happy," she said defensively.

"No," he said. "My return meant you were on the way out and I was in. Chet was securing his position. That was his reason for breaking the engagement. He wasn't sacrificing anything, only insuring it."

"So why did you hound him into admitting he was meeting me today?" challenged Dina.

"I didn't hound him. He was almost relieved to tell me."

"You have an answer for everything, don't you?" She refused to admit that anything Blake was saying made sense. She fought to keep that feeling of antagonism; without it, she was defenseless against him. "It's been like this ever since you came back," she complained, uttering her thoughts aloud.

"I knew when everyone discovered I was alive, it was going to be a shock. But I thought it would be a pleasant shock," Blake said wryly. "In your case, I was wrong. It was a shock you haven't recovered from yet."

Dina heard the underlying bitterness in his tone and felt guilty. She tried to explain. "How did you think I would feel? I'd become my own person. Suddenly you were back and trying to absorb me again in your personality, swallow me up whole."

"How did you think I would react when you've challenged me every minute since I've returned?" His retaliation was instant, his temper ignited by her defensive anger, but he immediately brought it under control. "It seems we've stumbled onto the heart of our problem. Let's see if we can't have a civilized discussion and work it out."

"Civilized!" Dina laughed bitterly. "You don't know the meaning of the word. You spent too much time in the jungle. You aren't even civilized about the way you make love!"

Black fires blazed in his eyes. The muscles along his jaw tensed visibly from his effort to keep control. "And you go for the jugular every time!" he snarled, rising from the chair in one fluid move.

Dina's heart leaped into her throat. She had aroused a beast she couldn't control. She took a step backward, then turned and darted for the door. But Blake intercepted her, spinning her around, his arms circling her, crushing her to his length.

His touch sizzled through her like an electric shock, immobilizing her. She offered no resistance as his mouth covered hers in a long, punishing kiss. She seemed without life or breath, except what he gave her in anger.

At last his head lifted a fraction of an inch. She opened her eyes and gazed breathlessly into the brilliant darkness of his. The warm moistness of his breath was caressing her parted lips.

His hand stroked the spun gold of her hair, brushing it away from her cheek. "Why do you always bring out the worst in me?" he asked huskily.

"Because I won't let you dominate me the way you do everyone else," Dina whispered. She could feel the involuntary trembling of his muscular body and the beginnings of the same passionate response in her own.

"Does it give you a feeling of power"—he kissed her cheek—"to know that"—his mouth teased the tips of her lashes—"you can make me lose control?" He returned to tantalize the curving outline of her lips. "You're the only one who could ever make me forget reason."

"Am I?" Dina whispered skeptically, because he seemed to be in complete control at the moment. She was the one who was losing her grip.

"I had a lot of time to think while I was trying to fight my way out of that tropical hell. I kept remembering all our violent quarrels and how they started over the damnedest things. I told myself that if I ever made it back, that crap was going to be a thing of the past. But a few hours after I saw you, we were fighting again."

"I know," she nodded.

As if believing her movement was an attempt to escape his lips, Blake captured her chin to hold her head still. With languorous slowness, his mouth took possession of hers. The kiss was like a slow-burning flame that kept growing hotter and hotter.

Its heat melted Dina against his length, so hard and very male. Her throbbing pulse sounded loudly in her ears as the flames coursed through her body.

Before she succumbed completely to the strength of her physical desire, she twisted away from his mouth. She knew what he wanted, and what she wanted, but she had to deny it.

"It won't work, Blake." She shook her head, hating the words even as she said them. "Not after the last time."

"The last time . . ." He pursued her lips, his mouth hovering near them, and she trembled weakly, lacking the will to turn away. "I hated you for becoming engaged to Chet, even for believing I was dead. And I hated myself for not having the control to stop when you asked me not to make love to you. This time it's different."

"It's no good." But the hands that had slipped inside her robe and were caressing her skin with such arousing thoroughness felt very good.

For an instant Dina didn't think Blake was going to pay any attention to her protest, and she wasn't sure that she wanted him to take note of it. Then she felt the tensing of his muscles as he slowly became motionless.

He continued to hold her in his arms as if considering whether to concede or to overpower her resistance, something he could do easily in her present state.

A split second later he was setting her away from him, as if removing himself from temptation. "If that's what you want, I'll wait," he said grimly.

"I . . ." In a way, it wasn't what she wanted, and Dina almost said so but checked herself. "I need time."

"You've got it," Blake agreed, his control superb, an impenetrable mask concealing his emotions. "Only don't make me wait too long before you come to a decision."

"I won't." Dina wasn't even certain what decision there was to make. What were her choices?

His raking look made her aware of the robe hanging loosely open, exposing too much cleavage. She drew the folds together to conceal her nakedness, though Blake didn't seem to mind. He turned away, running his fingers through the wayward thickness of his dark hair.

"Go to bed, Dina," he said with a hint of weariness. "I have some calls to make."

Her gaze swung to the bed and the quilted spread that concealed the rock-hard mattress. "The new box spring and mattress that I had Deirdre order for you came today, and she put it in here. I'll . . . I'll sleep in the guest room."

"No." Blake slashed her a look over his shoulder. "You'll sleep with me, if you do nothing else."

Dina didn't make the obvious protest regarding the intimacy of such an arrangement and its frustrations, but said instead, "That bed is like granite."

There was a wryly mocking twist of his mouth. "What's the old cliché, Dina? You've made your bed, now you have to lie in it."

"I won't," she declared with a stubborn tilt of her chin.

"Am I asking too much to want my wife to sleep beside me?" He gave Dina a long, level look that she couldn't hold.

Looking away, she murmured softly, "No, it isn't too much."

The next sound she heard was the opening of the door. She turned as Blake left the room. She stared at the closed door that shut her inside, wondering if she hadn't made a mistake by giving in to his request.

Walking over to the bed, she pressed a hand on the quilt to test its firmness. Under her full weight it gave barely an inch. Quite a difference from the soft mattress she usually slept on, but then, her bed partner was no longer the urbane man she had married. Dina wondered which she would get used to first—the hard bed or the hard man.

In her nightgown, the robe lying at the foot of the bed, she crawled beneath the covers. The unyielding mattress wouldn't mold to her shape, so she had to attempt to adjust herself to it, without much success. Sleep eluded her as she kept shifting positions on the hard surface, trying to find one that was comfortable.

Almost two hours later she was still awake, but she closed her eyes when she heard Blake open the door. It was difficult to keep her breathing even as she listened to his quiet preparations.

Keeping to the far side of the bed, she stayed motionless when he climbed in beside her, not touching but close enough for her to feel his body heat.

Blake shifted a few times, then settled into one position. Within a few minutes she heard him breathing deeply in sleep. Sighing, she guessed she was still hours away from it.

Chapter Seven

A hand was making rubbing strokes along her upper arm, pleasantly soothing caresses. Then fingers tightened to shake her gently.

"Come on, Dina, wake up!" a voice ordered.

"Mmm." The negative sound vibrated from her throat as she snuggled deeper into her pillow.

Only it wasn't a pillow. There was a steady thud beneath her head, and the pillow that wasn't a pillow moved up and down in a regular rhythm. No, it wasn't a pillow. She was nestled in the crook of Blake's arm, her head resting on his chest. She could feel his tawny chest hair tickling her cheek and nose.

Sometime in the night she had forsaken the hardness of the mattress to cuddle up to the warmth of his body. Her eyelids snapped open, and Dina would have moved away from him, but the arm around her tightened to hold her there for another few seconds.

A callused finger tipped her chin upward, forcing her to look at him, and her heart skipped a beat at the fond amusement in the craggy male face.

"I'd forgotten what it was like to sleep with an octopus," Blake murmured. "Arms and legs all over the place!"

Embarrassment assailed Dina at the intimacy of her position. Sleep had dulled her reflexes. When his thumb touched her lips to trace their outline, Dina was too slow in trying to elude it. As the first teasing brush made itself felt, she lost the desire to escape. He lightly explored every contour of her mouth.

It became very difficult to breathe under the erotically stimulating caress, especially when his gaze was absorbing every detail of his action. With one hand resting on the hard muscles of his chest, afraid to move, Dina felt and heard the quickening beat of his pulse.

The muffled groan of arousal that came from his throat sent the blood rocketing through her heart. The arm around her ribcage tightened, and his mouth renewed the exploration his thumb had only begun. With a mastery that left her shattered, Blake parted her lips, his tongue seeking hers.

In the crush of his embrace, it was impossible for Dina to ignore the fact that Blake was naked beneath the covers. It was just as impossible to be unaware that her nightgown was twisted up around her hips. It was a discovery his roughly caressing hands soon made.

As his hands slid beneath the nightgown, his fingers catching the material to lift it higher, Dina made a weak attempt to stop him. It seemed the minute her own hands came in contact with the living bronze of his muscled arms, they forgot their intention.

More of her bare skin came in contact with his hard flesh. The delicious havoc it created with her senses only made Dina want him more. Willingly she slipped her arms from the armholes as Blake lifted the nightgown over her head. His mouth was away from her lips for only that second. The instant the nightgown was tossed aside, he was kissing her with a demanding passion that she eagerly returned.

Blake shifted, rolling Dina onto her back, the punishing hardness of the mattress beneath her. He loomed above her, his elbows on the mattress offering him support. His warm, male smell filled her senses, drugging her mind. When he dragged his mouth away from hers, she curved a hand around his neck to bring it back. Blake resisted effortlessly, his burning eyes glittering with satisfaction at her aroused state.

At some time the covers had been kicked aside. As his hand began a slow, intimate exploration of her breasts, waist, and hips, Blake watched it, his eyes drinking in the shapely perfection of her female form. The blatant sensuality of the look unnerved Dina to the point that she didn't want it to continue. Again she had the feeling that a stranger's eyes were looking at her, not those of her husband.

Gasping back a sob, she tried to roll away from him and reach the protective cover of the sheets and blankets. Blake thwarted the attempt, forcing her back, his weight crushing her to the unyielding mattress.

"No, Dina, I want to look at you," Blake insisted in a voice husky with desire. "I imagined you like this so many times, lying naked in the bed beside me, your body soft and eager to have me make love to you. You're mine, Dina, mine."

The last word was uttered with possessive emphasis as his head descended to stake its first claim, his mouth seeking her lips, kissing them until passion overrode her brief attempt at resistance. A languorous desire consumed her as he extended his lovemaking to more than just her lips. She quivered with fervent longing at the slow descent of his mouth to her breasts, treating each in turn to the erotic stimulation of his tongue.

Overwhelmed by his sensuous skill, Dina forgot the strangeness of his arms and the rocklike mattress beneath her. She forgot all but the dizzying climb to the heights of sexual pleasure and the dazzling climax that made her want to cry.

Dina nestled in his arms, her head resting on his chest as it had when she had awakened. This time there was healthy sweat coating his hard muscles and dampening the fine, wiry hairs beneath her head. Dina closed her eyes, aware that she had come very close to discovering her love for Blake again. Its light still shone deep within her heart.

Blake's mouth moved against her hair. "I had forgotten how passionate you are." His murmured comment suddenly brought the experience down to a purely physical level. What had bordered on an act of love became lust. "I enjoyed it. Correction, I enjoyed you," he added.

Crimsoning, Dina rolled out of his arms, an action he didn't attempt to prevent. The movement immediately caused a wince of pain. Every bone and fiber in her body was an aching reminder of the night she had spent in the rock hard bed.

"How can you stand to sleep in this bed?" Dina was anxious to change the subject, unwilling to talk about the passion they had just shared. "It's awful."

"You'll get used to it." When Blake spoke, Dina realized he had slid out of bed with barely a sound while she had been discovering her aches and pains. Her gaze swung to him as he stepped into the bottoms of his silk pajamas and pulled them on. Feeling her eyes watching him, Blake glanced around. There was a laughing glint in his dark eyes as he said, "It's a concession to Deirdre and her old-fashioned modesty this morning."

Dina smiled. Even that hurt. "What time is it?"

"Seven," he answered somewhat absently, and rubbed the stubble of beard on his chin.

"That late?"

Her minor miseries deserted her for an instant, and she started to rise, intent only on the thought that she would be late getting to the office unless she hurried. Then she remembered she no longer had any reason to go to the office, and sank back to the mattress, tiredness and irritation sweeping over her.

"Why am I getting up?" she asked aloud. "It took me so long to get to sleep last night. Why didn't you just let me keep right on sleeping?" Then he wouldn't have made love to her and she wouldn't be experiencing all this confusion and uncertainty, about herself and him.

"You'd be late to work," was Blake's even response.

"Have you forgotten?" Bitterness gave her voice an edge. "I've been replaced. I'm a lady of leisure now."

"Are you?" He gave her a bland look. "Your boss doesn't think so."

"What boss? You?" Dina breathed out with a scornful laugh. "You're only my husband."

"Does that mean you're turning it down?"

"What? Blake, would you quit talking in riddles?"

"Maybe if you hadn't been so proud and stubborn yesterday morning and attended the meeting as I asked you to, you'd know what I'm talking about."

She pressed a hand against her forehead, tension and sleeplessness pounding between her eyes. "Well, I didn't, so perhaps you could explain."

"We're starting a whole new advertising campaign to upgrade the image of the Chandler hotel chain," he explained. "We can't possibly compete with the bigger chains on a nationwide basis, especially when most of our hotels are located in resort areas, not necessarily heavily populated ones. We're going to use that fact to our advantage. From now on, when people think of resorts, they'll think of Chandler Hotels."

"Great idea," Dina conceded. "But what does that have to do with me?"

"You're going to be in charge of the campaign."

"What?" Blake's calm announcement brought her bolt upright. There was wary disbelief and skepticism in the look she gave him. "Is this some kind of a joke?"

There was an arrogant arch to one dark eyebrow. "No." He walked around the bed to where she stood. "I put the proposal to the rest of the staff yesterday, along with the recommendation that you handle it."

"Is this a token gesture? Something for me to do to keep me quiet?" She couldn't accept that there wasn't an ulterior motive behind the offer. It might mean admitting something else.

"I admit that picking you to head the campaign was influenced by the tantrum you threw in the office yesterday." His gaze was steady. "But you can be sure, Dina, that I wouldn't have suggested you if I didn't think you could handle the job. You can interpret that any way you like."

Dina believed him. His candor was too typical to be doubted, especially when he acknowledged the argument they'd had earlier. It surprised her that he'd relented to this extent, putting her in charge of something that could ultimately be so valuable to the company. True, she would be working for him, but she would be making decisions on her own, too.

"Why didn't you tell me about this last night?" She frowned. "Your decision had already been made. You just said a moment ago that you told the staff yesterday. Why did you wait until now to tell me?"

Blake studied her thoughtfully. "I was going to tell you last night after we'd had our talk, but, um, circumstances altered my decision and I decided to wait."

"What circumstances?" Dina persisted, not following his reasoning.

"To be perfectly honest, I thought if you knew about it last night you might have made love to me out of gratitude," Blake replied without a flicker of emotion in his impassive expression.

She suddenly saw red. "You thought I'd be so grateful that I'd . . ." Anger robbed her of speech.

"It was a possibility."

Dina was overcome with indignant rage, but it didn't affect her aim. Her palm connected with the hard contour of his cheek. As the slap mark turned scarlet against his tan, Blake walked into the bathroom. Trembling with the violence of her aroused temper, Dina watched him go.

When her anger dissipated, she was left with a troubling question. If he hadn't made that degrading remark, would she still be angry with him? Or would this have been the first step toward reestablishing their marriage, with Blake recognizing her talent and skill?

At the breakfast table, their conversation was coldly polite.

"Please pass the juice."

"May I have the marmalade?"

That tender, sensual feeling they had woken up to that morning was gone, dissolved by doubt.

When they had finished breakfast, Blake set his cup down. "You can ride to the office with me this morning," he announced.

"I prefer to take my own car."

"It's impractical for both of us to drive."

"If you had to work late, how would I get home?" Dina protested.

"*If* that happens, you take the car and *I'll* take a taxi home," he stated, his demeanor cold and arrogant.

Dina was infuriatingly aware that Blake had an argument for everything. "Okay, I'll ride with you." She gave in grudgingly.

The morning rush-hour traffic seemed heavier

than normal, and the distance to the Newport office greater; the time passed more slowly, and the polar atmosphere between them was colder than ever.

Feeling like a puppy dog on a leash, Dina followed Blake from the parking lot to his office. There she sat down, adopting a businesslike air to listen to specific suggestions that had been offered by Blake and the staff for the campaign. It was a far-reaching plan, extending to totally redecorating some hotels to fit their new resort image.

Dina couldn't help a caustic comment. "I'm surprised I'm not limited to that. Decorating is woman's work, isn't it?"

His gaze pierced her like a cold knife. "Do you want to discuss this program intelligently? Or do you want to bring our personal difficulties into it? Because if you do, I'll find someone else for the job."

She wanted to flip him off, but common sense insisted she would ultimately be the loser if she did. The project promised to be a challenge, and Dina had come to enjoy that. Her pride was a bitter thing to swallow, but she managed to get it down.

"Sorry. That just slipped out." She shrugged. "Go on."

There was a second's pause as Blake weighed her words before continuing. When he had concluded, he gave her a copy of the notes from the staff meeting and a tentative budget.

Dina glanced over them, then asked, "Where do I work?"

"I'll take you to your new office."

She followed him out of the office and walked beside him down the long corridor until they came to the end. Blake opened the last door.

"Here it is."

The battered metal desk, chair, and shelves seemed to fill up the room, and the piles of folders only added to the cluttered feel. Three offices this size could have fit into Blake's office, Dina realized. And that wasn't all. It was cut off from the other staff offices, at the end of the hall, isolated. She could die in here and nobody would know, she thought to herself.

"Thanks for nothing," she said.

Blake saw the fire smoldering in her blue eyes. "This is the only office available on such short notice," he explained.

"Is it?" she retorted grimly.

"Yes"—he clipped out the word challengingly— "unless you think I should've moved an executive out to make room for you."

Dina knew that would have been illogical and chaotic, with records being shifted and working routines upset. Still, she resented the size and location of her new office, though she understood the practicality of his choice. But she didn't complain. She didn't have to, since Blake knew how she felt.

She looked at the bare desktop and said, "No phone? No computer?"

"The phone will be installed today. Getting a DSL hookup for a computer will take a little longer. And we have to patch you into the network."

"Fine." She walked briskly into the room, aware of Blake still standing in the doorway. "I look forward to spending time talking to the tech support guys."

"If you have any questions—" he began in a cool tone.

Dina interrupted, "I doubt if I will." The banked fires of her anger glittered in the clear blue of her eyes.

His gaze narrowed, his expression hardening. "You can be replaced, Dina."

"Permanently?" she said in a taunting voice.

For an instant she thought he might do or say something drastic, but instead he exhibited that iron control and pivoted to walk away. There was a tearing in her heart as he left. Dina wondered if she was deliberately antagonizing him or merely reacting to his attempted domination of her.

Pushing the unanswerable question aside, she set to work, taking an inventory of the supplies on hand and calculating a rough budget for the rest. After obtaining the required items from the supply room, she began making a list of information she would need before drawing up a plan of action for the ad campaign.

At the sound of footsteps approaching the end of the hallway, she glanced up from her growing list. She had left the door to her office open to lessen the claustrophobic sensation, and she watched the doorway, curious as to who was coming and for what reason.

Chet appeared, pausing in the doorway, a twinkle in his gray-blue eyes, an arm behind his back. "Hello there." He smiled.

"Are you lost or just slumming?" Dina questioned with a wry smile.

He chuckled and admitted, "I was beginning to think I was going to have to stop and ask directions before I found you."

"I don't think a lot of people will be stopping by to chat on their way someplace else. This is the end of the line," she declared with a rueful glance around the tiny office. "Which brings me to the next obvious question."

"What am I doing here?" Chet asked it for her. "When I heard you were exiled to the far reaches of the building, I decided you might like a cup of hot coffee." The arm that had been behind his back moved to the front to reveal the two Styrofoam cups of coffee he was juggling in one hand. "At least, I hope it's hot. After that long walk, it might be cold."

"Hot or lukewarm, it sounds terrific." Dina straightened away from the desk to relax against the rigid back of her chair. "I will love you forever for thinking of it."

She had tossed out the remark without considering what she was saying, but she was reminded of it as an uncomfortable look flashed across Chet's face.

"I guess that brings me to the second reason why I'm here." He lowered his head as he walked into the room, not quite able to meet her gaze.

"You mean about not meeting me yesterday and sending Blake in your place," Dina guessed.

"Yes, well"—Chet set the two cups on the desk top—"I'm sorry about that. I know you didn't want me to tell Blake, and I wouldn't have, either, except that he was in my office when you called and he guessed who I was talking to."

"So he said," she murmured, not really wanting to talk about it in view of last night's discussion with Blake.

"Blake didn't lay down the law and forbid me to go or anything like that, Dina."

"He didn't?" she asked skeptically.

"No. He asked if you sounded upset," Chet explained. "When I said that you did, he admitted that you two had your few differences and he thought it was best that I didn't become involved. He didn't want me in the position of having to take sides when both of you are my friends."

Friends? Dina thought. Just a few days ago, Chet had been her fiancé, not her friend. But he looked so pathetically sorry for having let her down yesterday that she simply couldn't heap more guilt on his head.

Instead she gave him an easy way out. "Blake was right; it isn't fair to put you in the middle of our disagreements. If I hadn't been so upset. . . . Anyway, it doesn't matter now." She shrugged. "It all worked out for the best." That was a white lie, since it almost had, until their blowup that morning.

"I knew it would." The smile he gave her was tinged with relief. "Although I wasn't surprised to hear Blake admit that the two of you got off to a rocky start." He removed the plastic lid and handed the cup to her.

"Why do you say that?" she asked.

"You were always testing each other to see which was the stronger. It looks like you still are."

"Really? Am I stronger? In your humble opinion," Dina qualified her question.

"Oh, I don't know." His laughter was accompanied by a dubious shake of his head. "Sometimes I want to say Blake, but I have a hunch I'd be underestimating you."

In other words, Dina realized, Chet wasn't taking sides. He was going to wait until there was a clear-cut winner. Meanwhile, he was keeping his options open, buttering up both of them.

The minute the last thought occurred to her, Dina knew it had been influenced by Blake's comment that Chet was always on the side of the one in power. But she immediately squashed the thought as petty and unkind to someone as loyal as Chet.

"You're a born diplomat, Chet." She lifted the coffee cup in a toast. "No wonder you're such an asset to this company."

"I try to be," he admitted modestly, and touched the side of his cup to hers. "Here's to the new campaign."

The coffee was only medium hot, and Dina took a big gulp. Chet's reference to the new project made her glance at the papers, notes, and lists spread over her desk.

"It's quite a project." She took a deep breath, aware of the magnitude of the image change for the Chandler hotel chain. "But I know I'll succeed."

"That's the third reason I'm here."

Her startled gaze flew to his face, her blue eyes rounded and bright. "Why?"

Had she made Blake so angry that he was already taking her off the campaign? Oh, why hadn't she held her tongue? she thought, angered by the way she had kept pushing him.

"Blake wants me to work with you on it," Chet announced.

Her relief that Blake hadn't replaced her didn't

last long. "Doesn't he think I'm capable of handling it by myself?" Her temper flared at the idea that he would doubt her ability.

"You wouldn't be here if he didn't believe you could," he said placatingly. "But after all, you're going to need some help. Blake knows how well we worked together as a team while he was gone."

Dina counted to ten, forcing herself to see the logic of Chet's explanation. But she wasn't sure that she liked the idea. There was still the possibility that Blake had appointed Chet as her watchdog and he would go running to Blake the instant she made a mistake.

She was doing it again, she realized with a desperate kind of anger. She was not only questioning Blake's motives, but making accusations against Chet's character, as well. Damn Blake, she thought, for putting so many doubts in her mind.

Chet took a long swig of his coffee, then set it aside. "Where shall we begin?"

"I've been making some lists," Dina focused her attention on the project at hand.

She went over them with Chet, discussing various points. Although Dina was still skeptical of Blake's reasons for having Chet assist her, she accepted it until she could prove otherwise. An hour later, he left her small office with a formidable to-do list of his own.

Dina spent most of the day getting the project organized. In itself, that was no easy task. At five o'clock, she was going over the master list again, making notes in the margins while various ideas were still fresh in her mind.

"Are you ready?" Blake's voice snapped from the open doorway.

Her head jerked up at the sound. Her reading glasses blurred his image, deceptively softening the toughness of his features. For an instant, Dina almost smiled a welcome; then his demanding question echoed in her mind. Recovering from that momentary rush of pleasure, she bent her head over the papers once again.

"I'll only be a few more minutes." She adjusted the glasses on the bridge of her nose.

Blake walked in, his dislike of being kept waiting charging the air with tension. He sat in the straight-backed chair in front of her desk. Dina was conscious of his scrutiny, both of her and her work.

"Since when did you wear glasses?" he asked.

She touched a finger to the nosepiece, realizing he had never seen her wearing them. "Since about a year ago."

"Do you need them?"

"What a ridiculous question!" she snapped. "Of course I need them."

"It isn't so ridiculous," Blake contradicted her. "They fit the image of a career woman who's turned her back on domestic bliss."

What a comment—snotty, patronizing, and absolutely infuriating. Dina chose not to rise to the bait. "All the reading and close work I have to do, was straining my eyes. After too many headaches, I put my vanity aside and began wearing glasses to read. They have nothing to do with my image." She lied, since the small frames had been chosen with that in mind.

"Then you do admit to having an image," he taunted her coldly.

It was no use. She simply couldn't concentrate

on what she was doing. It took all of her attention to engage in this battle of words with him. Removing her glasses, she slipped them into their leather case. Dina set her notes aside and cleared the top of her desk.

"You haven't answered my question," Blake prompted in a dangerously quiet voice when she rose to get her coat.

"I hadn't realized your comment was a question." She took her purse from the lower desk drawer, unconsciously letting it slam shut to vent some of her tightly controlled anger.

"Is that how you see yourself, Dina, as someone whose life is centered around her work, with no time for a husband?" This time Blake phrased it as a question. The office was so small that when he stood up, he was blocking her path.

"That's just not true." She faced him, her nerves quivering with his closeness.

"No?" An eyebrow lifted in challenging disbelief.

"Did you forget?" Sheer bravado made her mock him. "I was going to marry Chet, so I must have felt there was room for a husband in my life."

"I'm your husband," Blake stated.

"I don't know you." Dina looked anywhere but into those inscrutable dark eyes.

"You knew me well enough this morning, in the most intimate sense of the word," Blake reminded her deliberately.

"This morning was a mistake." She brushed past him to escape into the hallway, but he caught her arm to half turn her around.

"Why was it a mistake?" he demanded.

"Because I let myself listen to all your talk about long, lonely nights and I started feeling sorry for you, that's why," Dina lied angrily, because she was still confused by her tight cruel line, savage and proud. "Compassion is the last thing I want from you!" he snarled.

"Then stop asking me to pick up the threads of our life. The pattern has changed. I don't know you. The Blake Chandler that spent two and a half years in a jungle is a stranger to me. You may have had to live like an animal, but don't ask me to become your mate or satisfy your lust." The words streamed out, flooding over each other in their rush to escape. With each one, his features grew harder and harder until there was nothing gentle or warm left in them.

Blake gave her a push toward the door. "Let's go," he snapped.

Aware that she had roused a sleeping tiger whose appetites were ravenous, Dina quietly obeyed him. All during the ride back to his mother's house she kept silent, not doing anything to draw attention to herself. Blake ignored her. The cold war had briefly exploded into a heated battle, but once again the atmosphere was frigid.

Within minutes of entering the house, Blake disappeared into the library. Dina found herself alone in the living room with her mother-in-law, listening to the latest gossip Norma Chandler had picked up at the afternoon's gabfest.

"Of course, everyone was buzzing with the news about Blake," the woman concluded with a beaming smile. "They wanted to know every single detail of his adventure in the jungle. I thought they were never going to let me leave. Finally I had to insist that I come home, to be here when you and Blake arrived."

Dina was sure that Norma Chandler had been the center of attention. No doubt she'd reveled in it, even if the spotlight had been a reflection of her son's.

"It was thoughtful of you to be at the door when Blake came home from the office," she murmured, knowing that appreciation was expected.

"I only wish he had waited a few more days before returning to work," sighed Mrs. Chandler. "After all he's been through, he was entitled to rest for a while."

Of course. That would have given her a chance to dote on him, treat him like a little boy again. Dina wasn't sure if she was being blamed for Blake's decision to return to work so quickly. Just in case, she decided to set the record straight.

"It wasn't my idea for him to come back right away. But Blake has some great new plans for the company. I think he was eager to get back to work so he could put them into operation," Dina explained.

"I'm sure you're right, but he isn't giving us much time to enjoy the fact that he is back. There I go," Norma Chandler scolded herself. "I'm complaining when I should be counting my blessings. It's just that I can't help wondering how much longer I'll have him."

"That's a strange thing to say." Dina frowned. "You'll probably be moving out soon—into a place of your own, won't you? Then I'll only be able to see him on weekends," she pointed out.

"We've discussed the possibility of getting a place of our own," Dina admitted, choosing her words carefully. "But I don't think it'll happen in the near future. We'll both probably be too busy to do much looking. And we don't want to move into just any old place," she lied.

It wasn't that Dina was so focused on her career that she didn't long for a home of her own, as she'd led Blake to believe. At the moment, living in the Chandler house where his mother and the housekeeper could serve as buffers suited her fine. She wasn't ready to share a home with only the stranger who was her husband. Maybe she never would be.

"Well, I'm glad to hear you say that." Her mother-in-law smiled broadly. "You know how much I've enjoyed having you here, Dina. Now that Blake is back, my happiness has been doubled. Having a man around the house makes it seem more like a home."

"Yes," Dina agreed, if not wholeheartedly.

"I don't like to pry." There was a hesitancy in the older woman's voice and expression. "But I have the feeling that there's some tension between you and Blake. If I'm wrong, just say so or tell me to mind my own business. I don't want to become an interfering mother-in-law, but . . ." Her voice trailed off. She was obviously expecting a response from Dina.

It was Dina's turn to hesitate. She doubted if Mrs. Chandler would understand, but she felt a need to confide her fears in someone.

"That's true," she admitted cautiously. "It's—it's just that Blake has changed. And so have I. We aren't the same people we were two and a half years ago."

"It's Chet, isn't it?" Norma Chandler drew her own conclusions, not really listening to what Dina had said. "I know that Blake acted as if he understood and forgave, but it bothered him, didn't it?"

"Yes." She felt no need to say more.

"Well, it's only natural that he'd be upset to find his wife engaged to his best friend, but he'll come around. In a few years, you'll be laughing about it."

"Probably." Dina nodded, but she couldn't help wondering if they would be together in a few years. For that matter, she wondered if they would be together in a few months.

The housekeeper entered the living room. "Dinner is ready whenever you wish," she announced.

"Now is fine, Deirdre," Norma Chandler stated. "Blake's in the library. Would you please tell him?"

Dinner that evening was an awkward meal, since Norma Chandler seemed determined to convince Blake how properly Dina had behaved during his absence. Dina knew there was no way she could intervene, though Blake seemed indifferent to the praise his mother heaped on Dina, which only prompted Norma Chandler to pile on more.

It was a relief to escape to the privacy of the bedroom after coffee had been served. The tension of the day and the evening had tightened her muscles into taut bands. The sight of the bed and the thought of sleeping beside Blake another night increased the tension. She was a little crazy from confusion, torn between dreading the idea of Blake making love to her again and looking forward to the possibility.

Dina walked from the bedroom into the adjoining bathroom and filled the porcelain tub with hot water, adding a generous dollop of scented bubble bath. From her bedroom closet she brought her robe and hung it on a door hook. Shedding her clothes, Dina stepped into the tub and submerged herself up to her neck in the steamy mound of bubbles.

Lying back in the tub, she let the warm water soak away the tension and slowly relaxed in the soothing bath. The lavender fragrance wafted through the air, a balm to her senses. When the water cooled, Dina added more hot, losing track of time in her watery cocoon.

The bedroom door opened and closed. Dina heard it, but she wasn't unduly concerned that Blake had entered. The bathroom door was closed. She expected him to respect the desire for privacy it implied.

When the bathroom door opened anyway, Dina sat up straight in a burst of indignation. The sound of sloshing water drew Blake's gaze. Minus his suit jacket and tie, he had unbuttoned the front of his shirt down to his stomach, exposing a lot of hard, muscled flesh and dark chest hair.

"Sorry, I didn't know you were in here," he apologized insincerely.

The bubbles had been slowly dissipating during her long soak. Only a few bits of foam remained around the uplifting curve of her breasts. The fact did not escape Blake's attention. It kept him from leaving.

Dina grabbed for a washcloth, holding it self-consciously in front of her. "Now that you've discovered I'm in here, get out."

"I thought you might want me to wash your back, or wouldn't you consider that civilized behavior?" Blake mocked.

"I don't need my back washed, thank you." Dina wasn't sure why she had bothered with the washcloth. It was becoming wet and very clingy. "Please leave," she requested stiffly. "I'm finished with my bath and I'd like to get out of the tub."

"I'm not stopping you. The sooner you're out, the sooner I can take my shower." Blake turned and walked into the bedroom, closing the door behind him.

Not trusting him, Dina quickly rinsed away the bubbles drying on her skin and stepped out of the tub. After rubbing herself down with the towel, she slipped into her robe and zipped it to the throat. Another few minutes were spent neatening up the bathroom.

When she entered the bedroom, her senses were heightened to a fever pitch. Blake was sitting on the love seat, looking a little too relaxed. His hooded gaze swept over her.

"It's all yours." Dina waived a hand toward the bathroom.

Blake stretched out his long legs and took his time getting up from the love seat. "Thank you." His response was cool, almost taunting.

Dina suppressed a shudder at his freezing politeness and wondered whether their heated exchanges were preferable to this. As he crossed the room, she walked to the closet. At the door, she stopped to glance at him.

It suddenly became imperative to make him understand that she wasn't going to let him persuade her to make love, not until she was able to sort out her true feelings for him. She wanted to end this sensation that she was married to a stranger, before they got intimate.

"Blake, I have no intention—" Dina began.

"Neither have I," he cut in sharply, and paused at the doorway to the bathroom to pin her with his gaze. "I know I'm a husband in name only. Didn't you think I was capable of phrasing it politely?" Blake's tone was mocking. "Maybe if I'd kept my distance, promised never to tempt you, you would have been less afraid. Is that it?"

Dina chose not to answer his caustic challenge. "As long as we understand each other," she murmured stiffly, and turned away.

"Just so there isn't any mistake. I won't touch you again until you come to me. And you will come to me, Dina." There was something almost merciless in the controlled tone he used.

The sound of the bathroom door closing left Dina shaken. She changed out of her robe into her nightgown without being aware of her actions. She heard the shower running in the bathroom and tried not to visualize Blake standing beneath its spray, all sun-browned flesh, naked and hard, as virile as a pagan god.

Shaking away the sensual image, she walked to the bed and folded down the satin coverlet. Dina was between the silk sheets when Blake came out of the bathroom, a towel wrapped around his waist. He didn't glance her way as he switched off the light and walked around to the opposite side of the bed, unerringly finding his way in the dark. The mattress didn't give much beneath his weight, but she was aware of him. The sheets seemed to transmit the heat from his nude body.

A tidal way of longing threatened to swamp her. Dina closed her eyes tightly. Blake was fully aware of what he was doing to her. He had a motive for everything he did. She didn't believe that he was denying himself sex with her out of respect, any more than she believed he'd assigned Chet to the new project purely because she needed competent help. He wanted to undermine her confidence, no matter what. She silently vowed he wouldn't succeed.

But the remarks Blake had made about Chet's character haunted her over the next two weeks. Again and again she fretted over the doubts Blake had planted in her mind. The cold war between them grew colder without even a hint of a thaw.

A knock at the open door brought her out of her gloomy reverie. She had been staring out of the solitary window in her small office. She turned, settling her reading glasses on top of her head.

"Hello, Chet." She stiffened at the sight of him and tried to relax, but she had become too self-conscious lately in his company, not feeling the same freedom and trust she used to have with him.

"Okay. I finally got all the interior and exterior photographs of the hotels that you wanted." He indicated the stack of folders he was carrying with both hands. "I thought we should go over them together. Are you too busy to do it now?"

"No, bring them in." Dina began moving paperwork to one side of her desk. "Just give me a second to make some room."

Before the actual advertising campaign could begin, there was a lot of groundwork to be done. The most time-consuming part was improving the physical appearance of the hotels.

"I've already looked through them," Chet told her.

"Good," Dina nodded, and began to scan them herself.

The line of her mouth tightened. By the time she reached the bottom of the stack, she realized she'd seriously underestimated the amount of time and money this project would take.

"It's worse than I thought," she sighed.

"Yes, I know," Chet agreed, matching her expression.

"Let's take the hotels one by one and make notes." She sighed. "And keep in mind that each hotel should be different, its decor and landscaping inspired by its location. We don't want vacationers to think that if they've been in one Chandler Hotel, they've been in them all."

"That's right."

"Starting with the one in Florida"—Dina gazed at the photographs—"I think this has to be the most challenging. I didn't realize it looked so sterile. And the pink plastic flamingos have to go."

She flipped her glasses into place on her nose and reached for her notepad. "We can take advantage of the tropical environment. Light wicker furniture, airy colors, no carpeting, cool tile floors, and lots of potted plants and greenery."

"What about the exterior?"

Dina thought of the budget and winced. "I hope we can get by with some landscaping. I don't want to do a major face-lift unless there's no other way."

Down the list of hotels they went. The one in Maine would be done with a nautical flavor. The one in Mexico would have a hacienda look, complete with handmade tiles and an interior patio with brightly painted rustic furniture. The founding hotel in Newport already had an elegant yachting theme, which would now be stressed.

When the last photograph had been studied and set aside, Dina looked at her scribbled notes and sighed at the estimated amounts in the margins. She remembered her spiteful comment to Blake about interior decorating being women's work. Well, there was a mountain of it here, one that she doubted Blake would have the patience to tackle.

"Now what?" Chet questioned.

"Now"—Dina took a deep breath—"now we need to have these notes developed into sketches."

"Do you want me to contact some decorating firms?"

"With the scope of the work that needs to be done, I'm just wondering how we should handle it." She nibbled thoughtfully at her lower lip.

"In the past we've always used local businesses in the same city when we could," Chet reminded her.

"Yes, I know." Dina slid the pencil through the platinum-gold hair above her ear. "I checked the records last week. It makes sense and it's good business."

"But think of all the traveling our team would have to do," he observed. "That cost could eat into whatever savings we'd realize by using a local decorator."

"I'm afraid you're right," she agreed with a rueful nod. "We're probably better off with a major firm capable of doing all the work. In the long run it might save us hundreds of thousands of dollars."

"Tell you what"—Chet leaned forward, his blue-gray eyes bright—"first let's get these notes typed up and on a disk. I'll burn a few copies and contact two major companies to give us estimates on the work. To get a comparison, I can pick a half-dozen hotels fairly close to here and obtain bids from local firms. How about the hotel in Maine, the one here in Newport, the one in the Poconos—I can check the list."

"That might work," she agreed. It had been a half-formed thought in her own mind, but when Chet had spoken it aloud, it had solidified. "Excellent suggestion, Chet."

"I'll get started on it right away." He began gathering up the notes and the photographs from her desk. "Why waste time, right?"

"Before you go, there's something else I've been thinking about that I wanted to talk over with you," Dina said to stall him.

"What's that?" Chet sat back down.

"To keep the concept of every hotel being individual, I think we should carry it into the restaurants," she explained.

"But we're doing that." He frowned. "There'll be decor changes in the restaurants and lounges, too. We just went over them."

"No, I was thinking of extending the idea to the food."

"Do you mean changing the menus?"

"Not completely. We have to keep the standard items like steaks and chicken, but we could add some regional specialties. We do it already along the coast with the seafood."

"I see what you're saying." Chet nodded. "In the Poconos, for instance, we could feature Pennsylvania Dutch foods like shoofly pie. And genuine johnny-cake made out of white cornmeal here in Newport."

"Exactly," Dina nodded.

"I'll ask the restaurant managers of all the hotels to send us a list of three or four specialty dishes to include on their menus," he suggested.

"Yes, do that. We can initiate this change right away by simply adding a flyer to the menus until new ones can be printed."

"Consider it done, Dina." He started to rise, then paused. "Is that all?"

"For now, anyway," she laughed.

"I'll be talking to you. And I'll have my secretary send you a hard copy of these notes," he promised, and gathered the stack of notes and photographs into his arms.

As Chet walked out of the office, the smile left Dina's face and was replaced by a wary frown. She stared at the open doorway, feeling uneasy. Then, with a firm shake of her head, she turned back to the papers she had been working on.

Chapter Eight

Bent over her desk, Dina was concentrating on the proposals from the selected advertising agencies. Absently she stroked the eraser end of her pencil through her hair. Intent on the papers, she didn't hear the footsteps in the hallway or notice the tall figure darkening her open doorway.

"Are you planning to work late?"

The sound of Blake's voice got her attention. He stood there, so lithe and powerful, so magnetically attractive. The darkness of his tan seemed not to have faded, and was emphasized by the white turtleneck sweater. Through half-closed lids he looked at her, creating the impression of friendly interest, yet his expression seemed masked.

As always when he caught her unaware, her pulse accelerated. An odd tightness gripped her throat, leaving her with a breathless sensation. For an instant the room seemed to spin crazily.

It was at moments like these that Dina wanted to

let the powerful attraction she felt simply carry her away. But that was too easy and too dangerous. It wouldn't solve any of the differences that had developed in the years they were apart.

His question finally registered. She managed to tear her gaze away from his ever watchful eyes to glance at her wristwatch, surprised to see it was a few minutes before six o'clock.

Then she noticed the silence in the rest of the building. There were no muffled voices coming in from the hallway, no soft clickety-click of computer keyboards. Nearly everyone had left for the day, except herself and Blake.

"I didn't realize it was so late," she said in answer to his question. "I just have to clear my desk and I'll be ready to leave."

As she stacked the proposals one on top of the other without slipping them back into their folders, Blake wandered into the room. He suddenly seemed to fill every square inch of it. Dina was much too conscious of the sensuous impact of his presence, which annoyed her.

"How's the campaign going?" he inquired, his gaze flicking to the papers in her hand.

Dina had to search for the chilling antagonism that would keep him at a distance. "Hasn't Chet been keeping you in the loop?"

"No. Was he supposed to?" There was an edge to the blandness of his voice.

"I assumed he would," she retorted, opening a desk drawer to put papers away.

"If you didn't tell him to keep me up to date, Chet won't," said Blake, hooking a leg over the desk corner to sit on its edge. "He only does what he's told."

The desk drawer was slammed shut. "Will you stop that!" Dina glared at him.

"Stop what?" Blake asked innocently.

"Stop making remarks like that about Chet!" The antagonism was there; she no longer had to search for it.

Blake gave an indifferent shrug. "Whatever you say."

Impatiently she swept the remaining papers and pens into the middle drawer of her desk, leaving the top neat and orderly. Setting her bag on top, she pushed her chair up to the desk. Her sweater was lying on the back of the chair near where Blake stood.

"Hand me my sweater, please." Icy politeness crept into her voice.

Glancing around, Blake slipped it off the chair back and held it out to her as she walked around the desk to the front. "How are you and Chet getting along?"

"The same as always—really well." Dina gave him a cool look and started to reach for the sweater. "Did you expect it to be different?" It was spoken as a challenge, faintly haughty. A light flashed in her mind, and she forgot about the sweater. "You did expect that to change, didn't you?" she accused.

"I don't know what you're talking about."

"That's why you told Chet to give me a hand. I thought it was because you didn't think I could handle the job, but that wasn't it at all, was it?" Her anger was growing by the moment.

Completely in control, Blake refused to react. "You tell me."

"You planted all those doubts in my mind about Chet, then threw us together, hoping I would find something wrong with his work. That's what this was all about, wasn't it?" Dina was incensed at the way Blake had attempted to manipulate her thinking.

"I admit that I hoped you would see him as he really is." There wasn't a trace of regret in his expression or his voice that his motive had been uncovered.

"That is the lowest I've ever heard!" she hissed. Trembling with rage, she was completely unaware of her hand lashing out to strike him until it was caught in a viselike grip, short of its target. Without letting go, he straightened from the desk to stand before her, the sweater cast aside on the desktop.

"The last time you slapped me, I let you get away with it because I probably deserved it. But not this time," Blake said flatly. "Not when I'm telling the truth."

"But it isn't the truth!" Dina said, undaunted by his implied threat. "Not one word you've said against Chet is true. Not one!"

That darkly piercing look was back in his eyes as they scanned her upturned face. "You know I'm right, don't you?" he said in a low, satisfied voice. "You've started to see it for yourself—that's why you're so angry."

"No," she replied. "I haven't seen it."

"You have. Why don't you admit it?" Blake insisted with grim patience.

"No." Dina continued to resist and strained to break free of his hold. "And I'm not going to stay here and listen to you tear Chet down anymore."

He increased the pressure of his grip. "I'm not trying to make him appear less of a man. I'm trying to make you see him the way he is and not the way you've imagined him to be. Why can't you understand that what I'm saying is not a personal attack on him?"

Suddenly, unexpectedly, she did understand, and she believed him. The discovery took the heat out of her anger. Dina stopped fighting him and stood quietly.

"All right," she admitted.

"All right, what?" Blake lowered his gaze to her mouth, watching her lips as they formed the answering words.

"I have noticed a few things," Dina admitted.

"Such as?"

"The way he takes a suggestion and elaborates on it until you're almost convinced the idea was his in the first place."

"He's done that?"

"Yes. Today, when I mentioned an idea I had about adding regional dishes to the restaurant menus." She wished Blake would stop watching her talk. It was unsettling, heightening her senses. "He's already contacting the restaurant managers to see about starting it."

"Chet is very good at organizing and carrying out a suggestion," Blake agreed. "What else?"

"I don't know. A lot of little things." The compliment Blake had given Chet prompted Dina to mention another conversation that had bothered her. "When I didn't take a stand today about having a local or a national decorating firm redo the hotels, Chet didn't either. He suggested getting comparison bids from both and avoided offering a concrete opinion. In the last two weeks, I honestly can't remember Chet making a decision or offering a proposal of his own."

Looking back, she realized that his proposal of marriage had been an outgrowth of a conversation about whether she would marry again or not. When she had conceded the possibility, Chet had asked if she would choose someone like Blake. Her negative answer had then led to Chet's suggesting himself, after first testing out his ground.

That wasn't exactly the mark of the strong, dependable man she had believed him to be. His reliability was limited to the times when someone else told him what to do.

Lost in her thoughts, Dina was unaware of the silence that had fallen until Blake spoke. "I have another equally selfish reason for wanting Chet to work with you on this project." His fingers were lightly stroking the inside of her wrist, a caressing motion that was disturbing.

A tingling warmth spread up her arm, her nerves fluttering in awareness of how close she stood to him. "What is it?" There was a breathless catch to her voice. She looked into his eyes, nearly overcome by the sensation that she could willingly drown in the dark pools.

"Because I know that eventually this project is going to require a lot of traveling, and I wanted to make sure it wasn't my wife who had to do it."

"I see." She couldn't think of anything else to say.

"You might as well know this, Dina," he said. "You and I are never going to be separated for any reason."

The ruthlessly determined note underlying his

statement made her shiver. She felt a sense of being trapped, a feeling that his wishes were inescapable. Whatever Blake wanted, he got. But not from her, her pride protested—not unless it was her own decision to agree.

With a degree of reluctance, she pulled away, turning to the desk to pick up her sweater and handbag. "I'm ready to leave now," she said, all too aware of the conflicting magnetic currents between them, alternately pulling and repelling.

Blake didn't make a move. He just stood there looking at her, making her feel more uncomfortable and unsure of her own wants and needs.

"Sooner or later you're going to have to make a decision," he told her.

"I know. Sooner or later," she echoed softly.

"Why are you waiting? What's holding you back?" he questioned. "Chet's out of the picture, so what's left?"

"I don't know." Dina shook her head uncertainly.

Needing to move, she started for the door. With that animal silence she was beginning to associate with him, Blake came up behind her, his hands sliding over her shoulders. His mere touch stopped her in her tracks.

"Decide now," Blaked ordered in a low murmur. She felt the warm stirring of his breath on the exposed skin of her neck, sensitive and vulnerable. The sensuous pressure of his lips exploring that special pleasure point sent a delicious tremor through her.

His hands slid down to her forearms, crossing them in front of her as he molded her shoulders, waist, and hips to the hard contours of his body.

Dina was suddenly willing to be shaped into anything he wanted. A fierce passion scorched through her veins.

She struggled against her own desire, responding softly, "Blake, I can't!"

"You want to." His mouth moved to her ear, nibbling at its lobe. "You know you do."

"I don't know anything," she breathed raggedly. "Then feel," Blake told her.

That was the problem. She felt too much, and it kept her from thinking straight. She didn't want to make a decision in the heat of the moment, swayed by the physical need that was consuming her now.

"Blake, no!" She swallowed and pushed his hands from around her waist.

She took a step away from his tempting embrace and stopped, shaking and weak with desire. Her head was lowered, her chin tucked into her throat. She felt his gaze boring into her.

"Blake, no!" He mimicked her words with a biting inflection. "That's always your answer. How much longer are you going to keep giving it?"

"Until I'm absolutely sure that I know what I'm doing," Dina answered.

"And how long will that be?" Blake was striving for control. It was evident in the clipped patience of his tone.

"I don't know," she sighed. "I just know it's easy to surrender to passion now and not so easy to face tomorrow."

"Then you're a hell of a lot stronger than I am, Dina," he snapped, "because I don't give a damn about tomorrow!" He slipped a hand under her elbow. Her first thought was that he intended to ignore her uncertainties and kiss her into submission, something that wouldn't be difficult to do. Instead his hand pushed her forward. "Let's go," he muttered.

His long, ground-eating strides made it impossible for Dina to keep up with him without half running. He didn't slow down until he reached the parking lot, where she struggled to catch her breath as they walked to the Porsche.

Without looking directly at her, Blake unlocked the passenger door and held it open for her, slamming it shut when she was safely inside. Walking around, he unlocked his own door and slid behind the wheel. He put the key in the ignition but didn't start the car.

Resting his hands on the steering wheel, he stared straight ahead for several long seconds, a forbiddingly hard line to his mouth. Dina grew increasingly uneasy at the silence and felt pinned when his dark gaze finally swung to her. It wasn't a pleasant sensation.

"The first day I was back," Blake said, "you said we needed time to get to know each other again— that we had to become adjusted to each other. You felt we should talk."

"I'm surprised you remember," she remarked, and immediately regretted it.

"Believe me, I remember everything you've said," he replied with dry weariness, looking away. Dina shifted uncomfortably in her seat but kept silent. "The point is, Dina, that we aren't getting to know each other again. We aren't talking. The only place we spend any time together alone is in the bedroom. And we both know there isn't any communication taking place there, physical or otherwise."

"So what are you suggesting? That we should communicate on a physical level and work from there?" Dina asked uncomfortably, her pulse quickening at the idea.

"No, that isn't what I'm suggesting"—there was a cynical twist to his mouth—"although I know you're convinced that my instincts are primitive."

A slight flush warmed her cheeks. "Then what are you suggesting?"

"That we spend more time together."

"That's not easy with both of us working."

"Neither of us works on the weekend," Blake reminded her.

"You're forgetting we live in your mother's house." And Mrs. Chandler still hadn't gotten over her son's miraculous return. She hovered around him every possible moment she could.

"No, I'm not," Blake returned calmly. "The key word is *alone*—no friends, no relatives, just us. That's why I've decided we'll spend the weekend at Block Island together."

"Block Island." Dina repeated the name of the resort island off the Rhode Island coast.

"That's what I said. Any objections?" He turned his head to look at her, a challenging glitter in his dark eyes.

"None." How could there be when he had cornered her with her own words?

"There is one thing more, Dina." Blake continued to study her, aware of her reluctance.

"What's that?" She was almost afraid to ask.

"I want something clearly understood before we go. If you haven't made up your mind about us by

Sunday night, I'm not waiting any longer." She went pale, and he noticed. He smiled without humor. "And I don't care whether you consider that a threat or a promise."

"You can't set a deadline like that," she protested.

"I just did." Blake had already turned away to start the car, ignoring her now that he had stated his intentions.

"You can't force me to make a decision," Dina retorted.

"Whatever," Blake said indifferently. "Just pack a suitcase and bring it to the office with you Friday morning. We'll catch the ferry to Block Island after work."

As the ferry left the protected waters of Narragansett Bay for the open waters of the Atlantic, heading for the pork-chop-shaped island offshore, Dina stared at the Brenton Reef lighthouse without really seeing it. She and Blake had barely exchanged a word with each other since leaving the office, and the silence was growing thicker.

She knew the reason she felt so nervous. Blake's ultimatum had made her feel like he was pointing a gun at her head. How could she look forward to the weekend ahead of them? He had already determined the outcome and she should have refused to come. Why hadn't she?

Pressing a hand to her forehead, she tried to rub away the dull throb. The pills she had taken to stave off seasickness were working, but they clouded her thinking. At least she had been spared the embarrassment of being queasy, even if she did feel slightly drugged.

Sighing, she glanced at Blake, who was standing not far away talking to a fellow passenger. Their attention was on the low, dull gray clouds hanging overhead. There was nothing menacing about them, but they added to the gloom Dina felt.

The two were obviously discussing the weather, because Dina overheard the man remark, "I hope you're right about it being sunny and clear at the island. I don't know anything about ocean currents and how they affect the weather. All I know is that I want a weekend of good fishing."

Blake's prediction of fair weather on Block Island proved correct. The clouds began to thin, permitting glimpses of blue sky and a sinking yellow sun. When the ferry docked at the Old Harbor landing, there were only patches of clouds in the sky.

But the silence between Dina and Blake didn't break. Despite that, she felt her spirits lift as they drove off the ferry onto the island, named after Adrian Block, the first European to explore it. The sea breeze was refreshing, and Dina understood why it had been a fashionable health spa at the turn of the century.

She admired the scenery as Blake drove to the picturesque resort village of New Harbor, along the banks of the Great Salt Pond. It had once been an inland lake, but a manmade channel now linked it to the ocean, providing a harbor for pleasure craft and commercial fishing boats.

But the tension returned when Blake parked in front of a hotel. It seemed different somehow to share a hotel room. Just why, Dina couldn't say, since they'd been sharing a bedroom almost ever since Blake had returned. She felt self-conscious walking beside him into the lobby.

Blake glanced down at her, his gaze taking in the troubled look on her face. "How are you feeling?"

"Fine," Dina rushed out the answer.

"No leftover nausea from the ferry trip?"

"None. Actually, I never felt I was going to be sick. Except for a slight headache, I'm fine," she insisted. "Either the pills are getting stronger or I'm finally outgrowing my seasickness."

"Good." His smile was somewhat grim. "Excuse me. I'll go check on our reservation."

As he walked to the desk to register, she lingered near a rack of postcards, pretending to be interested until she saw a bellhop take their luggage. Blake walked toward her, and she immediately picked a card from the rack, as if about to study it more closely.

"Planning to send a postcard to someone?" The cynically amused query didn't help her fluttering stomach.

"No." She quickly returned it to the rack. "I was just looking at the picture."

"Tomorrow we'll take a look at the real thing."

Dina had to glance at the postcard. She had been so conscious of Blake, she hadn't noticed the actual picture. Now she saw it was a lighthouse.

"It looks interesting," she offered, just to be saying something.

"Yes," Blake agreed dryly, as if he knew that she'd had no idea what it was. "Shall we go to our rooms?"

"Rooms?"

"Yes, two," he answered. Dina was surprised by the gentle, almost tender expression of patience

on his usually hard features. "We have adjoining
bedrooms. I intend to prove whatever it is that you
feel needs proving, Dina."

She thought that over for a long moment.
Strangely, this seemed to be more of a concession
than all the nights when Blake had shared her bed
perhaps because he was granting her the privacy to
think without his presence to disturb or influence
her.

When he handed her one of the keys in his hand,
she managed a quiet "Thank you."

"A desperate man will try anything," Blake returned cryptically, but Dina thought she caught a
glimmer of humor in his dark eyes. It made him
seem more human.

They walked to their rooms in silence, but it was
no longer so strained. Blake hesitated outside his
door, catching her eye for an instant before he
turned the key in his lock and walked in.

Entering her room, Dina noticed her suitcase
lying on the luggage rack and walked over to it, in-
tending to unpack. Instead, she paused at the interior door that connected the two bedrooms. Blake
was on the other side of it. Unconsciously she
reached for the doorknob. It refused to turn; the
door was locked. Regret collided with relief as she
walked back to her suitcase and unpacked.

An hour later she had showered and was dressed
in a wheat-colored linen dress that was elegantly
casual. Blake hadn't said whether he would meet
her at the restaurant for dinner or go down with
her. She debated whether to wait in the room or
go to the restaurant, then decided to wait. She sat
down on the bed.

Instantly a smile curved her lips. The mattress was blissfully soft, sinking beneath her weight like a featherbed. It was going to be a wonderful change from Blake's rock-hard mattress at the house.

Just then there was a knock at her door, and Dina rose to answer it, the smile lingering on her lips. Blake stood outside, his eyes warming at her expression.

"You look pleased about something," he commented.

"My bed," Dina explained, a pair of dimples appearing in her cheeks. "It's soft."

His understanding chuckle was soft, almost silent—a disarming sound. Her heart skipped a beat, then refused to return to an even tempo.

"Shall we go to dinner?"

It was more of a statement than a question as Blake held out his hand for hers. Self-consciously she let her hand be engulfed in his, but he continued to block the doorway, not permitting her to step out. His hold on her hand shifted, and he raised the inside of her wrist to his mouth.

"Have I told you how beautiful you are?" he murmured.

"Blake, please," Dina protested, her lashes fluttering down at the heady touch of his warm lips against the sensitive skin of her wrist.

"It's only a compliment," he interrupted with a wry smile as he brought her hand away. "All you have to do is say 'thank you.' "

"Thank you," she repeated in a tight little voice, more aroused than she wanted to admit. He had quite an effect on her.

"That's better." Blake moved to the side, leading

her out of the room and reaching behind her to close the door.

Fresh seafood was the natural selection to make from the menu. Once that decision had been made, Dina sat in the chair opposite Blake's. Inside she was a bundle of nerves, but she forced herself to be still.

Without the steady chatter of Mrs. Chandler, Dina couldn't think of anything to say. It seemed like an indication of how far she and Blake had grown apart.

"I'm going to have to make a trip to the bookstore soon," Blake said idly. "I have a lot of reading to catch up on."

"Yes, I suppose you do." Dina wanted to cry at how stilted her response was.

But Blake either didn't notice it or deliberately ignored it. "It sounds a little crazy, I know, but reading was one of the things I really missed. More than good meals and clean clothes. I never considered it a necessity before."

"I doubt if I have, either," she admitted, forgetting her self-consciousness for a moment.

"Any new titles you'd like to recommend?"

Dina hesitated, then suggested, *Amazonia.* "It's a James Rollins thriller set in the jungles of South America. You'd like it."

Before she realized what was happening, she found herself becoming engrossed in a discussion of new books published in Blake's absence, and titles they'd both read in the past. From reading, their conversation drifted to movies and even reality TV shows. After all he had been through, he didn't understand how or why people would fake something as serious as survival.

When Blake later signaled for the check, Dina was surprised to discover that it was after ten o'clock. There hadn't been one awkward moment between them, not even a single argumentative remark. She hadn't thought it was possible. She wondered if Blake had noticed it, but was afraid to ask. She didn't want to risk breaking whatever kind of temporary truce they had established.

They both seemed to be in a reflective mood as they went up to their rooms. Dina was conscious of his hand lightly resting on the back of her waist, but she didn't object to it. In fact, she was beginning to enjoy his protectiveness.

"Do you know what this reminds me of?" Blake asked when they paused in front of her door.

"What?" Dina looked up, curious and thoughtful.

"All those times I used to walk you to the door of your sorority house and kiss you good night in a dark corner." He glanced around the hallway. "Of course, here there aren't any dark corners." His gaze returned to her face. "But I *am* going to kiss you good night."

His head bent and Dina lifted hers, welcoming his kiss—and his embrace. Each seemed to realize how little it would take to bring them together as lovers, surrendering to passion. Yet neither made the move.

Then, with obvious reluctance, they both took a step back, gazing silently at each other. Blake sighed, a closed look stealing over his face.

"Do you have your key?" he asked.

"Yes." Dina unfastened her clutch purse and took it out.

He hesitated a fraction of a second. "Good night, Dina." He moved toward his own door.

"Good night, Blake," she murmured, and entered her hotel room alone.

Chapter Nine

Dina didn't sleep well that night, ironically, because the mattress was too soft. She was awakened from her fitful dozing by a knock on the door and stumbled groggily across the room to answer it.

"Who is it?" She leaned tiredly against the door, her hand resting on the locked night latch.

"Blake," was the answer. "Are you ready for breakfast?"

Dina groaned. It couldn't possibly be morning already.

"Are you all right?" His tone was low and piercing.

"Fine," she mumbled, adding silently, *I just need some sleep*.

The doorknob rattled as he attempted to open it. "Unlock the door, Dina," he ordered.

She was too tired to think of a reason to refuse and too tired to argue if she had one. Slipping off the safety chain, she unlocked the latch and stepped aside as Blake pushed the door open. There was concern in his expression, but she didn't notice.

"I don't want breakfast." Dina was already turning to make her way back to the bed. "You go ahead without me."

Blake's arm went around her to turn her back. He pushed the tangle of cornsilk hair behind her ear and held it there, his hand cupping the side of her head and tipping it up. His strength was glorious, and Dina willingly let him support her weight, too weary to stand on her own.

"What's the matter, Dina? You look exhausted." Blake was frowning.

"I am," she sighed. "My fabulously soft bed was too soft. I barely slept all night."

He laughed softly. "Why didn't you take a pillow and blanket off the bed and sleep on the floor? Or was that too uncivilized for you?" His voice was gently teasing.

"I suppose that's what you did." Dina lifted her tired eyes to glance at him. He looked disgustingly refreshed and rested.

"Yes." He nodded.

"And probably slept like a baby," she added enviously.

"I didn't sleep all that well," Blake denied.

"Why not?" Dina slid her arms around his hard, warm body and rested her head against his shoulder, closing her eyes.

"I haven't liked sleeping alone since I met you."

His provocative statement sailed right over her head. Dina was only aware of how right it felt to be in his arms, so comfortable and so warm. She snuggled closer.

"Why don't you just hold me for a while and let me sleep?" she suggested in a drowsy murmur.

"I don't think so." The arm that had been around her withdrew. "If I hold you much longer, I won't be thinking about sleep," Blake stated, a half smile curving one corner of his mouth. "Why don't you shower and dress? I'll go get some coffee to help you wake up before we go to breakfast."

Dina didn't have a chance to agree or disagree. One minute she was in his arms, and the next he was walking to the door, leaving her swaying there unsteadily. The closing of the door goaded her into movement. She looked longingly at the bed but knew it was no use. Even if she could go back to sleep, Blake would be back soon. Following his suggestion, she walked to the bathroom.

It was midmorning by the time Blake and Dina finished their breakfast and started out on a leisurely tour of the island, dotted with freshwater ponds. It wasn't the first visit for either of them, but it had been several years since their last.

The island hadn't changed much, although more trees had been planted by property owners. Early settlers had long ago cut down the original forest for lumber to build their homes, and the windswept island needed all the help it could get.

Stone fences crisscrossed the rolling terrain. The rocks had been deposited on the island by Ice Age glaciers and stacked, probably long ago, by slave labor, to mark the boundaries of colonists' farms. They were a picturesque touch on the island once called "God's Little Isle" by an early Italian navigator.

On the southeastern shore Blake parked the car on Mohegan Bluffs. The lighthouse sat on the point of the bluffs, the rustic house and tower looking out to sea. Its navigational beacon was one of the most powerful on the New England coastline.

The salty breeze off the ocean was cool. Dina zipped up her windbreaker while Blake locked the car. Screeching seagulls soared overhead as they walked together past the lighthouse to the steep path leading down the headland to the beach.

A fisherman stood knee-deep in the surf, casting a line into the whitecaps. He nodded a friendly acknowledgment to them as they strolled by. Blake's arm was around Dina's shoulders, keeping her close to his side. She stepped over a piece of driftwood and turned her gaze up to his face. His expression was relaxed, almost contented.

"Why are we getting along so well?" she mused, more to herself than to him.

"Maybe it's because we've stopped looking at each other," Blake suggested.

"What?" A bewildered frown creased her forehead, confusion darkening the blue of her eyes.

"Sounds a little strange, doesn't it?" A faint smile touched his mouth when he looked at her. "But I think we've stopped trying to see the flaws in each other, the differences."

"I understand," Dina said, looking far down the beach in front of them. "At least I think I do."

"Why bother to analyze it?" he countered. "Why not just enjoy it?"

"That's true." She scuffed a canvas toe against a stone. "Except that I like to know the why of things."

"I remember," Blake murmured dryly. "Like the

time I gave you your engagement ring and you wanted to know what made me decide to propose to you."

Dina laughed. "And you said it was because I would make such a beautiful ornament in your home." The laughter died as she gave him a guarded look. "Is that how you see women? As ornaments?"

There was a hint of exasperation in his impatient glance. "You should know me better than that, Dina."

She was silent for several paces. "That's the problem, I guess—I'm not sure anymore how well I know you. You always seemed so sophisticated. Now"—she lifted her hand in a searching gesture—"you're so . . . earthy."

"Hey, I learned the hard way what's important and what's not. Basically, I don't believe I've changed."

"Maybe I didn't know you well enough then to understand that," Dina said thoughtfully.

"Maybe so." Blake flashed her a quick smile. "How did we get started on such a serious discussion?"

His lightning switch from a pensive mood to one that was lightly teasing was contagious. Dina responded immediately, "I don't know. You started it."

"No, I didn't. You did," he corrected her pleasantly, "when you asked why we weren't arguing."

"You didn't have to answer me, so therefore it's all your fault." She shrugged.

"Chick logic," Blake declared with an amused shake of his head.

"Learn to like it," she demanded in mock anger.

"Why?" he asked.

Dina gave him a sideways push with her shoulder. Knocked off balance, his arm slipped from around her and he took a step to one side to recover. Their aimless pace had taken them closer to the water's edge than they realized, and when Blake took that step, his foot—shoe, sock, and pant leg—landed in salt water. Dina had to laugh.

"Think that's funny?" He took a playfully threatening step toward her.

Unconsciously she began to retreat. "Honestly, Blake, I'm sorry." She was trying hard not to laugh more, but it bubbled in her voice. "I didn't know. I really didn't mean to push you in the water."

Blake continued to approach her. "Let's see if it's so funny when you get wet."

"Blake, no!" Dina kept backing up, shaking her head.

The wicked glint in his eye warned her that words would not appease him. Turning, she ran, sprinting for the rock bluff at a safer distance from the lapping ocean waves. Blake chased her, his long strides eating up her short lead. Any moment he would overtake her, Dina knew, and she spared a laughing glance over her shoulder.

A piece of driftwood in her path tripped her and sent her sprawling headlong onto the beach. Her outstretched arms broke most of her fall. Unharmed, she rolled onto her back, out of breath but still trying not to laugh, as Blake dropped to his knees beside her.

"Are you all right?" he asked, half smiling and half concerned.

"Fine," she managed to gasp.

Sitting on his heels, Blake watched silently as she caught her breath. But as her breathing slowed, her heartbeat increased. An exciting tension was leaping between them, quivering over her skin and bringing a rosy blush to her cheeks.

Blake moved forward as if to help her to her feet, but as he moved closer, arms bracing him above her, her moist lips parted, glistening. Dina lifted her hands to his chest to resist him, but instead they slid around his neck, pulling him down.

Fire ignited at the pressure of his mouth, hungry and demanding. No part of her was immune to the desire Blake was arousing so thoroughly.

Reeling under the tender assault, she knew she'd lost control. She made no attempt to get it back, allowing his lips to dominate hers for as long as he chose. With each breath she drew in the intoxicating scent of him, warm and male and magical. Never had Dina felt so alive.

"Hey?" She heard a child's voice, when previously she had only been able to hear his heartbeat and her own. "Hey!" This time the voice was more insistent, and Blake dragged his mouth from hers to roll onto his side with a frustrated groan. "Have you seen my puppy?"

A six-year-old boy stood beside them, knees dirty, a baseball cap on his light brown hair, staring at them innocently. Dina could feel Blake gathering the control to answer him.

"Uh, no, I haven't." His reply was terse to conceal the raggedness of his breathing.

"He's white and black with a red collar," the boy explained.

"Sorry, we haven't seen him," Blake repeated patiently.

"If you do, wouldja bring him back to me?"

"Sure."

"Thanks." And he trotted off, disappearing around a jumble of huge rocks on the beach.

Blake stared in that direction. "A few more seconds and it could have been embarrassing," he remarked grimly. "Come on." Scrambling to his feet, he caught Dina's hand to pull her along with him.

"Where are we going?" Her cheeks were an even brighter pink now.

"Back to the hotel."

"Why?"

"You're forgetting," he answered accusingly, flashing her a look that still had the smoldering light of desire. "I have a wet shoe, sock, and pants leg."

Slightly subdued, Dina offered, "I'm sorry about that."

"I'm not." His finger touched her lips, tracing their outline, warm and still throbbing from his possession of them. "If that's what I get for a wet foot, I wonder what would happen if I'd been drenched from head to toe." She breathed in sharply, wanting to tell him he didn't have to wait to find out, but she simply couldn't say the words. Blake didn't wait for her to speak, removing his fingers from her lips to encircle her hand. "Come on. Let's go"

Dina nodded in silent agreement.

The magic shimmered between them on their return trip to the hotel, there in the looks they exchanged, in the things they didn't say, and in the way they avoided physical contact with each other . . . if only for the moment.

Neither of them was willing to acknowledge the change in the relationship. But what would happen next wasn't clear.

After a late lunch in the hotel restaurant, they entered the lobby. Blake stopped and turned to Dina. "We're checking out and going home," he announced.

"It's only Saturday," she protested.

"I know," he agreed with a hint of impatience. "But I'm not looking forward to spending another night here."

Dina hesitated, unsure of his meaning. Finally she spoke. "The beds aren't very comfortable."

His mouth twisted wryly. "Yes, they're too soft."

"Do we have time to catch the ferry?"

"If you don't take forever to pack, we do," he told her.

"I won't," she promised.

"I'll check out while you get started," said Blake.

During the ferry crossing, neither mentioned the unexpected closeness that had them returning early. They talked around it as if unwilling to get into the reasons why. When the ferry docked in Newport, they stopped talking altogether, both absorbed in their own thoughts.

It was several seconds before Dina noticed that Blake had missed a corner. "You were supposed to turn at that last block," she reminded him.

"We aren't going back to the house right away," he said.

Dina waited for him to tell her their destination. When he didn't, she asked, "Where are we going?"

"There's something I want to show you," was all he answered.

After several more blocks, he turned onto a tree-shaded street, branches arching overhead, nearly touching. He slowed the car down, looking for house numbers as he drove, and Dina's curiosity grew with each second of his continued silence. Finally he turned into a driveway and stopped the car, switching off the engine.

Dina glanced at the large white house surrounded by a green lawn with lots of trees and flowering shrubs. She didn't recognize the place.

"Who lives here?" she asked.

Blake was already opening his car door and stepping outside. "You'll see."

She flashed him a look of irritation as he came around to open her door. He was carrying all this mystery business just a little too far. But she said nothing and walked ahead of him along the winding sidewalk to the front door.

There was a jingle of metal behind her, and she turned. Blake was taking a set of keys from his pocket. Selecting one, he stepped ahead of her and inserted it in the lock. Suspicion glittered in her eyes.

Pushing the door open, he motioned to her. "Go on in."

Dina moved forward to cross the threshold. On her right, carved oak posts ran from floor to ceiling to separate the foyer from the spacious living room beyond. Although the room was sparsely decorated, Dina recognized the furniture stored from their apartment.

"What's this supposed to mean?" Unable to look at

him, she thought she already knew the answer, and his high-handedness made her tremble with anger.

"Do you like it?" Blake ignored her question to ask one of his own.

"Did you buy this house without consulting me?" she demanded accusingly in a shaking voice.

"As I recall, you were too busy to bother looking for a place for us to live," he reminded her in an expressionless tone. "But to answer your question, no, I haven't signed any contracts or closing documents."

"If that's true, why is all our furniture here?" Her hand waved jerkily to the sofa and chairs.

"I got permission from the owner to bring it in to see how it would fit in the rooms . . . and to give the decorator an idea of what still has to be done."

Dina turned on him, her eyes flashing fire. "In other words, it doesn't matter what I want! You've decided on this house and if I don't like it, that's just too bad, isn't it?"

"Your opinion does matter." A muscle was twitching along his jaw, the only outward sign that he felt the lashing of her words. "That's why I brought you here."

There was a skeptical lift of her chin, disbelief glittering in her eyes despite his smooth denial. "Why not? Why not before? All this furniture wasn't just brought here and arranged overnight."

"No, it wasn't," Blake agreed.

"Then why now?" Dina asked.

"Because I had the impression you were ready to start looking for a place for us. Just us."

His narrowed gaze made her want to squirm. She focused her attention on the room, unable to admit that it might have been more than an impression.

"Was I wrong, Dina?" Blake asked.

She didn't want to answer that question—not yet, not until she had more time to think about it: She didn't want to be manipulated into a commitment.

"Since I'm here, you might as well show me through the rest of the house," she said with forced indifference.

Blake hesitated, then gestured for her to follow him. "The dining room and kitchen are this way," he directed.

As Dina toured the house, she realized it was everything they had ever talked about as far as a home of their own. Spacious without being too large, with plenty of room for entertaining, a study for Blake where he could work undisturbed in the evenings, a big patio in back, and lots of closets.

"Since you're working, we'll need a housekeeper. But not a live-in," Blake explained as they walked down the hallway from the master bedroom to the main living area of the house.

"Yes," Dina agreed absently. At the open doorway of one of the two empty rooms, she paused to look inside again. The spare bedrooms were smaller than the master bedroom but still quite large.

"There is one thing I haven't asked you." Blake stopped beside her.

"What's that?" She turned to meet his gaze.

"I haven't asked how you felt about having children."

Slightly flustered, Dina looked back to the empty room, visualizing it not as a guest bedroom but as a children's room. "We've talked about it before." They had discussed having two children, possibly three, she remembered.

"That was several years ago," Blake pointed out. "Now you have a career, and that's really important to you."

"Working women raise children." She hedged, avoiding a direct answer and speaking in generalities instead.

"Hey, some working women don't want to have children," he added. "I'm asking what you prefer, Dina."

He seemed to silently demand that she look at him. Reluctantly, she did, but she was unable to look any higher than his mouth. There were no soft curves to it; it was strong and firm and masculine. Dina had the impulse to raise her fingertips to it and trace the strength of its outline.

"I would like to have children, yes." Her reply was soft, almost inaudible.

"Do you have any objections to my being their father?" There was an endearingly husky quality to his voice.

The movement of his mouth when he spoke broke the spell, and Dina looked away, her heart pulsing erratically. She couldn't seem to speak. Something was blocking her voice.

"Do you?" Blake repeated. When she remained silent, his fingers turned her chin to force her to look at him. "What about this afternoon on the beach?" His steady gaze didn't waver as he looked deeply into her eyes, seemingly into her very soul. "Did you give me your answer, or was that just a moment of passion?"

"I don't know." Dina wanted to look away, but she couldn't. "I . . . I can't think."

"Just this once, don't think," Blake requested. "Tell me what you're feeling."

His hands slipped to her shoulders, tightening for a fraction of a second as if he wanted to shake the answer out of her, but they relaxed to simply hold her. Dina stared into the bluntly chiseled features, and those compelling dark eyes. This was Blake, a man, her husband, and not a stranger at all.

She swayed toward him and he gathered her into his arms, prepared to meet her more than halfway. Her lips parted under the plundering force of his mouth, taking the kiss she gave so readily. As if he had never been away, her soft shape molded itself to the powerful contours of his body.

His roaming hands caressed and pulled her ever closer to his solidly muscled flesh. His driving male need made Dina aware of the empty ache deep within her, which only he could satisfy.

Soon the torrid embrace was not enough. Bending slightly, Blake curved an arm under her knees to lift and carry her to the master bedroom and the bare mattress of their old marriage bed.

As he set her down, her twining arms around his neck pulled him down to join her. Nothing existed for either of them but each other—not the past and not the future, only the moment, eternally suspended in time.

The initial storm of their passion was quickly spent. When Blake came to her a second time, their lovemaking was slow and languorous. Each touch, each kiss, each intimate caress was enjoyed and prolonged, savored and cherished.

The beauty of it brought tears to Dina's eyes, jewel-bright and awesomely happy. Blake kissed them away, gently, adoringly, as he curved her to his side, locking his arms around her. Dina sighed in rapturous contentment and snuggled closer, not wanting to move, never wanting to move. Here was where she belonged, where she would always belong.

Chapter Ten

Blake stroked her hair, absently trailing his fingers through the silken strands, watching the fairness of its color glisten in the light. Her eyes were closed in supreme contentment.

"Would you say it now, Dina?" His huskily caressing voice rumbled from deep within his chest.

"What?" she asked with equal softness, not sure words could express anything close to what she was feeling.

"Welcome home." He supplied the words he wanted to hear.

Tipping back her head, she looked up to his face, love bringing a dazzling brilliance to the blue of her eyes. "Welcome home, Blake." She repeated the words in a voice that trembled with the depth of her meaning.

He lifted her the few inches necessary to plant a hard, possessive kiss on her lips. Then his trembling fingers moved over her lips as if to apologize for hurting them.

"I've been waiting so long to hear that." There was a sad look about his strong mouth. "Now it doesn't seem nearly as important."

"I often wondered what might have happened if I'd known you were alive before I saw you at the house," Dina whispered, her heart aching at the time together they had lost. "I thought at first it was someone's twisted idea of a joke."

"I should've made more of an effort to reach you before I came back," Blake insisted. "I knew it would be a shock. Chet tried to convince me to let him break the news to you, but I didn't listen. I was expecting too much to think that you would come to me as if nothing had changed."

"It wasn't just shock," she explained. "It was guilt, because I'd become engaged to Chet. And there you were, my husband. I wanted to run to you, but I couldn't. Then suddenly, you seemed so different—a stranger, someone I didn't know," Dina sighed.

"Guess I didn't want to admit I'd changed and so had you," he murmured with a rueful smile. "I wanted everything to be the way it was, as if I'd never been gone."

"Still, everything might have turned out okay if I hadn't been engaged to Chet." Dina turned to rest her head again on his chest and listen to the strong rhythm of his heartbeat.

"I don't know. It was painful. No getting around that," he insisted.

"Yes, but Chet—" Dina started to argue.

Blake interrupted. "He was no threat to our relationship. Even if I hadn't come back, I don't think you ever would've married him. You might've drifted along with the engagement for a year, but you're much too intelligent not to have realized eventually that it wouldn't work."

She relaxed, suddenly knowing he was right, and the last little doubt vanished. Smiling, she slid her hand over his flat, muscular stomach, patting him playfully.

"Weren't you just a little bit jealous of Chet?" The question was half teasing and half serious.

"No," he chuckled, and tugged at a lock of hair. "Me Tarzan. King of jungle never get jealous."

"Never?" Dina was almost disappointed.

"Never," Blake repeated. "There were times, though, when I was envious."

"Why?"

"Because you were so natural with him, so warm and friendly, trusting him, relying on him, and turning to him when you were confused. I wanted it to be me," he explained. "A man's instinct to protect is as strong as the maternal instinct in a woman. But you acted like you didn't need me."

"I did, though." Dina hugged him. "I love you, Blake. I've never stopped loving you."

"That's what I really wanted to hear." His arms tightened around her, crushing her ribs. " 'Welcome home' was just a substitute for 'I love you.' "

"I love you," she repeated. "You don't have to ask me to say that. I'll keep on saying it until you get sick of it."

"Never, my love." He shook his head.

There was a long silence as they reveled inwardly at the rediscovery of their love and the eloquently simple words that expressed so much.

"I hate to bring up something so mundane," Dina whispered, "but where are we going to sleep tonight?"

"I don't even want to go to sleep," said Blake.

"Aren't you tired?" Her sleepless night on the too-soft hotel mattress was beginning to catch up with her, aided by the dreamy contentment of his embrace.

"Exhausted," he admitted with a smile in his voice. "But I'm afraid if I go to sleep, I'll wake up and find none of this has happened. Or worse, that I'm still in the jungle."

"If you are, I'm going to be there with you," she declared, and poked a finger in his chest. "Remember, if you Tarzan, me Jane." Blake chuckled and kissed her hair. "Seriously, Blake, are we going back to the house tonight?"

"Not if the storage boxes in the garage have any blankets in them. Do they?" he asked.

"Did you take out everything that I had in storage?"

"Every single thing," he confirmed.

"Then there are blankets in the boxes in the garage," she promised. "As a matter of fact, there's everything we need to set up housekeeping."

"Is that what you'd like to do?" Blake asked. "Stay here tonight?"

"I thought you'd already decided that."

"I'm asking if that's what you want to do," he explained patiently.

"I must remember that and mark it on the calendar," Dina murmured. "A red-letter day. Blake asked me what I wanted to do instead of telling me what I was going to do."

"All right, troublemaker," he laughed. "You know what I'm really asking."

"You want to know whether I like the house,"

Dina guessed, propping herself up on an elbow beside him.

"Well, yeah."

"Yes. As a matter of fact, I love it," she smiled. "It's everything we ever said we wanted in a house."

"Good. That's what I thought, too. Monday morning I'll have the Realtor get the contract ready. In the meantime, I don't think he'll mind if we start unpacking the boxes in the garage."

"What if he sells it to somebody else?"

"He won't. I put earnest money down to hold it until you saw it and, I hoped, approved of my choice."

"Were you so positive I'd like it?"

"As positive as I was that you'd love me again," Blake answered.

"Conceited!" Dina teased. "It would serve you right if I hated it."

"But you do like it, and now you can take over the decorating."

"It might end up looking like a hotel," she warned.

"It better not," he laughed, and pulled her into his arms.

There was a scattering of snowflakes outside her office window, falling from pearl gray clouds. A serenely joyful light was in Dina's eyes as she still smiled, talking on the phone.

"Thank you, I'll tell him," she promised. "Merry Christmas." The season of comfort and joy was almost upon them, but the shortened days of December seemed to have passed her by in a blur of colored lights and festive decorations.

Hanging up, she let her attention return to the papers on her desk while absently humming a Christmas carol. The interoffice line buzzed and she picked up the telephone again.

She had barely identified herself when Blake ordered crisply, "I want you in my office immediately."

"Oh? What for?"

"We'll discuss it when you get here."

She arched an eyebrow at his sharpness. "Very well," Dina agreed calmly. "Give me about fifteen minutes."

"I said now," he snapped.

"You're forgetting it takes that long to walk to your office from here," she reminded him dryly.

"Now, Dina!" And the connection was broken.

Breathing in deeply, she stared at the phone receiver before finally replacing it on its cradle. She took a few seconds to put her desk into some kind of order, then walked into the corridor, closing her office door as she left.

Her estimated time was an exaggeration. Eight minutes later, Amy Wentworth glanced up from her typewriter and motioned her into Blake's office with a wave of her hand. Dina knocked once on the connecting door and opened it to walk in.

Blake sat behind his desk leaning back in his chair when Dina entered. His masculine features were drawn into cold, harsh lines to match the temperature outdoors. Anger glittered in his dark eyes, and Dina had no idea why.

"You wanted to see me, Blake?" She walked to his desk, smiling warmly at her husband, but it didn't thaw his expression. "Am I being called on the carpet about something?"

"You're damned right you are!" He reached forward to shove a paper across his desk toward her, his glittering and watchful gaze never leaving her face for an instant. "What's this all about?"

Dina reached for the paper and glanced over it. "This is the revised budget request," she answered, frowning as she recognized it. "Where did you get it?"

"From Chet," Blake snapped.

Her mouth became a straight line of grim exasperation. "He wasn't supposed to give it to you. I wanted to go over it with you when I submitted it."

"He didn't give it to me. I took it. And you can go over it with me now," he ordered. "This is the—what—third or fourth budget revision?"

"The third." Dina was determined not to match his biting tone. "And if you'd told me why you wanted to speak to me, I could have brought the P-and-L statements and—"

"I'm not interested in any of that; I want an explanation. Why the overrun?"

"It's a combination of things," she began. "We had to change advertising agencies for the campaign because the original firm wasn't able to meet deadlines. That meant an increase in the cost."

"You should've checked them out more thoroughly," he rebuked her.

"Well, they had a stellar reputation. Which tanked after we'd signed a contract with them," she replied sharply.

There was disbelief in his look, but he didn't pursue the point. "What else?"

"We had to revise the cost figures on revamping the hotels. The—"

"I knew it," he declared, interrupting her again.

"The redecorating costs for the hotels escalate every time you submit a budget. Are you redecorating them or rebuilding?"

The slow-burning fuse of her temper was finally lit. "There are times when I'm not so positive myself," she said, simmering. "Have you seen that hotel in Florida? We've tried landscaping and painting, but it needs a whole new facade."

"Why don't you just arrange to tear it down and build a new one?" he said nastily.

"Best suggestion I've heard yet!" she retorted. "Why don't you bring that up to the expansion department?"

"At the rate you're going, it might be the least expensive!" With controlled anger, Blake pushed out of his chair, standing behind the desk to glare at her. "I should have known this would happen. Put a woman in charge and she thinks she has a blank check!"

"I can't believe you said that. Is it possible to sue my own husband for sexual discrimination? Because I will!" Hot tears burned her eyes. "If that's what you think"—pain choked her voice—"why don't you take over? I never asked for the job in the first place! If you think a man can do so much better, go ahead!"

"And don't think I couldn't!"

"The great Blake Chandler. Oh, I'm sure you could nickel and dime the project to death," Dina said sarcastically, and turned away, filled with a mixture of disgust and hurt. "I don't know what ever made me think I'd want your baby."

"I don't know, either!" Blake snarled behind her. "Lucky for you that you have a choice, isn't it?"

"That's the whole point! I don't have a choice anymore," she cried bitterly.

Her sentence hung in the air for a long, heavy second before Blake broke the silence. "What did you say?"

"Didn't I tell you?" She tossed the question over her shoulder, her chin quivering with the forced attempt at lightness. "I'm going to have a baby."

In the next second his hands were on her shoulders to gently turn her around. Dina kept her chin lowered, still angry and hurt by his barbed attack.

"Are you sure?" he asked quietly.

"Yes, I'm sure." She closed her eyes to try to force back the tears. "Dr. Cosgrove called me a few minutes ago to confirm the test results."

"Why didn't you tell me?" His tension was exhaled with the question.

"How could I when you've been yelling at me for the past five minutes?" Her eyes widened to glare at him.

His fingers lightly touched her cheek before he cupped it in his hand. "I was, wasn't I?" There was a rueful twist to his mouth.

"Yes, you were." But her assertion didn't carry any sting of anger.

"I'm sorry—so sorry. I can be a total jerk sometimes."

"I know," she said sweetly.

"That's incredible news. Forgive me, Dina—I love you so much. I could lose everything I have and it wouldn't matter as long as I didn't lose you."

The glow radiating from his face was warm and powerful, and Dina basked in the love light. That serene joy she had known before their argument returned with doubled strength.

"You're forgiven," she said softly, and turned her lips to his hand to press a kiss into his open palm.

His head lowered, his mouth claiming hers in a sweetly fierce kiss that rocked her senses. She clung to him, reveling in his possessive embrace. A wild, glorious melody raced through her veins, its tune timeless, the universal song of love.

She was breathless when the kiss ended, and the sensation remained as Blake buried his face in her hair, his mouth trailing a blazing fire to the sensitive skin of her neck.

When he finally lifted his head, there was a disarming smile softening his roughly carved features. His hands moved to tangle his fingers in her hair and hold her face up for his gaze to explore. Dina knew this was a moment she would treasure forever in her heart.

"We're really going to have a baby?" There was a marveling look in his eyes as Blake turned the statement into a near question.

"Yes," Dina nodded.

"Are you all right?" He frowned.

"I'm fine." She smiled. With a sighing shake of her head, she asked, "Why do we argue so much, Blake?"

"It's our nature, I guess." He smiled wryly in return. "We'd better get used to the fact, because we'll probably do it the rest of our lives."

"Always testing to find out which of us is stronger." Dina couldn't forget Chet's explanation for their constant quarrels.

"Don't worry, honey, I'll let you be stronger once in a while," he promised.

"Blake!" She started to protest indignantly at his superior remark.

"Can you imagine what our children are going to be like?" he laughed. "Pigheaded, argumentative little rebels, more than likely. Especially the girls."

"No, you mean the boys," Dina said. "But we'll love every battling moment of raising them."

"The same as every battling moment you and I have together." He kissed her lightly and gazed into her eyes. "When's the baby due?"

"July."

"The new campaign will be in full swing by then. I can just see you directing operations from the maternity ward," Blake chuckled.

"You mean that I still have the job?" Dina arched a mocking brow at him. "And that blank check?"

"Yes," he saw with an arrogant smile. "I mean, no to the second part. But aren't you glad you have an understanding boss who'll let you set your own hours or work at home?"

"I'm very lucky." She slid her arms around his neck, rising on tiptoes. "And so are you."

"Oh, Dina . . ." Blake spoke her name in an aching murmur against her lips. "Think you can tame me?"

"I can try, tiger. And by the way, there's only one thing I want for Christmas. . . ."

She whispered into his ear, and Blake's face lit up.

More by Best-selling Author
Fern Michaels

DO YOU HAVE THE
HOHL COLLECTION?